For Pat, who makes it
all mean so much more.

Final Revelation

"Are you man enough to be a leader, Jared? Do you believe that even the dying serve the Lord?"

Jared looked up at Aaron. "I believe, Father."

"I will remind you that it was Divinely revealed to David Moses in the year 105 that the slaughter of men had not been punishment but was the Lord's way of revealing how we were to build our society."

Jared nodded. Everyone knew that.

"What you have never been told before is that at the same time it was also revealed to him how to maintain the necessary male minority."

Jared's brows went up. "The disease does that."

"No . . . it doesn't," Aaron said.

"Then"—Jared's mouth went dry,—"what does?"

"We do."

A Voice Out of Ramah

Lee Killough

A Del Rey Book

BALLANTINE BOOKS • NEW YORK

A Del Rey Book
Published by Ballantine Books

Library of Congress Catalog Card Number: 78-60976

ISBN: 0-345-28021-0

Manufactured in the United States of America

First Edition: January 1979

Cover art by H. R. Van Dongen

A voice is heard out of Ramah,
wailing and loud lamentation,
Rachel weeping for her children.
—Matthew 2:18

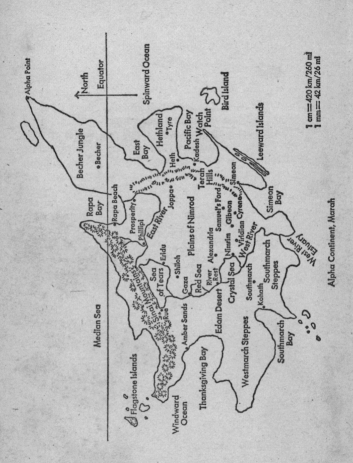

Alpha Point

North
Equator

Spinward Ocean

Becher Jungle

Becher

East
Bay

Hethland

Tyre

Pacific Bay

Heth

Kadesh Watch
Point

Bird Island

Terah
Hills

Leeward Islands

Rapa
Bay

Rapa Beach

Joppa

Simeon

Prosperity

Phillipi

East River

Plains of Nimrod

Samuel's Ford

Gibeon

Simeon
Bay

Median Sea

Eridu

Shiloh

Alexandria

Nimrim

Viridian Cyrene

West River

Sinai Mountains

River
Rue

Sea
of Tears

Gaza

Red Sea

River
Rest

Crystal Sea

Southmarch

West River
Estuary

Flagstone Islands

Amber Sands

Edam Desert

Kohath

Southmarch
Steppes

Thanksgiving Bay

Westmarch Steppes

Southmarch
Bay

Windward
Ocean

1 cm = 420 km/260 mi
1 mm = 42 km/26 mi

Alpha Continent, Marah

Chapter One

THERE WAS a new light in the night sky. Jared stood in the walled garden adjoining his rooms with his face lifted toward it. The light was small, no larger than a star, yet it was so bright it was clearly visible despite the full moons. It traveled east, passing close beneath the silver disks of Nightseye and its tiny attendant Tagalong, and within five minutes had disappeared beyond the Terah Hills.

A ship from Earth. Jared watched it in a turmoil of curiosity and trepidation. A ship from Earth. These were the people whose decadence and violence his ancestors had fled nearly six hundred years ago. Earth had been happy to see them go, too, or so the ancient diaries of the founders said. Why, then, had the Terrans come out to Marah? What did they want?

He sat down on a bench beside the pool in the middle of the garden. He would know, perhaps, in a few hours. The Gibeon flyer was bringing two people from the ship in from the Gahan ranch right now.

Jared could have wished differently. Eridu was the place for them to go, where the Bishop could deal with them. He was still not sure why, when he radioed the Bishop to tell him about the aliens, the Bishop had instructed they be brought here, to Gibeon, to Jared.

Jared had been dismayed. "But, Father, don't you want to see them yourself?"

"Not until after Thanksgiving. Courage, Jared. I know you are young for a Shepherd. I would indeed prefer they were in the care of someone more experienced, but Gahan ranch is in your parish. It's natural they come to you. Be careful; do not be seduced by their

1

godless ways, but talk to them, get to know them. I need you to look into their hearts and tell me what they are . . . and what they want of us."

No, Jared thought, but Elias Jamin was his spiritual leader. He said, "Yes, Father."

Jared bowed his head. The responsibility placed on him weighed heavily. Thank the Lord for his garden. It was his retreat, his salvation. Of all the temple, this was the place he loved most. Here he could walk without his staff or the beard tradition required he wear in public as a symbol of his manhood. Here he sometimes walked in just a loin wrap, letting the moonlight wash over the youthlike hairlessness of his body, erasing the lines three years of Shepherdhood had begun etching into his face. And here, beside the tranquility of the pool, amid the spicy sweetness of satan trees, he could always find strength for the hardest tasks, or peace from the most unsettling day.

He breathed deeply and waited for peace to come to him now. After all, there was nothing to fear. He was Kedar Jared Cloud Joseph, Shepherd of the Gibeon temple, spiritual leader and patriarch of a large portion of the south Nimrod Plains. He was touched by the Lord.

But peace did not come. The scent of the satan trees choked him and he was preternaturally aware of women's voices and low laughter beyond the stone-grilling that walled his garden. It was only temple guards passing time with each other, he knew. He had heard them like this on many other nights. Tonight, however, the sound irritated him. The Terran ship might be here for benevolent reasons, but even if it were, it was terrible in the awesomeness of its possibilities, and not an occasion for laughter.

He hunted down through himself for the source of his discontent. Close below the surface there was a plaintive strain of "Why me?" It felt more like an outgrowth, though, than a root. He followed the complaint deeper. Slowly, its origin emerged, reluctant and cringing. One of the Terrans was a man.

Jared folded his hands together so tightly they hurt. Marah could be death for any man that set foot on her. Only a few lucky immunes survived. If their emissary

2

died, what terrible vengeance would the Terrans in the ship wreak?

The temple clock chimed three o'clock.

Almost reflexively, Jared looked north, to where the capital Eridu sat broiling on the equator. His thoughts were not of the Bishop now, though. Instead, he wondered if Sky were awake tonight, too. Was the link that had existed between them as children still strong enough for her to feel her twin's distress?

He wished, as he often did in times of stress, that circumstances would let him ask her and her son to come live in Gibeon again. He wanted nothing as much as he wanted her here tonight, to help him talk out his fears. She could have listened sympathetically as she had done all the years of their growing up and been able, in the end, to tell him if his anxiety regarding the Terrans were justified. If not that, she could have given him some reassurance that would help him find peace.

He still remembered a time twenty-three years ago when he had particularly needed comfort. She had been there then. They had been fifteen years old. It was on a late October night, like this one.

After everyone was asleep, the two of them had sneaked out of the children's dormitory of the ranch house to go out on the prairie. They thought of riding but decided against it. The diurnal rapas were too prone to stumble in the dark. They were dangerous under the best of circumstances. One moment of inattention and a saurian, ill-tempered from being awakened, could club them with its stiff tail, take off an arm in one bite, or disembowel them with a sweep of a knife-clawed hind foot. Even a minor injury would have been awkward to explain in the morning. Jared was not supposed to be out on the prairie without a proper escort, certainly not at night on a creature no one but Sky was even aware he knew how to ride.

So they settled for walking. The autumn grass crackled under their boots. Silvered by moonlight, the grasslands rolled away from them to the horizon like some fabulous fairyland sea. Herds of rhinosaurs and leapers and flocks of the large flightless hooper birds moved across it in dark, misty patches. The light breeze, carrying the last warmth of the dying summer, brought them

3

the scent of dust and animal musk. Night birds whistled around them. Leapers barked in the distance, answered by the hoopers' whooping.

They walked without talking. Jared thought Sky was probably thinking about Gibeon temple and what it would be like for him attending Middle School there. He was thinking about dying.

The Trial, that deadly passage to manhood, was not a subject the family, not even his mother or Sky, would talk about. But how he wanted to talk. He longed to tell someone of this fear eating away inside him, this terror that he would not live to grow up.

Sky said, "When you finish Middle School you'll be a man. We'll take a cross-country ride, maybe as far as Viridian, and no one will be able to stop us."

If he came back. He turned toward her, starting to say that. But he was stopped by the fierce fire in her eyes. He realized, then, that she had not been thinking about Middle School at all; she had been thinking of death, too. And more than that, he saw she had guessed his thoughts.

"Of course you'll live to come back." Her voice accepted no other possibility. "We're twins. That means we're linked. My life strength is yours. It will flow to you when you need it and keep you safe. I won't let you die."

He desperately wanted to believe her. He threw his arms around her. She held him crushed against her. Gradually, he did believe she would keep him alive, and when his trembling stopped, they sat together in the grass. They watched Tagalong traverse Nightseye while they talked dreams and plans for the years ahead. It was something they had never dared do before. Jared found it the most wonderful experience of his life.

Jared the Shepherd, sitting in his garden, wondered if the Terran man had a twin somewhere to lend him life force.

Jared stood, rubbing his hands together. They felt cold. He still missed Sky after all these years. He knew now, of course, that Aaron Methuselah, Shepherd at that time, had been right to refuse him permission to go after her in Heth. He also knew it was unwise to ask her to rejoin him now. As Shepherd, he knew too many things lesser people could not be allowed to learn, things he might give away in the heat of passion or a tender moment of sharing confidences. Some of them he could hardly bear to think about in the privacy of his own mind. Between the terrible knowledge and the demands the office of Shepherd made on him twenty hours a day, he understood why it took a strong man to hold his position, and why many died years before their time of causes no healer or surgeon seemed able to diagnose or cure. It was for the best that Sky lived so far away, and yet—yet, how he needed her.

One of the guards laughed again.

Jared crossed the short distance to the wall and peered through the grilling. The two women, bows slung on their shoulders, stood with their backs to him at the gate on the far side of the courtyard. The position of one's hands, cupped a short way below her chin, suggested she was drinking a cup of tea.

"The Lord be with you, sisters," he called.

They started. The one dropped her cup and reached for her bow. The other had her bow off her shoulder and an arrow nocked before the cup hit the ground. They looked around to see where his voice was coming from.

"I'm here," he said, "in the Shepherd's garden."

The woman with the ready arrow looked in his direction. "Is that you, Father?"

"Yes." He tried to remember their names but could not. He actually saw these night guards very rarely, and could not ever recall speaking to them before.

They came toward him, slipping their bows back on their shoulders. The one returned her arrow to the quiver at her waist.

"You're awake early, Father. Sleeplessness causes weakness and disease."

He grimaced. That sounded like a quote from a healer. "Knowing the need for sleep doesn't make it come any easier."

The women exchanged glances. The tea drinker said, "Shall I send for a healer?"

Jared frowned. "I'm not ill. Today is an important day. We have guests coming from very far away."

"Oh? As far as Alpha Point or Amber Sands?"

5

"Much farther than that."

"But there's no one living anywhere else in the world."

Jared sighed. Why did he bother discussing such matters with them? He wanted to turn away but the thought of his empty sleeping room held him at the wall. "Tell me, what do you do when you can't sleep?"

The guards looked at each other again.

After a hesitation, the tea drinker said, "I meditate."

The other said, "I have my tanglemate hold me in her arms."

Neither sounded like a good solution to Jared. Meditation had not worked for him and he rarely found much release in sex. Sharing seed was a duty and a ritual to him, not a pleasure, not since Sky left.

When he said nothing more, one of the guards asked, "Do you need anything else, Father? We shouldn't be away from our post any longer."

"I hear someone coming," the other said.

Jared could no longer tell which one was speaking. He shrugged. Perhaps it was unimportant. "You may go."

"Thank you, Father."

Watching them hurry back across the courtyard toward the gate, he wondered at the relief in those final words. Were they actually uncomfortable talking to him? He had been uncomfortable talking to them. Women were charming, delightful for banter, but not for serious conversation as there would be between himself and another man. Sky had been the exception to that.

He had just turned away with the idea of going back to bed when he heard the beat of animal feet and hiss of buggy tires on street surfacing. His brows rose. That guard had sharp hearing. He listened as the sounds became louder. The driver of the buggy must be extremely anxious to get here. The buggy was hitched to a rapa. The swift one-two beat was nothing like the four-beat cadence of a rhino's gait. Jared peered back through the stone grill of the wall.

Moments later a covered two-wheeler, an outrider at the near wheel, swept through the gate and swung around to a halt at the temple door. Illumination from the candaglobe suspended in the portico showed both the buggy and outrider to be red with dust. On the rapa queen in the traces and the one carrying the outrider, lather had turned the dust to rusty mud. As they halted, both saurians dropped to their front legs and crouched with heads and tails drooping, sides working like bellows. The rasp of their breathing filled the courtyard. The guards approached the buggy with caution, but the rapas did not even hiss.

Jared had a brief vision of the lashing his mother would have given a ranch hand who abused an animal like this. It made him wince to think about. Someone must have wanted very much indeed to reach here. He strained to see who it might be.

The boots and breeches of the driver were visible, and a man's green knee-length tunic with trousers beneath on the passenger side. Jared had known there must be a man from the presence of the outrider. The clothing confirmed it, and its color, green—the color of peace and life—suggested his early visitor was an ecclesiastic. The face was hidden in the shadow of the buggy top, though, with only a suggestion of beard visible.

The outrider swung off her mount and said something short to the guards. The words were drowned out by the labored breathing of the rapas. One of the guards looked into the buggy. She offered the passenger her hand to help him down.

The face that came forward into the light was narrow and dark. Jared pressed his lips in a thin line. Raaman Midian. What was he doing back here? The Deacon was supposed to be visiting his family until after Thanksgiving.

Then the temple door opened and a stocky man stepped into the portico. That answered Jared's question. Forest Timna was ever Raaman's man. He had been here when the Gahan ranch station radioed of the Terrans found on their land. As a Deacon, of course Forest had learned about it almost immediately. He must have called Raaman as soon as Jared was out of the radio room. How many rapas had Raaman killed racing to be back here before the Terrans arrived?

Raaman stepped out of the buggy and into the por-

7

tico. He bent close to Forest, listening. He nodded, then the two went inside together.

The driver muttered something to the other women. The guards glanced toward the portico. One grimaced. The other went back to the gate. The remaining three women urged the rapas to their feet and off toward the stables.

Jared sprinted around the garden pool, through the doors into his sitting room, and across the sitting room to the outer door. He went up the corridor to a cross-corridor, and slowed to a walk just before intercepting Raaman and Forest.

The Deacons were startled to see him. After the first moment of wide-eyed surprise, Raaman quickly smoothed his expression into a bland mask, but Forest's eyes betrayed dismay.

Jared saw it with mixed satisfaction and anxiety. He liked confirming what he suspected, that Raaman had planned to appear without warning at the meeting with the Terrans. What worried him was, why? Raaman had hated him since Jared displaced Raaman as Aaron Methuselah's favorite to succeed to the Shepherd's office. He had been watching Jared with hungry eyes ever since. What did Raaman hope to accomplish that would discredit Jared?

Jared broke the silence first. "The Lord be with you, brothers."

Raaman managed a smile of greeting. "You're up early, Father."

"The noise of your queens blowing themselves to death woke me."

Raaman had grown up on a ranch, as Jared had. Jared watched Raaman's nostrils flare and knew his lean Deacon understood all the criticism expressed and implied in Jared's comment.

"It seemed to me to be of supreme importance to be here today."

Jared heard what Raaman left unspoken, too. Being back meant more than filial duty, more than sharing seed, more than his holiday, and certainly more than the lives of a few beasts whose only kinship with humans was that they both happened to be warm-blooded and live on Marah.

"Why was it left to Brother Forest to tell me about the Terrans?" Raaman's tone of puzzled hurt was masterful. Only the barest edge of his anger showed through.

Jared was tempted to reply that leaving it to Forest was the surest way he knew of keeping Raaman informed. He bit the words back. The momentary satisfaction of them was not worth starting open warfare with his Deacon. He had seen enough of cutthroat temple politics when Aaron Methuselah was Shepherd. Deacon election was this spring. Remaining polite now would make the intervening months more comfortable and simplify the process of replacing Raaman with a Deacon less hostile.

He made his voice placating. "I didn't call you because we aren't supposed to hold a formal meeting with the Terrans. The ceremonies will all be held in Eridu. We need to have them at ease so they will act natural while they're here and I can give the Bishop an accurate analysis of them."

Raaman's smile was righteous. "But you're so young, Father, and inexperienced, while these are violent, decadent people from a godless society. They may even be agents of Satan. You need the protection of your Deacons."

It was one thing to accept such a judgment from his spiritual superior, but quite another when a subordinate said it. Jared knew the duties of a Deacon often included telling a Shepherd just such facts, but hearing them galled just the same. Particularly from Raaman. When had Raaman last met Terrans? Jared wanted to ask. Who was Raaman to claim such expertise? Was it knowledge by Divine Revelation or only hand-me-down myths from their ancestors?

But he asked none of the questions. Jared bit down on his temper and smiled at Raaman. "I value your judgment and your concern, Brother Raaman; however, I don't want to converge on the Terrans with an assembly. There are only two of them and any suggestion of an inquisition will probably make them defensive. I can't have that."

Two spots of color darkened the skin across Raaman's cheekbones. "Then you're not going to use your Deacons for whatever insights they may have?"

"Of course I'll use you." Jared would take every opinion he could gather, even Raaman's. Despite his ambition, the man was highly intelligent, and an able Deacon. "I'd prefer to take Brother Levi to the first meeting, however. The rest of you will be introduced later, preferably one at a time in informal circumstances. They'll know everyone is curious. It would be suspicious not to let them meet you."

Forest Timna nodded, glancing sideways at Raaman.

Raaman, however, was not ready to surrender yet. "Whatever you judge best, but, Father, does it matter whom you take first? Brother Levi sleeps across town with his family, whereas Brother Forest, Brother Kaleb, and I are all here at the temple, at your service any hour of the day."

But Levi Dan had no vested interests at stake, no desire to help Jared make mistakes with the Terrans, and Levi was the oldest and most experienced man of them all. Jared was opening his mouth to give Raaman the last point as his excuse for the choice when a high whine stopped the words in his throat.

They all looked up, as if they could see through the ceiling. The flyer! The Terrans had arrived ahead of schedule. No time to send for Levi now. Jared started for the temple door.

"Father, your beard," Forest said.

Jared's hands went to his bare chin in dismay. He raced for his rooms. There was no time for a proper application. He spread on the thinnest possible coat of adhesive and pressed the beard into place. He took one more moment to peer at himself in the mirror, checking to be sure the beard was straight, ran his fingers through his hair so it would lie flat over his ears and neck, and slammed out of the room.

Raaman and Forest were in the portico well ahead of him, but the flyer was still settling the last few meters to the paving. He was in time after all.

Jared walked past his Deacons into the courtyard. The flyer's engines wrenched the air around the courtyard. The turbulence beat at Jared, flattening his tunic and trousers against his body, whipping his hair around his face into his eyes. He held on to his beard. The turbulence gradually faded as the whine of the engines wound down into silence.

A slit appeared in the flyer's side. It widened into a hatch and the interior lights switched on. Someone stepped out onto the wing and turned back to extend a hand.

That would be the pilot, Jared decided. He waited with held breath for the next person.

There were two. They came out one at a time and stepped off the wing onto the ground. They looked smaller than Jared had expected.

He began breathing again. The Terrans were not the giants he now realized he had been expecting, not monsters with horns and wings. They carried no awesome weapons, wore no outrageous, indecent clothes. They were only a few centimeters taller than himself, quite ordinary people, and plainly dressed in belted one-piece coveralls and short boots. They might not have looked alien at all but for their coloring. Except for the black curling cap of the woman's hair, they were the palest creatures Jared had ever seen, their skins and the man's hair albino-white, moon-white . . . death-white.

Jared forced himself not to stare. "The Lord be with you, brother," he said to the man. "I am Kedar Jared Cloud Joseph, Shepherd of Gibeon."

They came into the portico, and as the light of the candaglobe fell full on them, Jared felt his smile freeze. The woman had tired creases in her face, but the man—the man was little more than a boy, and his face sagged with a weariness not of exhaustion and was washed a muddy white. Jared felt his stomach knot.

The woman met his gaze with eyes green as a rapa's. "I'm Alesdra Pontokouros, liaison officer for the Intergalactic Communications ramjet *Galactic Rose*." Her words were hard to understand. The sounds were twisted, the rhythms subtly off. "This is Thors Kastavin. Is there a bed for him? I think he's fallen ill."

Ill. The knot in Jared's stomach went up into his chest and throat. The youth was not one of the lucky ones. Marah's curse had reached out for him, too. Jared's mouth was dry. The Terran was not just ill, he was dying.

Chapter Two

THE ROOM where they took Kastavin was spartan, with padded shelves for beds, globes of light supported in wall or table brackets, and chairs of animal hide woven in straps over or slung in wooden frames. The windows were narrow slits in the thick stone walls, running from the low ceiling to the carpeted floor.

Alesdra watched with relief the concern with which the three men put the boy to bed. This was a much better reception than she had been expecting. When those ranch hands rode Kastavin and her down to keep them away from the scout ship and then radioed for that flyer, she had wondered if the two of them were to be prisoners.

It was not an unheard-of reaction to strangers. There were several recorded instances of it in IGC's files. There were also worse findings: reports of colonists fallen into barbarism, of colonists even gone feral, of people hideously deformed by local mutagenic agents not detected by the unmanned bioprobes that discovered and analyzed the planet. There were stories, too, of croatoan colonies, disappeared without a trace. Ramjet crews never knew what could be waiting for them on a colony world.

Alesdra folded into one of the chairs. Her body ached as if this were a heavy- instead of light-gravity world. Invisible thumbs seemed to be pushing her eyes against the back of her skull. It made it difficult to concentrate on enough of the conversation the three men were having to follow it.

That was difficult anyway. She knew the old Terran language that the ancestors of this group had spoken, but five hundred Earth years of separation had given it new emphases, and different rhythms. She needed to pay close attention to understand anything of what they were saying.

It was an argument, low-voiced and with strained politeness, but an argument. She gathered they could not decide what to do with her.

"But, Father, women have never stayed in the actual temple," the stocky, red-brown man said. What was his name? Oh, yes,—Forest Timna.

"We've never had a visitor like this before, either," replied the yellow-brown one calling himself the Shepherd. He had light-brown, almost amber eyes. They slid anxiously toward her.

It went on. As the real point of the debate became clear, Alesdra was unsure whether to be annoyed or amused.

"Gentlemen," she said at last.

Their heads swiveled toward her.

She started to stand up but thought better of it. Her muscles seemed to have turned to low-test tissue paper. "I think we have a basic misunderstanding. I'm not here in a serving capacity to this boy. *I'm* the emissary. He's just a security officer riding shotgun for me. So as I see another bed over there, I'll stay in this room with Kasta-vin." She always tried to blend as much as possible with the local customs, but not to the extent it reduced her status of authority.

The men stared at her in openmouthed astonishment. *"You're*—but you're a *woman."*

"A *man* guarding a *woman?"* The thin man, the darkest of the three, looked as if she had uttered blasphemy.

"Mister—" What did she call this Midian Raaman Abram Midian? These people had a name system she had not figured out yet. The ranch hands' names had both started with Gahan, but they told her their names were something else, that Gahan was merely a family name.

The Shepherd came to her aid. "Brother Raaman is the customary address."

"Brother Raaman." Now she had forgotten what it was she was going to say. She looked at the Shepherd

13

instead. "Brother Jared, who is the highest authority in the colony?"

The other men winced at "Brother Jared" as the Shepherd answered: "The Bishop."

"Where can I find him?"

Raaman answered: "In Eridu, on the Sea of Tears. It's the large city up north on the equator. I'm surprised you didn't land there first."

She had not intended to make contact yet at all, only fly over. It was an accident that she and Kastavin had been caught down on the prairie. Seeing only three species of large land animals in the entire world had been too tempting; she had had to look at them from ground level. It was in coming back to the scout after looking that they had met those women . . . and come here.

"I need to see the Bishop. Can you arrange it?"

The Shepherd glanced at the other men. "The Bishop has been told you're here and will send for you when he's ready to see you."

She frowned. "When will that be?"

Damn. This was what came of messing up normal procedure. If the contact had been as usual, they would have made radio contact first, found out where authority was, and she, Captain Deyoe, and Constantine Melas, the technical crew foreman, would have gone down together in a delegation.

The Shepherd looked like a man feeling uncomfortable and trying not to show it. "The Bishop will want to present you to the Grand Council, I'm sure, and it's been recessed for Thanksgiving." He paused, obviously waiting for the next question.

She waited, too. He should not need to have her ask.

After a few moments, he went on: "Thanksgiving is a week away. The festival is three days long this year, then it will be another week before the solons are back in Eridu."

And in the meantime, no doubt, she was to remain a "guest" here. "Are any of the solons women?"

"Of course. We value the viewpoints of all members of Marahn society."

She regarded them thoughtfully. "But most are men?"

14

Forest said, "Certainly. It's the natural order of the universe for man to rule. It's the Lord's will."

She wondered what Captain Deyoe would think of that, or how the women of Hippolyte would react. For that matter, it irritated her, and most authority on Sahara had been male.

She closed her eyes. "I see. Thank you. I won't keep you any longer." She opened her eyes again. "There's just one more thing. Do any of you know what Kastavin and I might have?"

The instant shuttering of their faces told her they knew exactly what the disease was . . . and did not want to talk about it. Cold uneasiness trickled down her spine.

"Is it serious?"

The Shepherd shrugged. "It can be, but you'll probably feel fine in a few days."

Somewhere in the distance a clock chimed five and was quickly followed by a bell with a high, dinging tone. The Shepherd looked relieved.

"Brothers, we have morning prayers to say and today is a court day. Rest well, sister. I'll speak to you again later. When you're hungry, just ask anyone for directions to the kitchens."

He was gone, the other men following, before she could ask another question.

Alesdra stared after them, feeling exhausted. The bed beckoned to her. She remained in the chair, however, thinking. As liaison officer, all the responsibility of learning what the locals were and what made them that way was hers. She had had the decision of whether they even made contact taken out of her hands, but determining whether or not to offer the colonists a shuttlebox still rested with her. Space travel, even by ramjet, was a long, slow process. IGC had sent them a long way at great expense. She had to decide carefully before judging a planet, and this time, before she asked the captain and tech foreman down.

So what did she know so far? What they had *been* was members of a semi-fundamentalist, neo-Anglican religious sect, male-dominated, with strong back-to-the-soil and eco-conservationist beliefs as well. That much the charter application had told her. They had originally been well-educated, upper-middle-class people from several ethnic and racial groups. That probably accounted for the prevalence of dark hair and eyes among them and why their skins were all in shades of brown. She had noted with interest when she read the data on them that they had bought and crewed their own ramjet.

Given their origin, she was not surprised to find the men in firm control of a theocratic government. What puzzled her was that until she reached this temple, she had not seen a single man. The ranch hands were women, as was the pilot of the flyer. The pilot had made a side trip to a ranch station to pick up a woman in a difficult labor and bring her to the hospital across town before coming to the temple. Everyone Alesdra had seen at the ranch and the hospital was also female. Coming in, she had wondered if Marah were like Hippolyte, where women aborted all but a necessary few male pregnancies and kept their men in purdah. Now she knew that assumption was wrong, but where *were* the men?

The matter of the animal species made her uneasy, too. No planet had just three large land species. Those three could not begin to fill all the grazing, browsing, and predatory niches. There were thousands of species of birds, but what had happened to the other animals?

Kastavin had scoffed at her anxiety when she expressed it during the flyover. "What does that have to do with selling the colonists a shuttlebox?"

She had tried, and failed, to convince him it had everything to do with selling a shuttlebox. In liaison training a nineteenth-century poem had been drummed into them. "All things by immortal power/Near or far/Hiddenly/To each other linked are/That thou canst not stir a flower/Without the troubling of a star." Were the missing animals, were the missing men flowers or stars?

She popped the front of her belt buckle loose and turned it up to reveal two flat dials and a speaker diaphragm on the inner surface. She extended the antenna telescoped in one end.

"Pontokouros to *Rose*." It was a relief to shift back to the clean simplicity of Translan.

16

An answer came back promptly in the amused drawl of Dal Leboyne, the daywatch bridge officer. "You mean you haven't been eaten yet?"

She grinned. "Sorry to disappoint you."

"It isn't me. If anything happened to you, I could get stuck with liaison work. After that garbled transmission you sent a few hours ago Connie Melas and his *Wunderkinder* were ready to pile into a shuttle and set off on a rescue mission. I agreed with them in spirit; we're such a small group we can't afford to lose you or that pretty muscleboy, but after the skipper went into an I-am-god act and confined the lot of them to quarters, I was glad I didn't get involved. What *are* you doing—making early contact, sitting in jail, or what?"

"Or what. We're being treated well. Connie will be happy to know I've seen several portable communicators—not as compact as ours but still effective—and a very nice VTOL flyer. The natives have the capacity for high technology even though they seem to restrict its use."

Connie Melas' biggest fear was that his holy mission to unite the worlds of the galaxy would be blocked by colonies that lacked the ability to produce the high, steady source of power a shuttlebox needed.

Another voice came over the communicator, Captain Deyoe's. "What's going on, Ponto?"

Alesdra told her. The skipper's interested grunts punctuated the account. At the end, the captain said, "Well, I'm glad you're all right."

Alesdra pressed a hand to her aching head. "Whole, anyway. We're both sick, though."

"Do you want Doc?"

Alesdra stiffened. "No." She lowered her voice so Kastavin would not hear if he were awake. "The local shaman closed up like a blast door when I asked what was wrong with us, and then went right on to assure me it's nothing. Let's not let another person come down, not even for a look around the uninhabited continents, until I know more. The bioprobe may have missed something serious."

"Quite possibly. Very well, no one else comes down under any circumstances until you clear it. Keep me informed."

Leboyne's voice came on. "Take care of yourself, Ponto, and the kid."

She glanced toward Kastavin. "I'll try. Abermarle and I survived five contacts. I'd feel terrible if I lost Kastavin on his first planetfall."

She telescoped the antenna with a snap and clipped the communicator back on her buckle. Then she pushed up out of the chair to walk over to Kastavin. It was an effort to move. He was breathing in regular, shallow breaths. His color looked terrible but was probably not much worse than hers. While she was looking at him, he opened his eyes.

She smiled at him. "Hello. Have you been awake or asleep?"

His answering smile was weak. "Asleep mostly." His forehead wrinkled. "I didn't do a very good job of protecting you, did I?"

"A sleeper has never been a very effective weapon against bacteria."

He considered that. "No, but I didn't have to freeze when that animal charged and let myself be disarmed. If I'd used the sleeper on those women we could be back on board the ship by this time."

"Infecting everyone aboard. It's just as well we didn't make it back to the scout."

The creases in his forehead deepened. "Do you think it's that bad?"

Alesdra put on an offhand manner. She shrugged. "The Shepherd said we'd be all right in a few days, but one of my prime rules is never trust a shaman. How do you feel?"

"Made of jelly."

"Me, too. I'm going to see if I can find out more about this. You rest. I'll be back soon."

A very few minutes later, Alesdra was wondering if she would be able to find her way back. The temple was a labyrinth. She would never have believed a single building could be so complex. Corridors ran in every direction, and all looked alike with their walls of glossy, red marblelike stone and floors of bright mosaic tile. Courtyards appeared in her path without warning, with sundials in the center, or pools and sweet-smelling trees, or a swimming pool and game courts. One was built around a weathered stone statue. The translucent ivory of the stone and the style of the sculpture were so strikingly different from the solidity of the square-set red temple around it, Alesdra paused to stare.

She did not think it was intended to represent a human, though it was humanoid. It was abnormally slender for its height, almost delicate, almost childlike in its softness of line. The narrow face was all curves, brow into cheek into short, broad nose over soft, full mouth. The eyes looked as if they would have seemed wide and surprised if open, but the sculptor had chosen to create them with drooping lids, so the statue stared off dreamily through the spicy-smelling air, one three-fingered hand smoothing the oblique folds of the garment wrapping its torso. Alesdra wondered what fanciful vision had inspired its creator, and how it had come to occupy a place better held by one of those saint's statues, as on Earth. The dreaming face told her nothing, so presently she went on.

Not long after, Alesdra wandered through a half-open door and found herself confronted with the most incredible sight she had ever seen. She was in a library, a huge room lined from floor to ceiling with shelves filled by real books. Tables around the room were stacked with news sheets and periodical-like publications, but it was the books that captivated her. Books were such a joy, so *solid* and touchable compared to microfiches.

She was taking one of the books down from its place when a green-clad youth about Kastavin's age found her.

He regarded her with wide eyes for a moment, then said, "Are you one of the Terrans?"

She was no more Terran than he. She was second-generation Saharan and proud of it, but he would never have heard of Sahara, nor Kastavin's Nova Scandia, nor Arete, where IGC had its main offices, for that matter. So agreeing was easier than explaining, and she nodded.

"What's Earth like?"

Alesdra sighed. Standard Question One. She had never found the best answer. Perhaps some comparisons would satisfy him. "It's bigger than Marah but colder and more crowded. There's just one moon while the sun is whiter but smaller. The days are longer." That short Marahn day gave these people 382 days to 318 Earth days and crowded thirteen months into ten and a half Earth months . . . a long-sounding year that would virtually fly by. "Can you tell me where the Shepherd is?"

"Tuesday is court day. He's in the tabernacle."

That sounded like a church. When she followed the directions the youth gave her, she ended up somewhere that looked like a church, too, long and narrow with rows of benches and a broad altar on a raised dais at the far end. The only suggestion of a courtroom was the Shepherd and Deacons sitting behind the altar talking to two women who sat before them in chairs facing each other.

Alesdra stood at the back of the tabernacle, interested but afraid to sit down for fear she would not be able to get up again. If this were a courtroom, it was a very informal one. There seemed to be no lawyers for either side. The accused faced the witnesses for and against her while everyone on the dais—the Shepherd, the four Deacons, and the accused—took turns examining the witnesses. Everyone freely suggested lines of questioning to everyone else. The witnesses never hesitated to volunteer information nor to protest at having to answer some questions.

Alesdra watched three cases before leaving. The corridor outside ended in three sets of tall double doors that opened onto a broad courtyard filled with people, bicycles, and animals ridden and driven. Excitement rose in her, washing out some of the dragging weakness. This was what she liked best in her job, sitting somewhere central while the world went about the business of daily living. The streets and markets of a planet were where one learned about a people, not in the sterile corridors of its government. She leaned against one of the doors to watch the traffic.

Most of the people were women. Some of them were small but most, like the ranch hands she had seen yesterday, tall and muscular. The few men were about the same height but more slender, as well as longer-haired and more meticulously groomed. She saw many styles of clothing, but the men seemed to favor long tunics and wide trousers while the women wore shirts or short jackets and narrow pants. Many wore the boots and breeches of ranch hands. They streamed in and out of the temple, talking with each other, inquiring information of temple stewards at the door, pausing to read the notes and news sheets tacked to a huge public notice board.

Then, near the gate a bicycle cut in front of a copper-brown creature walking on its hind legs. It was like the animals the ranch hands had ridden the day before. It hissed and reached for the cyclist with a wide jaw full of terrible teeth. Trying to duck away, the cyclist over-turned her cycle and fell under the wheels of a buggy pulled by a triple-horned gray quadruped so thick-hided it looked armored. Alesdra had seen vast herds of the same species all over the grasslands of Marah's four major continents. The buggy driver hauled her animal to a stop with the wheel just short of the cyclist's head.

With a hiss, the biped now directed its attack on the quadruped. The quadruped retaliated by charging with head tilted so it could put all three horns into the other animal.

The melee lasted several minutes while the driver and rider shouted profanities at each other and beat their animals apart. It was a close contest. The biped moved with blurring swiftness, but for all its ponderous appearance, the quadruped was remarkably agile. It stayed away from both the teeth and vicious rear claws of the attacker and even scored once with its nose horn.

They looked reptilian but could not be, Alesdra decided. They were too quick, too active, for cold-blooded animals. They had to be endotherms. Incredible.

The fact of saurians did not amaze her. After all, dinosaurs had been tremendously successful for a long time on Earth, but why were there only three species? What were they, flowers . . . or stars?

Someone snorted near her. She looked sideways to see two bearded men in green watching the argument.

"Rapas don't belong in town," one said in disgust. "When are women going to learn that? We tell them and tell them. Rapas will go after rhinos and people every time."

21

"She should at least have it muzzled."

"Well, she'll be fined for that oversight, at least. Here comes a keeper."

A woman wearing a yellow tunic with a green triangular patch on the shoulder pushed her way into the crowd along with one of the guards from the gate. She reached the middle and began talking to the driver and rider. There was a great deal of pointing at one combatant and the other, some waving of arms, more pointing. The keeper listened, asked a few questions, then wrote on a pad she pulled from a pocket. She tore off the page and gave it to the rapa's rider.

The rider argued, but the keeper listened unmoved. After a minute, she walked away and left the rider protesting after her.

Only then did Alesdra realize that the cause of all the hubbub was missing. Sometime in the excitement the cyclist had picked up her machine and sneaked away.

Alesdra grinned. Planets might be different from one another, but people were not.

She wandered away from the doors back toward the tabernacle, and looked in. The Shepherd was adjourning court.

"Shandan Laila Rain Meran has appealed her verdict. She will be judged by public hearing on the afternoon of the second Thursday of November. Persons willing to serve as jurors will present themselves for impaneling at midday. Court is adjourned for this morning. The Lord be with you."

He picked up a crook-topped staff and walked down the long aisle out of the tabernacle, followed by the four Deacons. He stopped when he saw Alesdra. She had the impression it was an effort for him to smile.

"The Lord be with you, sister. Are you feeling better?"

"No," she replied, "but I'm more concerned about Kastavin. Will you please send for a doctor?"

She had been expecting the sudden rigidity that froze the Shepherd's features. What she wondered about was a gleam of satisfaction that appeared in the lean Deacon's eyes.

The Shepherd took her arm. "Come this way."

He pulled her down the corridor away from the

22

others into a benched alcove. He sat down and motioned for her to sit beside him. He looked down at hands folded around his staff.

"No healer or surgeon can help the man."

She bit her lip. "You mean you lied to me before?"

"Not exactly." He rubbed a thumb over a knob on the staff. "I said *you* would recover."

She digested that for a moment, growing cold. "What about Kastavin?"

He rubbed hard at the knob. "Not all men die. Some have a natural resistance. The disease is caused by a virus that turns one of the male hormones poisonous. There's no cure. We'll just have to wait. If the boy is stronger tomorrow, we'll know he's developing the resistance. If he's weaker . . ."

Alesdra thought of the courtyard full of women, of the ranch and hospital, staffed by women. Her throat felt dry. "Just exactly how many men do live?"

Now he looked up, meeting her eyes. "There were four hundred men on the ramjet that brought my ancestors here. Within two weeks after they landed, all but seventeen men were dead." He paused, struggling with something. "About ninety percent of our boys die as they reach puberty," he added.

There was a fine medical library back on the ship. "Let me take Kastavin back to the ship. Maybe we can help him there."

"*No.*" The Shepherd half-stood in his alarm. He sat back down. "You'll infect everyone. All of Marah is contaminated. Everything that breathes and doesn't die of the disease carries it: birds, saurians, reptiles, everything. You'll take it back to your ship."

Alesdra leaned back against a wall. It felt cold behind her. A world that breathed death. So that was where all the species had gone. Only the non-mammals survived.

"Where could the virus have come from?" she asked.

The Shepherd frowned at his staff. "We think the pre-Marahns engineered it for a weapon, only it turned on the makers, too."

Pre-Marahns? Oh . . . the statue in the courtyard. It was more than just a fanciful sculpture, then. The planet had been inhabited! The statue was an artifact.

23

Alesdra could have shaken herself. She had looked straight at that statue and never realized the significance of it. But could she really be blamed? She had never expected to find aliens here; humankind had met only one other race so far. Even in her distress she reflected it was a pity archeologists could not come here.

"If you had made radio contact before landing we could have warned you not to land. Now the boy will probably die here and you'll have to stay, too." His amber eyes were frightened.

A faint complaining whine in her—stay *here?*—stopped. She did not have to stay. The shuttlebox could put them in touch with the most advanced medical research facilities in the galaxy. Surely *they* could cure the disease so she could leave.

Alesdra thought of Kastavin, though, and felt her stomach knot unhappily. Not even the shuttlebox could help Kastavin. She was not looking forward to telling him.

Chapter Three

KASTAVIN TOOK the news hard. Alesdra told him everything, including the progress the disease would take, as outlined to her by the Shepherd. She felt Kastavin had a right to know the truth, to prepare for death with what dignity he could muster.

"Oh, no," he whispered. "Oh, no. It can't be true. It isn't. No, no, no, no."

Her heart twisted in her chest. It had to be a terrible thing to be so young and suddenly have no more future. She wondered if she had been wrong to tell him. Perhaps she should have lied, told him the weakness was a self-limiting thing and would improve eventually, fed him on hope until his mind was too dim for him to care any longer.

In the days that followed, though, watching him die, she decided she could not have lied. He would have guessed, and then, robbed of an outlet for talking about his fear, had to die completely alone.

It was hard staying with him. As he weakened and the creeping paralysis robbed him of more movement each day, the fear in his eyes approached panic. She felt helpless. She wished with despair either for help or for a quick death for him.

Sometimes his outward reaction was not terror but anger, anger at her, at his superiors on the *Rose,* at Dion Abermarle. "If Abermarle hadn't fallen in love with that girl on Schön and quit the crew to stay with her, he'd be here instead of me. He should be dying, not me. I'm too young. I should have a whole life left to live."

Or he begged for help. Those were the worst days. "Ponto, I'm scared. This can't be happening to me. Why is everyone just standing around? Do something to help me, please. Do *something.*"

All she could do was sit down on the sleeping shelf and take him in her arms, letting her nearness and warmth comfort him if it would. He clung to her like a child while he still had the strength. Later he just buried his head against her and cried.

She reported to the *Rose.* That helped her mood even less.

Constantine Melas swore at the news. He swore at the bioprobes. He swore at her. "Virus. Toxic androgens. Damn it, Ponto, if you'd just made a flyover as planned and not gotten out to go for a walk—if you'd made radio contact before you landed—"

The right to decide to land had been hers. She accepted the responsibility for the mistake, even though she felt she could hardly have been expected to suspect a disease like this from the available evidence. But she saw nothing to be gained from arguing about it. She let him yell on and made no attempt to defend herself.

Captain Deyoe's reaction disturbed her more. The captain sighed. "That's it, then." Her voice was resigned. "We have to pack our toys and go on."

Alesdra argued with that. "Don't leave yet. The virologists we can bring in could find these bugs and wipe them out. I'll be seeing the top man about the shuttlebox in another week. At least wait until then to leave."

"There's the problem of building the box, Ponto," the captain pointed out. "I don't think I have to remind you that half the tech crew are male."

"I'm not letting any of my crew down on that death trap, not men or women," Melas said.

Alesdra hissed in exasperation. "Captain, Connie, will the two of you please listen a minute? I'm not suggesting this blindly. My desire to leave hasn't interfered with my judgment. I've visited the library and read everything in it on this virus. The virus isn't indestructible; in fact, it can't live outside the body for more than fifteen minutes under the most favorable conditions. Almost anything will kill it: UV light, heat, cold, vacuum. The disease is spread only by breathing.

"We're mostly supervisors on these projects anyway, with the locals supplying the main labor. We should be able to rig telecommunications so as much direction as possible can be done from the ship. Supervisors who have to come down can wear life-supports and go through vacuum or a UV bath before reboarding the ship."

There was no immediate reply. She hoped that indicated they were considering the possibility.

She tossed in another argument. "At least give me a chance to avoid having to spend the rest of my life among a pack of amazons and their pampered studs."

"You still won't be able to leave with the *Rose*. Our new destination and the parts for the new shuttlebox will come through the shuttlebox here almost as soon as it's built. You'll have to remain until the disease is cured."

"But I'll be able to leave eventually, and IGC can put me on a new ship."

There was a long silence. Alesdra knew it was a radio silence only. Up on the *Rose* a great deal of fast talking was going on. The captain would be asking Connie's opinion. Connie was probably consulting his crew. Alesdra sat watching Kastavin whimper in his sleep and waited with fearful impatience for their answer.

After what seemed like eternity, Captain Deyoe came back. "Ponto? Connie's kids think it can be done. They want to try, anyway. You sell the shuttlebox and they'll work on a safe way to build it."

Alesdra sighed with relief. She might have been elated, too, but it was hard to feel any kind of real satisfaction with Kastavin dying by millimeters beside her.

Chapter Four

JARED WATCHED the boy die, too. Everything he could see of Alesdra's attitude showed him she was upset about the disease, but did not hold the Marahns responsible to the point she or her shipmates would want to avenge the boy's death. Nevertheless, Jared could not shake a certain uneasiness, and the progress of the disease itself also filled him with cold horror. He knew he was not obligated to take part in the deathwatch; that was a woman's duty. If he had needed an excuse not to, he could have claimed to be busy preparing for the rituals and ceremonies of Thanksgiving. But he was drawn to Kastavin by a fascination he could no more explain than he could resist.

He visited the Terrans' room every day with obsessive punctuality. He could not understand the boy's language, but he read Kastavin's expression very well. The terror he saw there reminded him of his own preadolescent days. With less luck, this could have been Jared.

He still remembered when his older brother was brought home from Middle School. Talmon had been put in their mother's room, though, and remained there until he died. Jared had not been allowed to see him.

Of the family children, only the girls had been allowed to visit. Jared looked at Kastavin and wondered, Was this what Talmon went through?

He tried to shrug off the question. Of course neither Talmon nor any other Marahn boy experienced what Kastavin was feeling. It was different now. Aaron Methuselah himself had reassured Jared the process was painless. Of course, Aaron might never have seen a boy die. Jared never had before, not as a student in Middle School nor as a teacher there. The boys were always sent home as soon as they showed the first signs. Aaron might only have been repeating what he himself had been told. He might also—the thought came too swiftly for Jared to shut it out—have lied.

Jared felt a choking constriction around his throat. He pulled open the collar of his tunic. He was usually careful to keep certain memories pushed down out of reach, just as he refused to think any more than necessary about some things he had learned. Now, however, he took one memory out—gingerly, reluctantly—and examined it.

It had been a November nearly ten years ago that Aaron Methuselah had asked Jared to accompany him on a drive out of town. They had parked the buggy, then commanded the outrider and driver to remain behind while the two men walked out onto the prairie. It was a windy day, Jared remembered. Their tunics flattened against their bodies and their hair blew around their eyes. Jared had kept touching his beard to make sure it stayed in place.

Aaron stopped well out of hearing of the women. Jared remembered the former Shepherd vividly. He had been a big man, nearly a head taller than any other man or woman in Gibeon. His brown coloring was infused with golden light. Even his eyes were gold.

He turned to look across the winter-brown land toward the blue northern horizon. "To be a man on Marah is a great responsibility." The wind carried away the words so that Jared had to strain to hear. "To be a leader, a man among men, is to bear burdens that break the body and try the soul." He looked down, his golden eyes seeing deep into Jared. "Are you man enough to be a leader, Jared? Can you accept the will of the Lord

28

without questioning, no matter how cruel it may seem? Do you believe that even the dying serve the Lord?"

Jared had known something important was about to happen. The temple was awhisper with rumors. The most popular seemed to be that Aaron Methuselah was going to back Jared for Deacon in the upcoming election. Jubilation boiled up through Jared now. The rumors must be true. Why else would the Shepherd be preparing to tell him ecclesiastic secrets?

Jared looked up at Aaron. "I believe, Father."

"I don't have to tell you the story of our ancestors' landing on this world. I will remind you, though, that it was Divinely revealed to David Moses in the year 105 that the slaughter of men had not been punishment but was the Lord's way of revealing how we were to build our society."

Jared nodded. Everyone knew that.

"What you have never been told before is that at the same time it was also revealed to him how to maintain the necessary male minority."

Jared's brows went up. "The disease does that."

"No . . . it doesn't," Aaron said. "By the fourth generation the immunity of those first seventeen men had bred through the population. The disease no longer killed anyone."

"Then"—Jared frowned—"what does?"

Aaron had not answered immediately.

Jared's mouth went dry. "What *does?*"

The remembered voice, deep and rich, boomed down through the years to Jared the Shepherd with echoes of brass. "We do."

Jared had stood stunned and horrified while Aaron explained how the ritual killing was carried out. David Moses had found a drug—it was never to be called a poison—which mimicked the signs of the disease. Every year the Bishop worked out the figures and told the local Shepherds how many boys must die in each parish to keep the male population at ten percent of the total. The drug was then administered randomly, perhaps once a week, one or two or three doses at a time, throughout the school year. It was given in the glasses of drink put out for the students at lunch.

"Which is why teachers are forbidden to take drinks from the student tray and why even boys who live in town are required to eat the noon meal at the temple," Aaron said.

Jared was speechless. This was the most monstrous thing he had ever heard. He looked up at Aaron. Incredibly, the Shepherd looked gilded and benevolent as ever. His golden eyes were wise and kind. He put gentle hands on Jared's shoulders and turned him to face out over the prairie.

"Keep your back to the women. Don't let them see your distress."

"*Distress?*" Jared managed to say. His voice was a grating gasp. "I'm not distressed, I'm—"

"Shocked? Horrified? Of course. So was I when I was first told. But stand back and consider. This was revealed by a Divine vision. It's the Lord's will, and the boys, who serve Divine purpose by dying, are twice loved in Paradise for their sacrifice. It's a painless, humane death. That I assure you. The boys just sink through increasing weakness into eternal sleep."

What shook Jared to the soul was realizing that this had been going on all the time he was in Middle School, all the time he taught at the temple, and he had never suspected. He thought suddenly of the times he had almost taken a glass from the student tray, thinking the prohibition made no sense. He shuddered at the memory.

"How—how many men know about this?"

"Very few. Not even all the Deacons know. It isn't knowledge we can trust to everyone; so few men have faith enough to bear it." His eyes bored into Jared. "Do you believe this is the Lord's will?"

How could such a barbaric practice ever be Divine?

But before Jared could open his mouth to say that, Aaron went on, "Because if you do . . . if you are man enough to take the responsibility of this knowledge, strong enough to act on faith, it will be your duty this year to administer the drug."

Jared's breath stuck painfully in the middle of his chest. No, oh, no, not him! "Father, I—"

"Don't decide now. Think about it. Remember, you aren't hurting anyone. You only drug the drinks. No one dies but as the Lord wills. If He desired everyone to live, the drug couldn't harm anyone. Reread Paul's episode with the snake in Acts 28 this evening." Aaron paused. "I'm placing a great faith in you, Jared. If you can't accept this responsibility, you may be man enough to teach, perhaps even to be a short-term Deacon, but you can never fully serve . . . and you'll never be man enough to be Shepherd." He paused again. "So think before you answer, my beloved son. Think carefully."

Remembering now, Jared wondered how the disease could be mimicked and not be at least psychologically painful. If all these generations the boys felt what Kastavin did, there was certainly mental anguish of the worst kind. How, then, could it be called painless, or humane?

With those questions eating at him, Jared watched Alesdra nurse the boy with tender patience. She was endlessly cheerful around Kastavin, optimistic and loving. Away from him, though, she was an angry, bitter virago.

She cornered Jared in his garden on the Sabbath eve. "I can't believe you've just let this go on generation after generation." Her green eyes flared like an angry rapa's.

He retreated around the pool. She followed him. How had she found him here? he wondered. How did she dare come into his private rooms uninvited? He considered walking out but there seemed to be nowhere in the temple he could escape from her if not here. No Marahn woman would have been so disrespectful. The men of Earth must keep very poor control of their women.

"We haven't just let it go on," he protested. A plump red satan fruit had fallen on the paving. He kicked it out of his path. A whiff of spicy sweetness rose to him from it. "The first generations tried to find a cure and failed. That's why they named the planet Marah. Marah is Hebrew for 'bitter.' "

"Did they even find out why the resistance of those surviving men didn't breed through the rest of the population?"

Ice chunked up in Jared's gut. What could he answer to that and not lie? "As the Lord will, so things are."

31

This was how society must be, many women ruled by a few men. It had been Divinely shown and the insight handed down from Shepherd to Shepherd for nearly five hundred years. It must be true. Jared believed that firmly; he had to.

Alesdra spat a short word. Her use of the Marahn language seemed to improve hourly, but in stress or anger, as now, she fell back into her own tongue. She took a breath and said in his language, "Do you really believe some supernatural force maneuvered the pre-Marahns into creating that virus and setting it loose? Nonsense. It's no more a result of Divine will than any other senseless killing in war."

If it were not Divine will, it was murder. Jared took refuge in cant. "Who is Man to say what shape the Lord's plans may take? It might be that this planet was scoured clean just for us, and that we are now being tested by fire before being allowed to build our new Eden here."

Her look should have cremated him on the spot. "Do your women believe that? I'm only fond of Kastavin, yet I feel like I'm being torn apart inside. If he were my son, I'd lose my mind. I can't believe that thousands of women every year suffer through this and still think that any god could want it."

Jared never thought of the mothers, and he avoided thinking of them now. "That's because you don't have the strength or faith our women do. They know the Lord will sustain and succor them no matter how heavy the burdens He gives them to bear."

She repeated the curse again and spun away from him.

He scowled after her. What an exasperating female. Why did he lower himself to arguing with her? He was a man, and a Shepherd. He had no need to be defensive. "The virus exists and our boys die," he said. "What should we do, let it break us, or bury our dead and our grief and go on?"

She turned back, smiling. She was a handsome woman, Jared suddenly realized, very attractive in her own pale-skinned, alien way. Her green eyes were as fascinating as they were unique. "Now that's an honest answer, and one I can stomach. But I'm sure there's a cure. It's only a matter of having the means to find it. IGC can provide the means."

"A machine?" She had mentioned the shuttlebox a number of times in the past days. "My ancestors left Earth to escape machines."

She arched a brow. "You have machines on Marah, too, and I notice you don't hesitate to use *them* when you need them."

He could not deny that. He shrugged. "Very well." He sat down on a bench. "How can a machine help us?"

This was more than curiosity, he reassured himself. He was not being seduced by Terran gadgetry. This was information to pass on to the Bishop.

Alesdra sat down beside him. "The shuttlebox makes it possible to communicate with any other planet that also has a shuttlebox. The trouble with space travel is it's slow and expensive, and mostly one-way, thanks to time dilation. The shuttlebox eliminates space travel."

He blinked. "How can it do that?"

"The space inside a shuttlebox—or Equipotential Transfer Portal, if you want IGC's terminology—has potential identical at every point to the potential at the same points in another box. We use generators which produce—well, call it a sixth force. Our technical crew foreman can explain all about lines of thermonuclear flux and the like but I won't try. What it amounts to is, we have two boxes which are exactly alike in every respect, except location, and since they're *exactly* alike, they're essentially the same box. If you climb into one, you can step out of the other."

Jared found what she had said highly improbable. He frowned. "It sounds more like magic than technology."

She looked at him a moment. "Magic is in the eye of the beholder."

She stood and walked into the temple. He heard a drawer open. A moment later she reappeared carrying a candaglobe.

"Do you consider this magic?"

He frowned. "Of course not." Candalight was simple chemical reaction.

She set the globe on the coping of the pool and sat

33

down beside him again. In the darkening evening, the globe glowed with gentle yellow light. "There are worlds where cold light would be considered magic."

"But we just copied the process the candalilies use."

"And the shuttlebox lets us move people and merchandise instantly from one planet to another. And that's how we can help save lives here." She turned, leaning toward him. Her voice was rich with urgency. "With a shuttlebox, you could bring in the finest medical minds in the galaxy to find a cure for your disease."

Jared bit his lip. What they would find was that no one on Marah could possibly be dying of the disease.

Her words echoed in his mind long after she had gone back to tend Kastavin. They haunted him through the evening and as he went to bed. They even followed him into sleep.

He dreamed he was Kastavin. He was slowly choking to death because his lungs were too weak to work. The door opened and Alesdra and his twin sister Sky walked in, dragging a huge trunk.

Kiri Sky! His heart jumped joyfully. He tried to call her name and sit up to hug her, but he could not move.

They set the trunk beside his sleeping shelf and opened it. Out climbed a score of healers and surgeons.

"Is this the victim?"

They poked at him. He tried to protest but he was too weak even to talk. He could only lie motionless while they prodded and thumped.

"Can you help him?" Alesdra asked.

The healers and surgeons stood straight and backed into a neat row. Their faces folded into scowls.

"We can't help him," one said.

"Because he isn't ill," said another.

"We find no sign of illness."

"He's a fake."

"A fake."

"A fake."

"A fake."

Suddenly Raaman, Forest, Kaleb, and Levi appeared, wearing long robes that looked like Testament illustrations. "Will you give him to me, then?" Raaman asked.

Raaman was looking not at the healers, but at a man

34

in the doorway. Jared managed to turn his head enough to see. His breath caught. The man was . . . himself.

"Take him," he said.

Jared stood in his own skin in the doorway, watching the Deacons drag Kastavin out of bed. They gave him to the healers, who now wore the crested helmets and metal cuirasses of old Roman armor. They led Kastavin away.

Jared turned and walked out into his garden.

The garden had changed. It had become a roof garden, and instead of a wall, it had a low parapet. Beyond it he could see the skyline of a biblical city. Looking over the edge, he saw the soldiers hurry Kastavin out into the dusty street below.

Behind him, Sky's voice said, "That man is innocent. Have nothing to do with this."

Jared watched the soldiers. He was amazed by them. Imagine, *men* doing guard and keeper duty. "As the Lord wills, so let it be," he said.

Then, from the midst of the guards, the prisoner looked up, and instead of Kastavin's face, Jared saw a pale, gentle face, infinitely sad beneath its crown of thorns.

Jared woke with sweat cold on his forehead and temples. He sat up on his sleeping shelf, hugging his knees. His heart was pounding. *Pilate?* He shuddered. Merciful Lord, whatever had brought him to dream of himself as Pontius Pilate?

It was while he sat there shivering and searching his soul for enlightenment that a temple page slipped into the room and, seeing him awake, announced in a quiet voice that the Terran man had died.

Chapter Five

JARED SAID RITES over Kastavin's body on Thanksgiving eve, after the Sabbath evening Praying, and stood with his Deacons and Alesdra while the body was cremated. As he waited through the ritual, Jared regretted not having been able to speak the boy's language and not having offered any real comfort to him. He wondered if he even knew how to comfort Alesdra. She stood stiff and dry-eyed, and when he touched her arm, she moved a step away.

She wanted to scatter the ashes on the prairie. Jared had a temple steward hunt up a driver and an outrider to hitch a rhino to a buggy and drive them out of town. As the rhino trotted its slow way down a road lined by the pale glow of candalilies, Jared tried to talk to Alesdra, but she answered only in monosyllables.

"Isn't there anything I can do for you?" he finally asked.

"You stopped being able to do anything for me when your people gave up trying to fight this damned virus of yours."

He sighed. That again. "We didn't give up, we—"

"You gave up. I've read about it in the library. After three generations, when you were still fighting the other elements of the planet just to survive from day to day, your ancestors gave up. So now Kastavin's dead and I'm an involuntary guest for god knows how long."

An intake of breath told Jared the driver was listening with amazement. Rather than treat the woman to a scene of another woman being disrespectful and getting away with it, Jared fell silent.

He let the buggy continue until they were several

kilometers from town, then called for the driver to halt. With a beam from a tube of candalight picking out a path before them, he and Alesdra walked away from the road onto the prairie. The outrider started to follow.

"Wait here," he commanded.

"But—yes, Father."

They walked to the top of a knoll. There, Alesdra uncapped the funeral urn and spread the ashes on the wind in the broadcasting motions of a farmer sowing seed.

"It should be over water," she said. "He loved water. His father was a sea captain on Nova Scandia. He used to tell us about growing up on the ship."

When she finished, she recapped the urn, but made no move to return to the buggy. Instead, she stood looking up at the night sky. Jared followed her eyes to the tiny bright light of her ship arching overhead. He tried to imagine how it would feel to be forbidden to ever return to his family's ranch. How terrible it must be for her to see home when it was inaccessible.

She must have seen him watching her. Her attention shifted to the moons. They were silver ellipses, Tagalong in transit across Nightseye's face.

"You do have beautiful moons." Her voice had lost its anger. She sounded as if she felt she needed to find something good in Marah.

She turned back toward the buggy. They rode to town in peaceful silence.

The peace did not last, for him. He dreamed of himself as Pilate again. He woke shaking, to spend the rest of the night pacing his garden. It was an early beginning for a day which began early anyway. Thanksgiving First Day was filled with ceremony, from the dawn Praying to a blessing of family men and a passage ritual for eighteen-year-old boys who had survived puberty, to the First Day Praying in late afternoon.

He usually liked ritual. He loved the rhythm of chanting, the patterns of countering voices. Today, however, there was little pleasure in it. His flawless recitations were said by rote. And today the Litany of Thanksgiving almost choked him.

"For drought, and famine, and barren herds . . ."

"PRAISE THE LORD," replied the congregation.

The tabernacle was full. Looking out over the rows of heads, he reflected that twice a year, at least, Prayings were well attended, the two or three days of Thanksgiving and the three days of New Year's in the spring.

"For temptations that strengthen, and sorrows that teach . . ."

"PRAISE THE LORD."

"For pestilence, and death . . ." Jared almost spat that one.

He saw his Deacons glance curiously at him.

"PRAISE THE LORD."

"For travail, and tribulation . . ." He wondered what Alesdra was doing. He hoped she was all right.

"PRAISE THE LORD."

"For the tests of fire, and trying of souls . . ."

"PRAISE THE LORD."

"As the Lord wills . . ."

"SO LET IT BE."

Kaleb Eshban took over the last prayer. Jared finished with "The Lord be with you," and it was over. He led the Deacons out up the aisle. Outside he turned his Shepherd's staff over to a steward so he could go mix with the Gibeonites setting up the First Day Feast in the courtyard.

That was the real event of the day. Most people in town and from the nearby farms and ranches came, all bringing food. Ten long tables sagged with the bounty.

The Deacons broke away to join the festive crowd in the courtyard, even Raaman, after a narrow-eyed look at Jared. Levi Dan, though, stayed near and, after a few minutes, edged Jared aside.

"You look troubled and tired, Father."

Jared looked into the wise dark eyes that so often seemed troubled themselves. "I haven't slept well for several nights."

Levi's forehead creased in concern. "You've been too involved with this Terran boy's death. I think you've seen more of the woman than is wise, as well."

"I'm trying to learn as much as I can about her people."

"A few casual talks would have served that purpose. It's no reason to have made daily calls on the boy."

Jared shrugged helplessly. "I couldn't seem to stop myself."

Levi laid a hand on Jared's arm. "In that kind of temptation lies madness." His voice was haunted.

A chill washed over Jared. "You know, too, then? You've seen it? You know the dying isn't as we've been told?"

"I know. I'm still a family man. I've stood by the sisterwives and watched Roshdan boys die for fifteen years."

"And you've just continued here at the temple year after year? How do you bear it?"

Levi's voice lowered. "Remember this is a public court, Father."

Jared glanced around. No one appeared to be paying attention to them. "Let's go to my rooms."

"No. This is the First Day Feast. You have duties here. Put on a smile and come mix with your flock, Shepherd."

Jared frowned. "I don't feel like it. I'd rather—"

"Don't feel like it?" Levi kept his voice low, but that did nothing to lessen the cutting edge of it. "You have duties, Father. They're required of you by your office, regardless of your personal preferences. Fulfill them or resign the office."

Jared felt one moment of rage at being scolded like a child, then realized the Deacon was right. He sighed. "Thank you for reminding me."

Levi nodded. "It's my honor to serve you as I can."

Jared smiled into the haunted eyes. "You're a good Deacon."

He turned and dutifully moved out into the crowd. His smile felt like part of a mask. It touched nothing inside him, where he stood apart from the gaiety and laughter around him. When he spoke to this person or that, it was the Shepherd in him that talked. Jared himself paced around the back of his mind thinking of Kastavin and Alesdra and the terrible dying.

A woman touched his arm. "Father."

He recognized her, he thought, as one of the Sharon family.

"I'm Patience Amalek, Father. I'm planning another

39

child, and as I've admired you for several years, I wanted to ask you if I may have seed from you."

He nodded. "Call the hospital and make an appointment with AI clinic. Don't forget the law requires you have seed from two men. Have you chosen the other man yet?"

"Yes. He's our family man. Thank you so much, Father."

"I serve as the Lord wills."

He walked on, amused. The birth rate was always highest in September and early March, eleven months each after Thanksgiving and New Year's. He never failed to marvel at the breeding urge festivals stimulated.

He passed Raaman, regaling a group of admiring women with some anecdote of his visit home. He was portraying the locals with subtle differences of voice and posture that cleverly caricatured each. Jared watched a grin light the dark face. Raaman could be so charming—he was socially and sexually in demand—it was a waste that the two of them were enemies.

People started moving toward the tables and lining up. Jared's stomach lurched sourly at the sight of the food. He knew he could not eat. He had had enough of the festival atmosphere, too. If he left, perhaps everyone would merely assume he was talking to someone somewhere else.

Under the pretext of making his way toward someone in the back of the line, he edged toward the door. As soon as no one was looking, he slipped through it, into the temple.

The building was deserted. All the civic offices were closed, the four women city commissioners and their staffs gone outside with everyone else to join the feast. The pages, stewards, and a half-dozen Middle School instructors who lived in were also gone. He met no one as he made his way through the corridors toward his rooms. The pre-Marahn statue stood alone in its courtyard, dreaming inhuman dreams amid the scent of satan trees. As he passed the library, though, he saw a line of light beneath the door.

He stopped. Who could be missing the First Day Feast to read? Someone using the library earlier must have forgotten to take down a candaglobe and put it away when he left. Jared opened the door and went in.

Alesdra Pontokouros was there, sitting cross-legged on the floor, books and news sheets piled around her. She looked up. Her face seemed strained but calm. "Good evening, Jared. Is the party over so soon?"

"Not yet. What are you doing?"

"Just reading. I'm delighted by the names you've given some of your animals." Her finger traced the words in the book open in her lap. *"Rapasaurus rex* and *Rhinosaurus tricornis* are beautiful. Tell me, this *Kangasaurus*—that's the jumping animal I saw in big herds, isn't it?"

"The leapers, yes." He frowned. How could she be so interested in mere animals at a time like this?

She glanced up and stopped, her brows lifting. She closed the book and laid it aside. "What's wrong?"

He sighed. "The boy haunts me. Whatever I'm doing, I see him."

He was astonished at himself for saying it. He rarely confided in people that way, and never in a woman except, years ago, Sky. Why had he opened himself to an alien?

He knew why, on thinking about it. She reminded him of Sky. Why, he was not sure. The two women looked and sounded nothing alike. Perhaps it was her frankness. Since he had passed puberty, no woman except Sky had talked to him as Alesdra did.

She looked at him now with something of the same concern Sky used to. "Who does a Shepherd talk to when he needs a shoulder to cry on?"

"His Deacons."

"Like Raaman of the Cassius look?" She shook her head. "Not my choice of confidants. Talk to me tonight instead."

He regarded her a moment, first with surprise, then gratitude. She was a fine person. "All right."

They dropped the candaglobes into the light drawer and closed the library. He led the way to his rooms and out into the garden. Sitting down on a bench there, he reflected that this was much better than the feast.

The temple clock chimed six.

"I kept worrying about you all day," he said. "What did you do?"

"Called the ship." She looked up at the branch of the satan tree above her head. It was heavy with fruit. "I read. I stood at the back of the tabernacle during the service." She reached up and picked a fruit. "Do these taste as good as they smell?"

"No! Please put that down and don't try it."

Her brows went up.

"It's so acid it'll burn your mouth and throat."

She held the fruit away from her, looking at it, then gingerly laid it on the ground under the tree and stepped back. "Lovely. If they're so dangerous, why do you have four trees of them in your garden?"

"Satan fruit has its uses. The acid breaks down with decay, so many animals live the winter on fallen fruit. The pulp makes good compost, too. And there is an edible nut inside the seed, the patience nut, that we grind for spice. We have them around the temple, though, because they smell good."

"But"—she frowned—"I've seen these trees in the public courtyards, too. Isn't the fruit a terrible temptation for children?"

Jared shrugged. "They've been warned about it. Yes, some are tempted, but so are we all throughout our lives by dangerous things with the appearance of good, and whosoever yields will surely suffer."

She stared at him in disbelief. "One of the temptations that strengthen, no doubt. You have a very different idea of what to be thankful for than most people I've met."

He started to frown at the implied criticism, then decided she could not really be blamed for her attitude. It was only a result of her godlessness. He needed to explain the value of the Litany. "It's easy to be thankful for good things. Anyone can do that, just as it's easy to like people who are kind to you. But to see Divine reason in adversity, to accept it without understanding it, is an expression of true faith."

"As the Lord wills, so let it be?"

He beamed at her. "Exactly." She understood, after all.

Alesdra walked to a bench around the far side of the

42

pool and sat down. She pulled her legs up crosswise, rested her elbows on her knees, and put her chin in her hands. "Under all the righteous sanctimony, who and what are you, Kedar Jared Cloud Joseph? What is it like to be a boy on Marah? Do you know who your father was? Do you wonder about the children you've sired? Has anything but Thors Kastavin's anguish ever broken through the insulation of complacent acceptance of everything to pluck a chord of rebellion in you?"

Anger burned the smile off his face. He was a fool to waste time on her. He started around the pool in the opposite direction, toward his sleeping-room door. "You may go, sister."

She unfolded from the bench. "I came because I sensed you needed someone to talk to, but all I've heard is cant, platitudes, and dogma. Is there a man under those vestments or only more priest?"

He stopped. Her taunt triggered the memory of a shriller voice, Sky's, delivering the last accusation she had thrown at him before running away to Heth sixteen years ago.

"The temple is the most important thing to you now, isn't it? Your time is taken up washing Aaron Methuselah's feet. There's none for me any longer. Everyone kept warning me, even Mother. I should have listened. Boys are fine as friends, they said, but boys don't stay that way; they grow up into men, into untouchable, insufferable priests."

He was appalled at how unreasonable she had become in the past weeks. "Sky," he snapped, "stop it."

"Is 'sky' some kind of curse?"

Jared realized he must have echoed the memory aloud. He sighed. "Sky is my twin sister, Ashasem Kiriathaim Sky Joseph." He saw her thinner, darker figure superimposed over Alesdra. A need to defend himself against both overwhelmed him. "I do what my office demands of me."

Alesdra's voice softened. "Can't you ever lay the office aside?"

Tension ran out of him. "I will right now."

He walked into his sleeping room. Without bothering to close the door behind him, he stripped away his beard and pulled off his surplice and tunic. He was unfastening his trousers when he turned to find her watching him from the doorway with unabashed interest.

"Do you shave every morning before pasting on your beard?"

"I don't shave. I don't have a beard, or any other hair except what's on my head. I had my body depilated when I was seventeen."

She blinked. "All over? Why?"

"We—the older boys in Middle School—thought it would make it harder for the younger boys to tell who had Passed. We thought if they couldn't see how few of us there were, they would be less afraid."

"What a kind thing to do. Do all men wear false beards, then?"

"No. It was a short fad. We found it didn't help."

She came into the room to sit on the edge of his sleeping shelf. "A boy's childhood must be a fearful thing."

"Yes." He told her how fearful while he took off his trousers and put on a robe. He wondered in passing if he were in any way offending her by exhibiting his body, but she seemed to accept it. Undressing before her did not bother him, not when he had spent his childhood undressing every night in a dormitory filled with any assortment of visitors and blood and fraternal siblings. "Growing up male is never daring to plan, never looking beyond puberty until it's past." He sat down on the sleeping shelf beside her. "It's having nightmares week after week and growing more scared each year but never being allowed to talk about it. It's having a mother who can't decide whether to cling to you while she has you or hold you off in hope of making your loss more bearable."

Alesdra grimaced. "That's horrible."

Being male was more than fear, of course. He went on to tell her about being protected, spoiled, given special treats girls were not allowed to have. Protected meant being imprisoned on the ranch station even when lessons were over, kept "safe" while his fraternal and blood sisters went out on the prairie to ride and learn range duties. Jared had found one solution to that frustration. He dressed up in Sky's clothes. As long as the two of them were not together in sight of anyone else,

44

people mistook him for his twin. He had learned to ride a rapa, to herd leapers and rhinos, and to throw a bolas.

And of course he talked about Sky. He could hardly have said a word about his life without mentioning her. While the temple clock chimed the hours and half-hours, he talked about her far more than he needed or intended to. He wondered what he was doing even as he talked. However, the alien woman listened with such rapt attentiveness that the words just kept coming. Only when he reached the last year they spent together did he falter.

Alesdra moved in to fill the silence. "You even lived together here in town while she became a keeper and you a teacher? Are many Marahn men as close to their sisters as you are?"

"Yes." He saw her brows twitch as she started and stopped a frown. He wondered why that offended her. Out on a ranch three or four days' ride from anywhere, who else was there to be friends and lovers with?

"Obviously she doesn't live with you any longer. Where is she?"

"She lives in Eridu." He picked at the fabric of his robe where it tightened over his crossed knees. "She's an investigator for the peacekeepers there. She's a member of the Ashasem family and has a son."

He looked sideways at her when she did not respond. She was staring straight ahead, face taut. She turned her head to look at him. "I hope her son is luckier than Kastavin."

Jared felt as if he had been stabbed. Isaiah was fifteen; he would be starting Middle School next week. Jared had forgotten that until Alesdra's remark reminded him.

"Jared?" Alesdra's voice was sharp with concern. "Are you all right?"

"I will be." That was the closest he could come to truth. He stood and walked out through the sitting room to the door. "I'm tired. Will you go now?"

She continued to look concerned, but she left, promising to talk to him in the morning. He nodded. It was only as he was closing the door behind her that he noticed the wide-eyed page standing out in the corridor.

He sighed. Tomorrow's gossip would no doubt be

filled with the news that the Shepherd, so long, so unnaturally celibate, had bedded the alien woman. He shrugged. Let them say what they liked.

His concern was Sky. What would the anguish of watching her son die do to her? There must be some way to save her from it. He immediately dismissed the idea of advising her to keep the boy out of school and give him lessons at home. Temple attendance was required by law. He wondered about giving the boy special attention. There was nothing that could not be accomplished through temple politics. He was a Shepherd, after all, and the point of having power was using it.

He began to feel better. Isaiah would probably attend Eridu temple. The Bishop was sure to radio soon to hear Jared's report. Jared would ask then what could be done.

Chapter Six

JARED WAITED OUT the last two days of Thanksgiving with impatience. He knew there was no chance of a radio call from Eridu until after the holiday. The Bishop was even busier with rites and ceremonies than the Shepherds. So Jared waited. He played his role; he recited dawn prayers, blessed mothers, dedicated children, rededicated adults to the Lord's service, and continued the daily Prayings . . . all with his mind ahead, anticipating the Bishop's call. He appeared at each evening's feast, at least long enough to greet people and make agreements for sharing seed. After that he slipped away into the temple to find Alesdra.

He came to morning Praying the day after Thanksgiving in a flush of expectation that drove out the exhaustion of three days of praying and three nights of talking until dawn. Around him his Deacons, except for Levi Dan, looked as tired as he should have felt. Kaleb Eshban would have fallen asleep during Forest Timna's scripture reading if Jared had not surreptitiously rapped the Deacon on the ankle with the lower end of his staff. There were few celebrants, virtually no women and only the most devout or ecclesiastically ambitious men.

Jared began the Litany. The rhythm of it exerted its magnetism on him and he fell into it, chanting the words with pleasant contentment. It was then, looking down the length of the tabernacle, he saw Alesdra Pontokouros enter at the back.

Her pale skin showed in the dimness as if she were standing in a beam of sunlight. She came closer while the Litany went on and stopped about halfway to the altar beneath a candaglobe. From there she listened with what looked like remote, rather clinical interest.

Suddenly Jared felt self-conscious. How must this sound to her? He was aware, after having forgotten for several days, that she was not just an exotic woman. She was foreign, *alien*. She was born on another world, raised under a different sun. She came from a society with other ethics, different ideals. Alesdra was not here this morning as a celebrant but as an observer, noting the local customs and no doubt comparing them to similar or totally dissimilar rites she had seen on other worlds.

He stumbled over "sorrows" and could not remember what came next. While eyes snapped toward him and the Deacons' expressions sharpened, he went back to the beginning of the phrase and repeated it without a mistake, but for the rest of the Litany and Praying, the words sounded quaint, even ridiculous, and tasted sour in his mouth. He was relieved when the ritual was over, and even more relieved that she left before he and his Deacons did. If she had stayed, he felt he would not have known what to say to her.

The Shepherd and Deacons traditionally ate breakfast at a table by themselves at the head of the dining hall. Most times the meal was quiet. The temple leaders always tried to set a good example for the boys and other men. Right now, however, with school dismissed and most of the live-in instructors home visiting, there was no one else but a group of stewards, pages, and kitchen help at a table at the far end of the hall. Alesdra was there, too, but seated at a table next to the temple staff, eating by herself.

Jared saw Raaman glance from the woman to him, and sighed. He waited for whatever poison was brewing on Raaman's tongue.

Raaman waited a moment too long before speaking, though. Kaleb spoke first. "I hate leap years." He yawned. "Three days and three nights is too much thankfulness for the human body to tolerate."

Levi smiled at him paternally. " 'They that wait upon the Lord shall renew their strength.' "

"You can talk, having spent your nights in your own bed no busier than usual." Kaleb sprinkled ground patience nut across the top of his boiled rice and fruit. "May all your family's children be boys."

The curse was not meant seriously, Jared realized, but it stung. Mothers of girls never had to watch their children die. Jared snapped, "Kaleb, I don't ever want to hear you say that again, not ever." He said it far more harshly than he intended to.

Kaleb turned in annoyance. "Who dropped satan juice in your tea?"

There was a moment of shocked silence, then Kaleb flushed and said swiftly, "Oh, Father, I'm sorry. I forgot who I was talking to. You see how tired I am? Please forgive me."

"I expect the Shepherd is tired and needs to ask forgiveness, too." It was Raaman at last, a barb on every word.

They looked at him.

"I can understand his weariness, after three nights with that godless Terran."

Jared ignored the bait. To deny what Raaman was implying would only seem defensive. Instead, he fought the anger rising in him by thinking how appropriate it was that Raaman had been cast as the High Priest Caiaphas in his nightmares. He amused himself for a moment imagining how Raaman might react to being told. It helped control the anger and kept his voice mild. " 'Thou shalt neither vex a stranger nor oppress him; for ye were strangers in the land of Egypt.' "

Levi added, " 'Be not forgetful to entertain strangers; for thereby some have entertained angels unawares.' "

Jared silently applauded. He wished he had thought to use that one.

Raaman's answering smile was thin and cold. "I doubt if the scriptures intended that we should go to such great lengths as the Shepherd has in that entertainment. I for one am very disturbed that while he has refused his bed to many deserving women of his own kind, consigning them to the AI clinic for his seed, he now yields to lust with an alien whose relationship to angels must be considered with great skepticism."

Anger won after all. Jared snapped, "Until you manage to put a spy inside my sleeping room itself, don't presume to know too much of my relationship with the woman. She is a woman, and only that, not some succubus or demonic manifestation. She's alone among us, cut off from her own people, perhaps for the rest of her life. She deserves your compassion, not scorn."

"Then how do you account for the fact that the mere sight of her at the Praying caused you to falter on a Litany you've said for years without fault, even half asleep? I say your reaction to her isn't natural."

Jared's anger evaporated in a wicked flash of mischief. He grinned. "Perhaps I'm in love."

That startled even Raaman into silence.

Levi's was the first mouth to close. He cleared his throat. "With—ah—Middle School resuming this week, we need to plan orientation for the two new instructors and the incoming boys. Father, you'll want to see the class rolls. I have them in my office."

Raaman's eyes dropped to his bowl. He became intensely busy eating.

Jared eyed him. He found that act suspicious, nor did he like the flicker of expression he caught before Raaman averted his face: a smugness, a glint of triumph, a gleam of anticipation. Jared felt a stir of uneasiness in himself. Raaman was busy plotting, and Raaman had learned intrigue from Aaron Methuselah himself.

Jared regretted the remark about spies now. That

was what came of letting his temper overcome prudence. He had never intended to let Raaman know how much he was aware of the Deacon's agents. He pledged himself to be more careful. Arousing Raaman's suspicions would only make removing him from the Deaconship more difficult.

From breakfast he went to his office. The antechamber was crowded with petitioners. His scribner had them divided into two groups, those with spiritual requests and those with secular requests.

"The Lord be with you, Father," the scribner said.

The petitioners echoed the scribner.

"And with you, my children." Jared always felt strange calling them that. Many were older than he was. "I'll see them the usual way, Ethan." One from each group alternately.

The parade began. Many were small matters easily decided. A woman who had not been able to see him at Thanksgiving wanted seed. He referred her to the AI clinic. A woman wanted her blind son exempted from Middle School. He refused the petition. A healer wanted use of the flyer for two pregnant women whose family was moving to Philippi but who had a history of miscarriage and were afraid to try the long journey overland. That was harder to refuse, but the flyer was an emergency vehicle and a flight to Philippi would take over a day to go up and come back. Jared could not risk having it gone so long on a non-emergency flight.

Some petitions were referred elsewhere, or set aside for study. Some he scheduled for discussion with the city commissioners.

Near the end of the morning the scribner put his head around the door not to announce another petitioner, but to bring the message Jared had been waiting for. "You have a radio call from the Bishop, Father."

Jared jogged the half-kilometer of corridors to the radio room. The operator nodded as he came in. He handed Jared the headphones and the microphone and left without being asked, closing the door behind him.

Jared depressed the speaker switch on the microphone. "The Lord be with you, Father."

Elias Jamin's thin, precise voice came back to him through the headphones. "And with you, my son. Well, have you done as I asked? Tell me all you've learned about the Terrans."

"They're people, Father. It's honorable to deal with them. They aren't really from Earth, however."

He told the Bishop all Alesdra had told him about the corporation she worked for, about its headquarters planet Arete, about the worlds she and Kastavin had come from. He described Kastavin's death at some length.

Midway through the description the Bishop interrupted. "Yes, yes, but that is not what we're discussing now, Brother Jared. Tell me about the woman."

Jared characterized Alesdra as thoroughly as he could, mentioning her intelligence and self-confidence, her attitude of authority, her sympathy, even her tendency to irreverence. He repeated everything she had told him about her education on Earth, what that planet was like, and about her liaison training and six previous planetary contacts.

"She is not a young woman, then?"

"No, Father. She's a bit older than I am, I think."

"Attractive?"

Jared frowned. That was a strange question . . . irrelevant, he would have thought. "In an exotic way, yes, Father. She's very pale but she has striking eyes green as a rapa's."

He waited for the Bishop to explain the question, but Elias changed the subject. "Now, why are they here? The purpose must be commercial if it's a corporation ship."

"Their employers make a machine they call a shuttle-box to send people and merchandise instantly between planets."

There was a long silence at the Eridu end of the radio. Finally the Bishop said, "And they want to sell us one of their machines."

"Yes."

There was another silence. "It's impossible, quite out of the question for any of us to leave Marah. Can they still be interested in selling to us in light of what happened to their man?"

"They're still interested. The woman says we can bring in virologists to cure our disease."

The Bishop's intake of breath was audible even over the radio. *"What?* Brother Jared, this is no subject for discussion over the air, but surely you know what result that would bring. It's a violation of Divine will. We're winnowed for a purpose. To try escaping that purpose risks damnation."

"Shall I tell her you won't see her, then? What do I do with her after that? She can't go back to her ship."

"Can you tell her?"

Warning gongs reverberated in Jared's head. That was the second off-note question. "What do you mean, Father?" He scented the sour traces of intrigue.

"I have had communications from Gibeon concerning this woman and you. A letter arrived just before Thanksgiving, and I received a radio call early this morning."

"From Raaman Midian?" Jared could not think of anyone else so well qualified. So that was what the man was up to.

"Yes. The man is no friend of yours. You should rid yourself of him as soon as possible. He claims the woman has bewitched you, seduced you to Terran ways. The radio message this morning said you have spent every Thanksgiving night with her."

"That's true. We've talked at great length."

"He also expresses the opinion that you're too weak to be a Shepherd. He warns you have been irrationally concerned by the Terran male's death."

Jared thought before answering. "It was the first of that kind I've ever seen. It was much . . . different than I expected."

"But you're not one to argue with the Lord, I hope. Aaron Methuselah—the Lord keep him in Paradise forever—thought highly of you. He loved you like a son. I would hate to see you betray his faith."

Jared felt as if he were being squeezed into a corner. He hunted for a near-truth. "I never question the Lord's ways, Father."

"I'm relieved, my son."

Jared noticed for the first time that though the pitch and inflections of the Bishop's voice were different from Aaron Methuselah's, the quality was the same. It soothed, cajoled, pressured.

"I will see the woman after all, if only to tell her we have no need of her machine. Have your flyer bring her as soon as can be scheduled."

"She'll be on her way by dawn tomorrow." Now was the time to ask about Sky's boy. "Father, my sister's son begins Middle School this year. Ashasem Isaiah Cloud Joseph. He should be attending Eridu temple. If he is, I have a favor to ask."

"I will have my education Deacon check the class rolls."

Jared sat back to wait for the reply. It would take a while, he knew. Eridu's temple was almost twice the size of Gibeon's, with the Grand and High Council chambers and work space for all the solons there. The Bishop would have to send a page all the way back to the offices for the school roll.

While he waited he switched through other radio frequencies, listening to the air traffic. On some channels were snatches of transmissions from ranch base stations. The low-powered portable units the ranch hands carried were too weak for him to hear, though. On other channels were conversations between keeper stations and between the keeper base in Gibeon and its portable units. He picked up transmissions from the public radio office, too. It reminded him of the times as a boy he sat on watch duty at the Kedar base station, and of the times as a teacher when he could not sleep and whiled away the night hours sitting in here with the night operator.

The operator looked in. His brows went up. "I thought you'd be through by this time, Father."

"Do you have requests piling up?"

The operator shrugged. "Nothing I can't postpone."

The radio crackled. "Gibeon temple, this is Eridu temple."

"That will be all, Benjamin," Jared said.

The operator backed out and closed the door.

Jared depressed the transmission button. "Go ahead, Eridu."

The Bishop's voice came back to him. "I've had the school roll checked. The boy was scheduled to come here but a notice of transfer was put against his name just before Thanksgiving."

53

"Transfer? To where?"

"I did not bother to check that far. I suggest you ask your sister."

As if that would be easy. Jared sighed. "Yes. Thank you, Father."

He came away from the radio room feeling defeated. Transferred. Now why had Sky done that? He could go ahead and send a message asking her where the boy was, but he had wanted to be an invisible protector. He had no desire to make her think he was trying to obligate her to him for anything.

He was almost back to his office before he remembered there was a more immediate task than protecting Sky's son. He spun around and went to tell Alesdra she had been summoned.

Chapter Seven

ALESDRA AND the pilot were the only occupants of the flyer on the flight to Eridu. She was happy to accept the pilot's invitation to sit in the empty co-pilot's seat, where she had a fine view of the brown prairie streaming beneath them. It reminded her of the last time she had flown over this country. That hurt. It also reminded her of the drive onto the prairie behind an ambling rhinosaur to scatter Kastavin's ashes. She waited for the lump in her throat to dissolve before asking how fast they were going.

"Three hundred twenty kph," was the reply. "We'll reach Eridu in approximately seven hours."

That made Eridu twenty-two hundred klicks. The same time on the ground would not put much more than thirty-five or forty klicks behind a person. It was like two different worlds. She was amazed that the

Marahns did not seem to realize how small the difference between their ground and emergency transportation was.

She amazed the pilot by reporting to the ship on her buckle communicator. In Translan she told Captain Deyoe, "I'm finally on the way to see the head shaman."

"Sell him on the shuttlebox," the captain came back. "The tech crew has come up with a plan for building it without exposing themselves to the virus."

That was good to hear. "How is everyone tolerating looking down on this untouchable jewel?"

"Impatiently. But having survived the enforced intimacy of the eleven months it took to get us here, we'll manage a few more days before we start killing each other. How are you tolerating looking up at this untouchable jewel?"

Alesdra tried to laugh but the sound would not quite come. She took several deep breaths before answering: "Well enough, as long as I believe I'll sell the shuttlebox. It's the nights I doubt, that I start feeling claustrophobic."

"But we're the ones in the small enclosed space."

"You'd have to be here to appreciate the circumstances."

"Well, keep believing, then, and good luck selling the box."

"Skipper," Alesdra said wryly, "you'll never know how good it is *not* to hear someone say, 'As the Lord wills, so let it be.' Pontokouros out."

She reattached the communicator to her belt and sat watching the country pass. The land grew browner as they flew north, then began greening up again. Woods appeared and hills steepened.

"Are you hungry?" the pilot asked. "The kitchen packed some lunch for us." She pointed to a box sitting in one of the passenger seats.

Alesdra brought it up. Inside were sandwiches of thick slabs of hooper meat and a bottle of fruit juice. She and the pilot shared the juice.

The sun reached zenith as the flyer neared the equator and the woods below thickened and darkened to tropical forest. The glitter of sun on water appeared on the horizon, then swiftly broadened into a huge inland sea. To the north of it an awesome range of mountains rose into the sky. Alesdra stared at them. To look that tall at this distance, they must be some of the most gigantic peaks she had ever seen.

"What are those?"

"The Sinai Mountains, 'washing their toes in the Sea of Tears,' to quote Ishmael Maacah. There's Eridu."

The capital was on the eastern shore. Like every other Marahn town she had seen, it lay along streets radiating out from the sprawling labyrinth of the temple. But—she stared, frowning—was this what had been described that first night as "the large city up north on the equator."

"How many people live there? Ten thousand?"

"Oh, no, over twelve. It's more than twice as big as Gibeon. Impressive, isn't it?"

Size was relative, of course. Twelve thousand would be a large city to a people who had a population of some three million scattered over a continent larger than Earth's Africa. "It's a metropolis," Alesdra agreed. "What's that beyond it?"

A complex filigree design was cut into the earth.

"That?" The pilot shrugged. "That's the Old City. The street design is pretty from the air, isn't it?"

Alesdra's brows went up. "You mean you had another there before you built—oh!" She understood suddenly what the pilot meant. "You mean a pre-Marahn city." She studied the area covered by the pattern. It would have swallowed several Eridus. "It's being excavated for study?"

"No, mined."

Mined? Of course . . . for the metal. Alesdra smiled, thinking of the archeologists who would die of apoplexy at the idea of melting down alien artifacts. It gave her a queasy feeling, too.

The Seeker probes had not mapped inhabited worlds and the Egkharen were the only other known spacing race. As a vanished race who had left traces to be studied, the pre-Marahns were so far unique. There must be other cities, though, buried and untouched.

"We're going down," the pilot said.

The flyer slowed almost to hover. It drifted, swinging around until it was aligned with a large courtyard on the perimeter of the temple, then settled vertically to the ground. The landing was so soft it was almost undetectable. When the whine of engines had died away, the pilot unlocked the door and they stepped out over the wing onto the ground.

The air smothered Alesdra in hot, humid folds on her first breath. She pulled open the collar of her coverall. The tropics of worlds with as little axial tilt as Marah had *really* warm weather. She was a little surprised the colonists had come this far north at all. Then she remembered some of the history she had read in Gibeon's temple library. Eridu was the site of their first landing. They had just stayed here, despite the heat.

She glanced around the courtyard as they crossed it toward the three men waiting for them in the portico. It looked much like Gibeon's temple, except that it was built of a cream-yellow stone instead of red. But as in Gibeon, women guards stared at her from their posts at the gate and three bearded brown men in long green tunics and trousers came to meet her.

She bowed her head to the leading man. "Bishop?"

"No," he replied. "I'm Chief Steward Adam Dishon. With me are Brother Jonathan Temah and Brother Pinna Obal. We welcome you to Eridu. The Bishop has asked me to be your guide. I'm to show you to your quarters and answer any questions you may have."

She wanted to snarl. She was still being put off. She smiled instead. "I have a question. When may I see the Bishop? I've come a very, very long way to see him."

"Yes, sister, I know . . . from Gibeon."

She gave up smiling. "No, brother . . . from a planet named Sahara, and one called Earth, and most recently, from Schön."

The steward blinked but said, "The Bishop is a very busy man. When he has time to see you, he'll send for you."

"He *has* sent for me. I waited in Gibeon eight days for the order to come here." She studied him. Diplomacy was wasted on officious nulls like this. Maybe a smart goose would help. "I'm only a member of the crew of my ship. I haven't any control over what my superiors will do if they lose patience or think they're being mocked."

The steward's brown skin went muddy. "I—I'll—ah—see if the Bishop will receive you now." He backed toward the door.

Alesdra followed. "I'll go with you."

The men looked shocked at her behavior. The pilot hid a grin.

Inside, the temple was dim and cool. The steward hurried through the maze of corridors like one pursued by devils. He kept looking over his shoulder at her, as if hoping she would have vanished between one glance and the next. At a door on the far side of a crowded anteroom, the steward spoke to another green-clad man and ducked through so fast Alesdra could not follow him. Biting back a smile, Alesdra leaned against an empty piece of anteroom wall, nodded to the Marahns staring at her, and waited.

A few minutes later the door opened and the steward looked out. "The Bishop will see you."

She gave him her most gracious smile in thanks and left him nonplused as she strode past him into the Bishop's office.

The Bishop sat in a high-backed wicker-looking chair, his hair and the papers on his worktable stirred by a breeze coming through the screened window slits behind him. He was an old man, small and withered, with the silken white of his hair and beard an interesting contrast to the aged-wood brown of his skin.

"Father, it's kind of you to see me."

He looked up at her with eyes that glittered like obsidian. "Had I a choice? I'm honored, of course, to greet a visitor from so far away. You are Liaison Officer Alesdra Pontokouros and your world is called Sahara, is it not? And Arete is where your employers have their headquarters?"

She wondered if Jared had reported their conversations verbatim or just given the highlights. "You're well informed."

"It is my business to know what goes on in my world. I am—"

"Jemuel Belam Elias Jamin, Shepherd of Eridu, Bishop of Marah."

He was taken aback for a moment. "You are in-

58

formed, too, I see. Did Brother Jared tell you my full name?"

"No. I read it in the library. I learned more, too. Jemuel Belam Elias Jamin, born in 500 in Rapa Beach to Korah Esther Mary Jamin, youngest of five children, only survivor of three boys. Became page at Rapa Beach temple in 518, temple steward in 525. Joined the Jemuel family in 526. Elected Deacon in 538. Left family and Rapa Beach to become Deacon in Eridu in 540. Elected Bishop on the death of Joseph Bethuel in 551. In the forty-one years of your tenure, your notable accomplishments have been—"

"That is quite enough, thank you. I am impressed." He sounded sincere. "You show unusual initiative for a woman."

She let that pass without comment.

He smiled at her. It was, she noted, very professionally paternal. "Please accept my apologies that there was only a delegation of stewards to meet you. If I had known you were coming I would have met you myself."

She sat down in a chair facing him. "But you did know; you sent for me."

"I told Brother Jared to send you as soon as his flyer was free to bring you. I never expected it would be this soon. I confess, with great shame, that I am totally unprepared for you at this time. I had intended a formal reception, and to present you to the Grand Council. After all, what you have to say should be heard by representatives of all Marahns. But the solons will not be back before the end of the week. This is not Earth, where every person has a personal flyer. Our people have to travel by train, or ride animal-back or in buggies."

He was still putting her off, no matter how logical, how reasonable he made it sound. Her temper beat at the lid she closed over it. He had called her at this time. She was convinced of that. So why was he making her sit around waiting some more? What did he hope to accomplish?

"What do you suggest I do until you're prepared?"

"Well, you can tell me why it is you have come to Marah, then make use of Brother Adam to guide you around the city. It is no doubt small and simple by

59

your standards, but it is a lovely city, refreshing to the soul. I'll have you come before the Grand Council when it assembles."

She leaned back in her chair. "Jared has probably already told you why I'm here."

"He said there was a machine. But he did not say how it works or how much it costs."

"It doesn't cost you anything. It earns you money. We don't actually sell the shuttlebox. What we do is lease land to build it on. Intergalactic Communications operates the box as a service, charging users a fee, as a railroad charges for tickets. You, as local government, may of course tax goods or travelers, set up trade tariffs, whatever you please."

The Bishop frowned. "It is impossible, I'm afraid. I would not want to risk spreading contamination to the rest of the universe. And what of the lives of the people who would build this machine?"

"We have a way to build it without being infected by the virus. After that, the first transports would be medical scientists to study the disease and develop a cure."

She expected a reaction to that, but not the sudden shuttering of his face. She was reminded of Jared's change of expression that first night when she asked if he knew what might be wrong with Kastavin. She assessed his mask and came to the conclusion there was nothing more to be gained here now.

She stood. "I've taken enough of your time. We can talk again when it's more convenient. Where are my quarters?"

His face relaxed. "Across the street from the temple in Solon House. I'll have Brother Adam show you the way."

The solons' building proved to be like a huge dormitory. Corridors lined with sleeping rooms radiated out from the central common room and dining hall. The temple steward gave her to a house steward, who showed Alesdra to a room.

"If you need anything, you can summon someone with this bell cord," the house steward said.

Alesdra nodded. The steward left her.

Alesdra looked over the room. It seemed comfortable by Marahn standards, but uninviting. Like rooms in the south, it had a low ceiling and floor-to-ceiling window slits. In deference to the climate, the windows were screened rather than glazed and the tile floor was bare. The two chairs and table were of the wicker-type construction. Even the pad on the sleeping shelf was a stack of grass mats rather than a material which would mildew in the humidity. It was no place just to sit for a week. So now what?

She called the ship.

Captain Deyoe was not happy hearing about more delay. "They don't sound very interested in a shuttle-box."

"Well, the men have their precious position to lose if the disease is cured, but when I have the chance to talk to them, I'll make the travel tax and tariff opportunities sound too good not to want."

"I keep wondering why we're bothering with them if they can't see the obvious advantages. Add their reluctance to the conditions down there and it makes me doubt putting a box on Marah is worth the trouble."

Alesdra experienced a spasm of desperate anxiety. "Skipper, don't give up yet!"

Her sigh came over the communicator. "Don't worry, Ponto. I don't want to abandon you."

But signing off, Alesdra was not reassured. The captain was just that, not a sales rep. She thought in terms of crew safety and convenience. She did not have the persistence or thick hide of a rep, nor Connie Melas' feeling of holy mission. The captain could very easily become disgusted and decide to try the next colony on their route rather than waste more time here. Perhaps that was what the Bishop wanted. Alesdra considered the interminable days until the Grand Council convened, and she hissed in angry frustration.

To help distract herself, she went exploring through Solon House. The activity helped but was short-lived entertainment. Each wing was the same as all the others, and just as empty. She seemed to be alone in the building. She finally found a small group of women in the kitchens, drinking tea and playing a game using a die with representations of animals carved into the twelve sides.

They stared at her and stood, forgetting their game.

61

"You must be the woman from Earth," one said. "I'm Ruth Noah, house steward. You didn't need to come all the way back here. If you need something, you can pull any bell cord."

"I wanted the exercise and company. Can someone tell me the time? I know we came enough west to make a time difference."

"The temple clock rang three not long ago."

Alesdra set her wrist chronometer. The women stared at it. With reason. It was a precision instrument, a combination calculator/multichron model that could be programmed for any length of day.

"Would you like some tea?" Ruth asked.

Alesdra nodded.

One of the women poured her some. She sat down with them, and the questions started. What was Earth like? How many worlds had she seen? Were other worlds sinks of iniquity?

Outside thunder boomed and rolled. The narrow stips of Marah Alesdra could see through the windows disappeared in a deluge. The rain had stopped by the time the women ran out of questions, though.

Tropics, she thought. She had spent time in them, acclimated herself to them when necessary, even come to admire the lush beauty of them, but she could never quite feel they were the "right" climate for living in. She still found herself longing for the dry heat of Sahara's flats and savannahs. She was going to have to find something to keep her occupied this week or she would start getting homesick . . . and that would be torture. She wished Marah's capital were in Gibeon; she preferred the country there.

Thought of Gibeon kicked her mental processes into a quantum jump. Jared Joseph's sister Sky lived somewhere in Eridu. She was—oh, yes, an investigator for the local police. Alesdra had plenty of time. Why not look up this sister?

She finished her tea and looked across at the house steward. "Where is the peacekeeper headquarters?"

"You mean Peace Hall? It's on the other side of the temple. Just follow the road around the temple's outer wall."

The heat enfolded her the moment she stepped out

of Solon House. Within a few hundred meters sweat was running down her face and torso. Her coverall plastered itself to her chest, back, and shoulders. She needed to exchange her clothes and boots for some of the sandals and loose pants and blouses she saw the Eridunians wearing. Or perhaps what she really needed was gills. The humidity, now much worse for the rain, made her feel she should be swimming instead of walking.

Not only the keepers were on the city center, she discovered. Everything important was, and all built on one level of the same yellow stone as the temple and Solon House. There was a school, a rabbit-warren-like block of city offices, a machine shop where she could see a woman turning a buggy axle on a lathe, a combination hospital-veterinary clinic, a print shop exuding the sounds of machinery and the smell of ink. A row of shops stretched down a radial street across from the main temple gate.

Traffic was moderate. Street traffic passed her at frequent intervals, mostly bicycles, but interspersed with occasional rhino-drawn buggies and ridden rapas. The rapas, she noticed, were different colors here, patterned instead of the solid brown and blue-gray she had seen in the south. They looked much smaller, too. The walkways were crowded with pedestrians, women alone or in groups, mixed groups of children, occasional men accompanied by one or two women. They stared at her as they passed. Turning to watch Alesdra, one woman went off the walkway and fell on her face in the street.

All of it helped her forget the heat, but none of it was like the relief of stepping into the cool dimness of Peace Hall. Inside, the building was simple, for once, just a single corridor stretching ahead. Near the door was a desk with a young woman behind it. She wore a loose green shirt with a triangular patch of darker green high above the left breast.

"May I help you?" Her voice was professionally polite. If she found Alesdra a strange sight, it never showed by as much as a flicker of expression.

"I'm looking for an investigator named Sky Joseph."

"Third door on the right."

The third door on the right opened into a room of

63

moderate size furnished with four worktables, a number of chairs, and filing cabinets. Green-shirted women sat at two desks, writing. A third sat talking to a fourth who wore a long stick on her belt.

The woman closest to Alesdra looked up and after one blink asked in brisk, clipped syllables, "Help you?"

"I'm looking for Sky Joseph."

The woman turned her head and called back to the two talking at the rear of the room. "Sky. Visitor."

The woman without the stick looked around. She left her companion and stepped forward, smiling. "May I help you?"

There was no question in Alesdra's mind she was Jared's sister. She might have been a centimeter or two taller than her brother but she had the same slim build, the same dark hair, yellow-brown skin, and amber eyes. There were fewer lines in her face, but her features looked so much like Jared's when his beard was off that Alesdra could easily understand how they could dress in the same clothes and fool people into believing Jared was Sky.

Alesdra introduced herself.

Sky Joseph's eyes widened. She exchanged quick glances with the small woman at the desk. Alesdra could see questions forming behind their eyes, but their expressions quickly changed when Alesdra explained why she was looking for Sky.

"You've talked with Jared?" Sky's face lighted. "How is he? Is Shepherdhood aging him? Obviously he mentioned me to you. What did he say?"

The small woman's face creased in concern. "Forget the priest, Sky."

Sky shrugged. "I can't, Daria. He's still my brother and I still love him. It's my life's trial."

"Which we all share."

Sky leaned down and gave her a quick hug and a kiss on the forehead. "For which I love you." She straightened. "This is Daria Hanoch, my sisterwife as well as my colleague."

Alesdra exchanged nods of greeting with the small woman.

"Where are you staying here in Eridu?" Sky asked.

"Solon House."

Sky was horrified. "But no one lives there when the Council is recessed. You must be all alone. What fool put you there?"

"The Bishop."

Daria snorted. "Predictably."

Sky looked distressed. "You shouldn't be so disrespectful. He's a man."

"Exactly." A sly grin tugged the corner of Daria's mouth.

Sky sighed and turned back to Alesdra. "Solon House has to be dreadful right now. Please, come stay with my family."

Daria straightened. "Sky, this is a special visitor. Alien. Needs to be accessible, twenty hours a day."

"I'll leave our address with the house steward so she can send a runner when the Bishop wants Alesdra. That way she can be reached and we don't need to bother trying to get permission from the temple for her to visit us."

That statement startled Alesdra. Sky was concerned when Daria was disrespectful of the Bishop, but Sky was proposing to do something that could be more serious, taking away Alesdra behind his back.

"Do we have room?" Daria asked.

"She can have Isaiah's sleeping shelf."

Daria shrugged. "All right."

Sky looked at Alesdra. "Will you come?"

"I don't want to get you in trouble, or to impose."

"You won't. It'll be an honor to have you, won't it, Daria?"

"An honor," Daria said.

Alesdra grimaced in an agony of indecision. On the one hand, she wanted to do it. Knowledge of how a Marahn family functioned could give her invaluable help understanding Marahn psychology, and help her sell the shuttlebox to the Grand Council. On the other hand—"What if the Bishop disapproves of my leaving Solon House?"

Even Daria shrugged that off. "The steward will see he never finds out."

Alesdra arched a brow. These women were not as servile as they seemed.

Sky stuck her head into the corridor. "Runner!"

A young woman appeared. Sky wrote on a sheet of paper Daria handed her. For all its haste, Alesdra noticed the writing was neat and legible. Was that one of the benefits of a leisurely, machine-limited society? Sky folded the note, sealed it with a sticker, and handed it to the runner.

"Deliver this to Sabrina Malchiel at Ashasem House on Charity Street."

"Today is Sabrina's home day," Daria said to Alesdra. "Sky's warning her to expect another for dinner and put sheets on Isaiah's sleeping shelf."

That puzzled Alesdra. "Sky's son won't be there?"

Sky said, "No. He's left for school."

"He's not just a day student?"

Sky smiled. "He isn't going to school *here.* I'm surprised Jared didn't tell you. Just before Thanksgiving he sent me a radio message asking me to let Isaiah come to Gibeon for Middle School. I've always wanted Jared to have the chance to know Isaiah, so I asked for permission to transfer him and put him on the train for Gibeon yesterday morning. Also I—" As she hesitated, Daria flung her a quick look of concern. She finished, "I thought Gibeon might be lucky. Jared survived there."

Alesdra's throat squeezed tight. When she tried to talk, her voice emerged husky. "Good luck."

They looked at her a moment without speaking, then Daria said, "You've seen?"

"A young man landed with me."

Sky reached out to touch Alesdra's arm. "You poor thing. What a terrible welcome for you. I was just eight when my brother Talmon came home from school, but I still remember almost every minute of the time I sat with him."

"We start early," Daria said. "Watching. To get in practice for our own sons."

Alesdra stared at them in horror. Children had to watch a thing like that? What a hellish world.

Chapter Eight

A STACK of radio messages lay on Jared's worktable waiting for him after breakfast. He unfolded the top one and read it. It was a reply from Shiloh to the query he had sent the day before. No, it said, there was no boy named Isaiah Joseph enrolled at Shiloh temple. He worked his way through the stack. They were all replies. He had queried every temple within a thousand kilometers of Eridu, and even radioed the Shepherd in Heth. That was a long gamble, but since Sky had lived there for a time after running away from Gibeon and Isaiah had been born there, Jared had thought it worth a try.

He read the last reply with a deep scowl. Negative, like all the others. He tore it into a half-dozen pieces and tossed them into the air. He walked to the window and stood staring through the slit into the courtyard beyond. If Sky were not sending the boy to Eridu or Heth, where could he be?

A half-dozen boys followed a page across his field of vision. They would be some of the early boarding arrivals from the ranches. From their wide-eyed stares around them he judged them to be first-year boys. The white-faced stillness of terror in several confirmed it.

Somewhere Isaiah must be doing this same thing, following a page on a tour of a temple and moving into a dormitory room. If he were to help the boy and not let him risk the Trial, Jared decided he would just have to ask Sky where the boy was.

His scribner came in with the mail.

Jared reached for the handful of letters. "Ethan, will you please send a message by radio to—" He broke off as he saw the return address on the top letter: Ashasem House, Eridu.

"By radio to whom, Father?"

"Never mind." He dismissed the scribner with a wave.

Laying the other letters on the worktable, he turned Sky's over in his hands. It was thin. Sky's infrequent letters were usually thick. He broke the seal on the envelope, took out and spread the single sheet of paper flat on his worktable.

He read quickly. Halfway through, he stopped, puzzled, and went back to the beginning. This time he read with more care. What was this about a radio message? He had never sent her a message, and it had certainly never occurred to him to ask that the boy attend school here. It was a fine idea, though. It would make saving the boy very much easier.

He took the letter up the corridor to Levi Dan's office and showed it to his Deacon.

Levi read it in silence, then looked up with a frown of concern. "Why did you ask her to send the boy here?"

"I didn't. Is he registered here?"

Levi nodded. "The transfer notice came by mail just now. If you didn't send the message, who did? You ought to find out because this is a very dangerous—"

But Jared was on his way out before Levi could finish. Sky would have wanted the boy to arrive a couple of days before school began. There had been a train from Eridu today, the one that brought Sky's letter and the transfer notice. There would not be another until day after tomorrow, so if Sky's son were to come here, he must have arrived this morning!

Jared headed for the school wing and found the dormitory steward. "What first-year boys have checked in?"

The steward showed him the list. Isaiah's name was written at the bottom in a different shade of ink. Opposite it was the number 135. Jared returned the list with thanks.

The school dormitory was busy and noisy. New boys were trying to find which of the tiny cubicles opening off the corridor were theirs while older boys greeted friends they had not seen for the month-long holiday. Jared could never walk down the long U-shaped corridor without remembering his own school days here. The echo of boys' voices off the hard, glassy walls and floor was still almost deafening, but then it had actually been painful. He remembered putting his hands over his ears and wondering how even the busy parts of the rest of the temple could be quiet when it was so noisy here. Then he had forgotten the sound in the wonder of seeing so many boys together all at once and having a room of his own. The cubicle was small, just large enough for the sleeping shelf, a bookcase, a small worktable and chair, but to a boy who had spent his life sleeping in a dormitory with all his fraternal and blood siblings, plus assorted cousins and guests, the room was as good as a mansion. Only adults had rooms by themselves. It almost made him forget the terror inside him.

Years later, teaching here, he had discovered the reasons for the separate rooms and sound-reflecting corridor. In a common room the boys would have been impressed too harshly, and therefore frightened, by the growing number of empty beds. Alone in their rooms with the voices of classmates and upperclassmen amplified to sound like many times the actual number, the missing boys were less noticeable.

Jared stopped at the doorless archway of 135. Was it mere coincidence Sky's son had this room, he wondered. Through the opening he could see a boy kneeling by the drawers beneath the sleeping shelf, putting away his clothes.

Jared knocked on the wall. "The Lord be with you, Isaiah."

The boy looked around. The face was Sky's, or his own, as Jared remembered them at fifteen. The boy's eyes widened and he jumped to his feet. "The Lord be with you, Father."

Jared felt a jolt of surprise. "You know me? I've always thought that without my staff I look just like an instructor, or a steward."

"You do." The boy's blunt honesty made Jared wince even as it amused him. "But Mother has a portrait of you in her room. I recognized you from that."

So she still had it. It gave him a sharp pang of pleasure, though he wondered that it should. She had made a joke of painting it, making him wrinkle his face so she could see where the lines were going to be, then painting him older than he was.

"This is how you'll look years from now when you're a senior instructor beloved by all your pupils," she had said.

"May I come in, Isaiah? Your mother wanted us to get acquainted."

"Yes, Father." The boy sat on the sleeping shelf.

Sitting in the chair, Jared noted that although the room looked smaller than it once had, it had otherwise changed very little over the years. There was still a black stain under the worktable where he had dropped a bottle of the dye used to paint ranch brands on saurian hides. Jared could no longer remember the practical joke he had been planning, only his horror as the bottle fell, and the hours of fruitless scrubbing to remove the evidence of the accident.

"This used to be my room when I was in school," Jared said.

"Did it?" The boy licked his lips. "Maybe—maybe it will bring me luck."

He had forgotten the superstitions. They came back to him now, all the magic they so desperately hoped would keep them alive. See the full moon over your left shoulder with Tagalong exactly in the middle and you would live. Carry a lock of hair from an adult man and the disease would not affect you. There were dozens more.

Jared changed the subject. "How is your mother?"

"Fine, Father."

Jared waited for him to say more, but the boy said only that and waited with an expectant look for the next question. "She didn't—did she give you any messages for me?"

"Messages?" The boy frowned. "No, Father."

"Tell me about her. It's been a long time since I've seen her. Does she still paint? How is her work?"

"She doesn't talk about work at home. She does paint. Last month she painted a picture of a statue miners found in the Old City. It was an animal, Father, very strange. It was as tall as a rapa but standing on four legs all the same size, like a rhino, and it had a short, skinny tail. Mother said from the roughness of the metal surface, she thought it had had hair all over its body. The historical society wants to keep the statue but the mining company wants to melt it down. They have to argue it before the temple this month."

Jared was more interested in the boy than in historical artifacts. "How was your train ride here?"

"Fine."

"Who brought you?"

The boy grinned with pride. "No one."

Jared stiffened. "You can't mean you came alone?" What could Sky be thinking of, sending a boy forty-six hundred kilometers without an escort for protection?

The boy's grin faded. "Almost alone. Mother asked the train stewards to look after me, but they let me do what I wanted and never fussed over me. They treated me almost like a girl."

Jared was shocked. That was outrageous. "The world is full of women, but we can't afford to take chances with a man."

Isaiah looked past Jared, his face pale. "I'm not a man yet."

His fear stabbed Jared. Jared was suddenly very glad the boy was here. He could erase that fear. He touched the boy's shoulder in reassurance. "You *will* be a man, though. That I promise you. Your mother sent you here for my protection, and I'll give it to you."

He left the boy staring after him with wild hope.

Before visiting Levi again, Jared stopped in the dormitory steward's room. "How did you happen to give 135 to Isaiah Joseph?"

The steward's brows rose. "I assigned it at your request." He opened a drawer and rummaged through it. In a few moments he turned back to Jared with a sheet of paper.

It was written in the precision hand of a scribner. "A boy named Isaiah Joseph will be entering Middle School here, a transfer student from Eridu. It will please me if he is given room 135, my old room." The signature was Jared's own, and the seal.

"I had to move another boy out of the room to do it, too," the steward said.

Jared folded the note and put it in his pocket. "I appreciate your trouble. Thank you. The Lord be with you."

He left the school wing with a cold chill settling into his bones. Someone had forged that note from him. Why? Who could benefit from Isaiah Joseph occupying room 135?

He passed Forest Timna in the courtyard, sitting in a circle of new pages. They looked up and greeted him as he passed. He replied.

Then Forest said, "Are you getting your sister's son settled into the dormitory?"

It took all Jared's control to keep his face expressionless. "Yes," he said.

He walked on. Now how had Forest known Sky's son was coming to school here? It occurred to him that anyone could sign a name to a radio message. He doubted that Forest had sent the message to Sky. If Forest knew about it, however, there was only one other person likely to have done it. Once the matter of Isaiah's safety was taken care of, Jared thought, he would take a close look at Raaman's recent activities.

Jared found Levi still sitting in his office, hands in his lap. He looked as though he were waiting.

"You've met the boy now?"

Jared nodded. "And I have a favor to ask of you."

A muscle twitched in Levi's jaw. "What is it, Father?"

Jared sat down opposite him and leaned forward so he could keep his voice too low for the scribner in the anteroom to hear. "You're in charge of all matters pertaining to the Middle School. I'd like you to take special care of my sister's son."

"I try to treat every boy here as if he were a member of my own family. Your sister's son will receive no less care."

"But I mean . . . unique care."

"I don't think I understand, Father."

Jared leaned farther forward and his voice sharpened. "I mean that when the time comes to"—his voice dropped almost to a whisper—"to start the Trial, will you see that my sister's son has a safe glass?"

Levi sighed. "I thought you might ask me that. I'm sorry, I can't help you."

72

Jared frowned. "There must be a way."

Levi tented his fingers and brought them to his chin. He spoke with great deliberation. "I mean, Father, that I *won't* help you."

"Won't?" Jared stared at him in disbelief. "Why not? It was a request. I'll make it an order if you prefer."

Levi's fingers laced together. "I still refuse, Father."

Jared found himself on his feet, shouting in rage. "Who are you to refuse me? I'm the *Shepherd.*"

Levi's knuckles were white. "Which is not, fortunately, the same as a king." He sighed. It was a sad sound. "Let me try to explain."

Jared sat down and leaned back in his chair, lips pressed into a thin line. "Explain, then."

"Don't think you're the first man to come to me like this. At first I was tempted to help, but after much soul-searching I decided I must always refuse. If there are to be choices, they should be the Lord's, not ours. Can't you see that?" His voice pleaded. "The moment we interfere, it's no longer impartial. When we start choosing who lives, we'll also be choosing who dies, and then it becomes not Divine will but murder."

Jared bit his lip. "But there must be something I can offer you that will change your mind. This is my sister's son, *Sky's* son."

Levi shook his head. His hands twisted in his lap. "You drugged the drinks one year because Aaron Methuselah wanted you to become an active part of the Trial, to commit you and harden you in preparation for making you Shepherd. It tortured you, I know; I heard you crying in your room one night. Yet you continued drugging the glasses and stood without interfering while the boys chose their glasses."

Jared nodded. He had wanted to be Shepherd.

"I've done it for twenty years. I've stood without interfering, knowing exactly what would happen to those boys. I've watched boys from my own family take drugged glasses." A muscle twitched in his jaw. "Your mother had two sons out of three survive. My family had nine boys, and all of them, all nine, died. I watched them seal their death, too."

Now Jared understood the haunted pain so often in Levi's eyes. "And you never tried to save even one?"

The Deacon closed his eyes. "How could I save one and not the rest? There was no way for me to choose which son I loved more than the others."

Jared's skin drew up in chill-pimples. "Son?" Men had no sons.

Levi's eyes opened. "Son. Our ancestors have done all they could to destroy the bonds between men and boys. Children take their mother's name, inherit her property. By custom women must receive seed from two men for a pregnancy. Even the words for relationships between men and boys are gone. A woman calls her sister's sons nephews and they call her aunt, but you and I can only call them our sisters' sons and they call us their mothers' brothers. It took determination for me to remain a family man after I became Deacon, when I was being pressured to follow the custom and leave my family to live in the temple." He sighed. "But in spite of it all, our ancestors were not entirely successful. Fatherhood is an attitude, an emotion, not a mere biological circumstance. The sons of my family were my sons, too, no matter whose genes they carried. So—" he looked into Jared's eyes with a hard, direct gaze "—having let my own sons die, I can think of nothing anyone can offer me for the lives of their sons."

"Then I'll have to save him myself." Jared started to stand up.

"I'll interfere." Levi's voice was deadly calm.

Jared felt his anger rising. Refusing to help was annoying, but understandable, under the circumstances. Preventing Jared from doing anything was unforgivable. "Just what would you do, Deacon?"

"Start a petition for a Shepherd election and throw my support to Raaman Midian."

Jared stared at him in dismay. Levi would go that far?

As if reading Jared's mind, Levi said, "I would go that far to keep you from corrupting the Trial to your own advantage. You're an intelligent man, an excellent administrator, and a compassionate priest, but Raaman has been right all along, I'm afraid; you're not hard enough for a Shepherd. You let yourself become involved with both the Terrans and now you've given in to fear for this boy's life. A Shepherd can't afford personal emotions."

A terrible, heretical thought forced its way into Jared's mind. He looked at it and shuddered, but voiced it. "Levi, do you really believe the Trial is the Lord's will?"

Levi looked down at his hands. He considered the question for several minutes. Finally he lifted his eyes again. "I believe that the practice exists, and that there is little you or I can do about it except see that until every boy can be saved, they are all treated impartially."

Jared carried that thought with him the rest of the day. He thought about it throughout the afternoon meeting with the city commissioners. He had to be continually called back to the questions of whether the damage by buggy tires and iron-rimmed prairie wagon wheels was enough to justify hard-surfacing the streets or whether the bimonthly grading took care of the problem, of whether repairs on the building where the girls attended Middle School should be done now or in the spring.

"Father," Raaman said, his voice smooth, dry, and amused, "you seem rather preoccupied today." Raaman looked very pleased by it.

Esther Heber, one of the commissioners, resumed reading proposals. Jared tried to listen, mindful of Raaman's eyes on him, but found himself considering his heretical thought. It was not a new idea, he realized, only one he had kept buried out of sight and asking for ten years. He wondered how many other men had also had the same thought. There must have been others, when they became personally affected by the Trial. There was no written record of them, though. Did that mean their questions had been answered, their doubt silenced? The lack of argument against the Trial, the lack of attempts to stop it, could indicate the custom was Divinely supported. Still, Jared could not help but wonder what would have happened to him if he had refused to drug the glasses when Aaron Methuselah ordered it. What if he had proven too weak to remain silent under the burden of the knowledge entrusted to him?

At the end of the meeting the commissioners left without comment, but the Deacons closed around him with frowns.

"Father," Levi said, "are you all right?"

"I'm fine."

Jared pushed through them out of the room. Raaman followed. "You seem troubled. Is it something discussion would help?"

Not with Raaman. "I think meditation will be sufficient, thank you, brother."

"It isn't due to the Terran woman leaving, is it?"

"No."

Raaman still pressed. "Is it—"

"When I choose," Jared cut him off, "I'll talk about it." He switched the subject to the old controversy of whether salvation was through faith, good works, or both. He kept Raaman and the other Deacons, and his own thoughts, at bay with it until evening Praying.

He came close to losing control at supper, when he addressed a welcome to the new and returning boys. He could see Isaiah at the back of the dining hall between an instructor and an older boy. New boys were always scattered out so they would not, through the year, find themselves with empty places on either side of them. He forced his mind back to Shepherd's business and held it there, even through the social time with the instructors and stewards after supper.

Someone produced a die and for a time, they were no longer priests but boys again, involved in a lively game of hierarchy. Most of the stewards and instructors joined, along with Forest Timna and Kaleb Eshban. Jared contented himself with watching, and from the corner of his eye, watching Raaman watch him.

"Leaper!" Kaleb groaned. "I would start that high."

He shook the twelve-sided die and rolled it again. The picture on the upper side was a rapa. Jared smiled at his Deacon's sigh of relief. But the next roll brought a firebeetle and with a sniff of disgust, Kaleb passed the die to the next man.

It was then that the memory of the morning session with Levi broke through the barrier Jared had put up against it. *How could I save one and not the others?*

76

Until every boy can be saved, they should be treated impartially. Every word stabbed.

"Father," Raaman said, "what's wrong?"

Jared pulled his face straight. "The leaper we had for supper feels like it's still jumping."

"I'm very concerned about you, Father."

"That isn't necessary, but thank you."

Kaleb left the hierarchy game. "Shall we call a healer?"

"No." Jared stood. "I think I'll just go to bed."

Instead of heading for his rooms, however, Jared made his way through the corridors to the school wing and toward room 135. Most of the boys were sleeping, restless humps under the sheets of their sleeping shelves. A few of the older boys were sitting up reading, canda-globes shielded from spilling light into the corridor. Two boys noticed him passing and bowed their heads in respectful greeting.

Jared stopped at several rooms before reaching 135. He was attracted to one because the boy in it was whimpering in his sleep. Jared stood watching him for a long while, remembering his own fears at that age. *How could I save one and not the others?* Very slowly, Jared went on to Isaiah's room.

The boy was awake, sitting up on his sleeping shelf staring at the wall. He looked around as Jared came into the cubicle and smiled. It was Sky's smile.

Jared smiled back. Having Isaiah here was like having part of Sky. It gave him a warm feeling.

"How are you doing?" Jared whispered.

"Fine, Father."

Father. Jared had been called that countless times, but this time, from this particular boy, the word had a strangely different sound. The intended *you who are my Shepherd, the caretaker of my soul* became *you who are part of me.* Jared began to understand what Levi meant by saying fatherhood was an attitude. It was unimportant whether Jared's seed had actually given this boy life; through his bond to Sky, Jared was also bonded to the boy. The realization gave him an odd pain in his throat.

"I just wanted to make sure you were all right," he said around the pain. "Good night, Isaiah."

He backed into the corridor and stood leaning against a wall. The stone felt cool and slick behind him. The boy must not be allowed to risk the Trial. He must not. And yet, Levi's voice still whispered: *How could I save one and not the others?* How could Jared turn away from the boy who whimpered, or let any of them suffer the anguish Kastavin had felt?

Turn away? With a shock, leaning there, he understood why he had dreamed of himself as Pilate. He knew who it was he, like Pilate, had washed his hands of. And he knew who that one condemned man represented.

Jared pushed away from the wall and walked slowly back through the temple to his rooms. He could no longer turn boys over to the Trial and ignore their fate. He had to save Isaiah, and he had to save the rest, too. The question now was . . . how?

Chapter Nine

THE MIDDLE SCHOOL boarders sat in the first rows of the tabernacle for the Sabbath Praying. Jared watched them. The best way to save all of them was to stop the Trial, of course. He wondered what would happen if he stood up and told everyone how their sons had died.

He stood up, but only to begin the Litany. "As we are the Lord's faithful servants, perfectly submissive to His will, in blessings or adversity, let us now join together to praise Him for all He has brought to our lives."

Telling everyone was an insane idea, of course. He did not seriously consider it. These people were unprepared for that kind of burden. Their reactions were not predictable. If the Trial were to be stopped, it would have to be done quietly, and logically, so that no one beyond the informed circle would know the real reason, as no one beyond the informed circle now knew the true nature of the Trial. It would have to be done the way he had spent the night planning it.

He saw the boys stiffen as he reached: "For pestilence, and death." Isaiah alone looked trustingly up at him. He smiled down on them all.

After the Praying, as he and the Deacons stood in the courtyard chatting with members of the congregation, Jared whispered to Levi Dan, "Invite me home to spend the day with you and your family."

Without as much as a blink, Levi replied in a voice that could be heard halfway across the courtyard, "Father, will you do me and the Roshdan family the honor of spending the day with us?"

Jared accepted with formal grace.

After he changed out of his vestments, he joined Levi and a part of the family for the walk to Roshdan House. Levi made introductions as they went. Jared had met most of them several times: Sinai Dan, Levi's blood sister; Constance and Bird Rosh, Levi's fraternal sisters; and four other women who had become friends and joined along the way. There were new members, though, several very young women whom Jared did not know . . . until he realized they were daughters of the original sisterwives. The Roshdans were evidently becoming a linear as well as a peer family.

Sabbath dinner was a loud, lively event. It took Jared back to his childhood, and made him homesick for the Kedar ranch. If he had not given in to Aaron Methuselah's arguments and had gone after Sky, if he had brought her back to Gibeon, if he had insisted, as Levi had, on remaining a family man, this could be what his life would be like now. Listening to the conversations cross and clash and blend around him, he wondered if being Shepherd were really what he should have striven for. Perhaps he should have remained a simple religion and law instructor. At the very least, he would still have Sky. But then . . . he would never have been told the truth about the Trial, and he would be on the brink of losing Isaiah instead of saving him.

79

After the meal he excused himself from the women and took Levi for a walk in the yard. They sat down in the shade of a satan tree, on the bench built around its trunk. He leaned back against the smooth bark and breathed the spicy sweetness around him.

Levi looked expectantly at him.

Jared looked up at the mellow sunlight filtering down through the leaves. "You said yesterday there was nothing anyone could offer you for the lives of their sons, but . . . what if I offered you the lives of your grandsons in exchange for Isaiah?"

Jared glanced at Levi. If the Deacon had turned to salt he could not have been more still.

"Levi, I want to stop the Trial."

Life began seeping back into Levi. He licked his lips and regarded Jared thoughtfully. "Elias Jamin has strong support, but we can try. I have a few friends who will be helpful."

Jared blinked. "What are you talking about?"

It was Levi's turn to blink. "Aren't you planning to challenge Elias in a Bishop election?"

"No. Why should I?"

"Isn't that how you're going to stop the Trial?"

Jared shook his head. He wondered what had made Levi think that. Oh! "You were going to stop it that way, weren't you?" he said in sudden understanding.

"Once upon a time." Levi sighed. "As Bishop I would have had a 'vision' that told me the Trial should stop. But my plan had a flaw. I forgot to allow for Aaron Methuselah's fickleness." His voice grew bitter. "A necessary step to becoming Bishop was becoming Shepherd here, and though I slaved for our late Shepherd, he never once noticed me. First his favorite was Winter Talmai, then David Amalek, then Raaman Midian, then you. I was never in his consideration for the next Shepherd." His eyes raked Jared. "How do you plan to do it?"

"Blackmail."

Levi's breath was an in-drawn hiss. "How?"

"It came to me in a dream." Last night he had dreamed the dream of Pilate again, only Alesdra Pontokouros had stood on the roof garden with him rather than Sky. She spat at him, her green eyes flaring. "Think of some way to save them, because if you don't, I'll just have to do it myself, my own way."

"Alesdra will do it for me. She wants to sell us her company's machine. Helping us will accomplish that. I'm going to fly to Eridu and tell her about the Trial. I'll ask her to get a private audience with the Bishop and tell him she's found out. He won't dare harm her because of the reprisal that might come from the ship. Then she can threaten to reveal the truth to the world unless he buys her machine and stops the Trial. He won't dare order any deaths with alien virologists coming, because they'll learn right away that we're immune."

Levi stroked his beard as he considered the plan. After several minutes he said, "It might work. How will you explain going to Eridu?"

"Why bother to explain? I'm the Shepherd."

Levi nodded. "When will you leave?"

"Tomorrow morning."

Levi looked toward a group of young children chasing one another around the house next door. "If your scheme works, there will be no Trial this year. That would be . . . wonderful." He watched the several boys among the children for a few minutes, then brought his gaze back to Jared. "Perhaps I've underestimated you. You've absorbed something of Aaron Methuselah's tutelage after all, though I'm sure he'd be outraged by your use of it."

Jared grinned. "Shall we rejoin the women?"

Much later one of the younger women escorted them back to the temple for the evening Praying. At the door, as they were about to go in, the sisterwife held Jared a step or two behind Levi and whispered, "I've never seen Levi looking as happy as he looked when you came back this afternoon. For the first time I can recall, even his eyes were smiling. I don't know what you said to him out there under the satan tree, but in the name of the Roshdan sisterwives, I thank you, Father."

She hurried ahead into the tabernacle.

Jared watched her go before turning off toward his rooms. Levi was to be envied. He had women in his family to whom he was more than a family priest. They not only obeyed and respected him, they cared about him. No wonder Levi resisted all ecclesiastical efforts to separate him from them.

While he was in Eridu, Jared decided, he would go to Sky and ask her to come back with him. There was no longer any reason for living without her.

He heard a hiss. "Father."

Jared looked around to see Kaleb Eshban beckoning to him from a doorway.

"Come here," Kaleb said.

Jared stepped over to see what the Deacon wanted. Kaleb pulled him inside and closed the door.

"Raaman is stirring up trouble against you."

Jared bit his lip. "What kind?"

"Ever since you left today he's been telling everyone—in the most solicitous manner, of course—that you're ill, that you should be given a rest. He hasn't said it, but he's implying you're unfit to be Shepherd."

"Is anyone believing him?"

Kaleb nodded. "His arguments are very persuasive. We've all seen the way you've been acting. You can't deny spending hours of your time watching that Terran boy die, nor the agony it caused you. Why did you act that way? He isn't the first person to die of the disease."

Kaleb had never been told about the Trial. Jared did not feel now was the time to enlighten him, either. "Go on."

"You spent the Thanksgiving nights with the woman instead of with your own people. Everyone in Gibeon knows how you felt about your sister, and it looks sentimental for you to have sent for her son to come to school here. You even had the boy put in your old room. A Shepherd has to belong to everyone, Father, not just one or two people, or even one family. Sentimentality is weakening. Not only that, but your mind is off the-Lord-knows-where most of the time. You haven't done justice to your duties since the Terrans came."

It was a damning list, all the worse for the half-truths. He had not sent for Isaiah, of course, but now he knew why Raaman had. He debated telling Kaleb about that and decided against it. It would sound defensive. Better to wait until he could prove something, and better still to seem calm and unworried by Raaman's plotting.

"Perhaps I haven't. The problem is solved now, though. What does Raaman preach in the way of giving me a rest?"

"He's suggesting you be given a thorough examination by healers and a long holiday, perhaps go into retreat for a year."

"A year. I'd have to resign. Can't people see Raaman is doing this because he's hungry for Shepherdhood?"

"We see it, but just because he wants your office doesn't mean his arguments aren't true. You're going to have to fight him. Is there some way I can help? I can put pages to spying on him for you."

"In a while, perhaps, but not just yet. Thank you for the warning."

Kaleb smiled. "My mother was fraternal sister to yours."

Jared nodded. Not blood kin, but their mothers had been daughters of sisterwives, kinship enough to explain Kaleb's concern.

"Raaman pretends to worry about you but I really do. Maybe you should rest. You could go out to the ranch for a couple of weeks. Levi Dan and I can keep Raaman under control while you're gone."

"Again, perhaps later. I have something I have to do first."

The prayer bell began its high dinging, summoning the devout to the evening Praying.

Kaleb said, "You'd better go dress, Father. I'll see you at the tabernacle."

Jared made sure he said one of the best Prayings of his life that evening. He saw Isaiah in the front row and smiled at him once, then made sure he smiled at other boys, too. To his great satisfaction, Raaman looked annoyed.

"You seem much more yourself this evening," Raaman said as they left the tabernacle for the dining hall. "I'm so glad." He did not look it.

"I think spending the day away from the temple with Levi's family was a good change."

Raaman's eyes gleamed. "You know, a change would be—"

"Now," Jared cut him off, "I'm looking forward to beginning the school year and to resuming a normal routine again."

"That's good to hear, Father."

Jared kept his face solemn. "But coming back I started thinking, Brother Raaman. You've been working very hard. A change would be good for you. Have you considered going on retreat? Simeon has a beautiful temple." It was also fourteen hundred kilometers away.

Raaman's expression froze. "Retreat?" His voice sounded strangled.

"Yes. I'll contact the Shepherd in the morning and make arrangements for you to retreat there for two or three months. You can leave on the next southbound train."

He walked ahead before Raaman had time to close his mouth.

Jared passed Kaleb to reach his chair at the head table. Kaleb caught his eyes and said, "That might not have been wise."

Jared glanced back toward Raaman. The lean Deacon was talking to a steward. "He needs to be kept on the defensive for a while."

By the time he took his seat and the meal began, Raaman had recovered his composure. Smiling, he started the scripture game. He recited a piece of scripture. Whoever could identify the passage could then recite a passage of his own.

Jared had always liked the game. It was certainly preferable to listening to a reader. At the same time, it kept other conversation to a minimum.

The men let the boys identify as much scripture as possible. If no boy knew a passage, one of the men would name it.

No one seemed able to identify: "Have I not commanded thee? Be strong and of good courage; be not afraid, neither be thou dismayed: for the Lord thy God is with thee whithersoever thou goest.' "

Jared said, "Joshua 1:9. My scripture is: 'A false witness shall not be unpunished, and he that speaketh lies shall not escape.' "

84

Raaman regarded Jared with narrowed eyes for a moment, then smiled. "Proverbs 19:5."

Jared did not hear Raaman's scripture. That smile boded no good. The thought put an uneasy twist in his stomach.

A few minutes later Jared realized that the trouble with his stomach was not entirely emotional. There was something else happening. It was twisting with increasing strength, sending darts of pain down through the rest of his abdomen.

Not long after that he recognized the steward serving them as the one Raaman had spoken to earlier.

Somehow Jared sat through the rest of the meal without giving in to the rising pain. The darts turned into knives. He felt perspiration break out under his arms and across his upper lip. Kaleb had been right; he should not have threatened Raaman. It had only spurred the Deacon into panic measures against him. Jared was sure whatever had been given to him was not lethal, just something to make him ill. If he showed it was affecting him, however, he would find himself in bed with a healer at his side and no way to arrange a retreat for Raaman in Simeon or to leave for Eridu tomorrow.

Standing up at the end of the meal took the greatest act of will in his life. His body wanted to curl in agony on the floor. Somehow, he forced himself out of the chair and straight upright. He let himself be stopped every meter on his way to the door for a few words with a boy, instructor, or steward. He smiled and endured the wrenching, stabbing, tearing pain that warned him he needed to reach his room as quickly as possible.

"Father, will you join us swimming this evening?" one of the instructors asked.

"I'd better not. I have some reading to do."

Then Raaman accosted him. "Father, may I speak to you?"

"In the morning, please. I would like solitude tonight."

He continued on to his room in a dignified stroll while pain tore at him. Temple doors had no locks and never before in his life had Jared cared. Now he wanted one desperately.

He looked around the room for something to block the door. There was a chair of hide straps over a frame that looked about the right height. He wedged it under the doorknob, then he fled to the bathroom and was explosively, violently ill.

Chapter Ten

HE COULD NOT spend the night in the temple. Jared was coldly certain of that fact. Raaman's plans were coming to fruition and the Deacon would not dare let himself be sent on retreat. If he did not act now, he might have to wait months, even years more. Jared thought Raaman had waited all he was willing to.

Still shaking from the aftermath of his poisoning, he stripped off his clothes and beard. He showered. Afterward, he put on a clean tunic and trousers. He never stopped worrying about Raaman the entire time.

Since the poisoning attempt would not appear to have worked, Raaman would have to try something else tonight. Jared kept expecting to hear the door being battered in. That was foolish fancy, of course; Raaman would do nothing that crude, or violent. Still . . .

What it meant was, Jared would have to leave for Eridu tonight, before he could be stopped. And it meant he could not leave openly. Raaman would certainly do something to prevent his departure. In effect, Jared would have to escape from the temple.

He would have to take Isaiah with him, too. Without the use of the flyer, the only ways open to Eridu were slow. It was unthinkable to leave Isaiah here where the boy was in Raaman's power. Another frightening possibility was that the Trial might be ordered started before Jared was able to stop it. Isaiah had to come with him, at least far enough to put the boy out of danger.

The problem was getting them both out of the temple undetected. The gates were all guarded and no man ever left without a woman to escort him. The point in his favor was that the guards were there to keep people from coming *in*. They were not likely to be looking over their shoulders for men trying to get out.

He was debating whether to reapply his beard when there was a knock on his door. Forest Timna's voice said, "Father, may I come in?"

Jared went cold. "Not tonight, please."

"But I need—" The knob turned. The door moved inward a few millimeters before it was stopped by the chair. "It's jammed." The last comment was low and did not sound directed at Jared.

There was just the one door out. The sitting and sleeping rooms' other exits were into the garden. Stuffing his beard in his pocket, Jared crossed toward the sitting room garden door. He moved in long, quiet strides. Easing the garden door open, he slipped out.

There was a murmur of voices in the corridor, then Forest said, "I'll leave you then, Father."

Getting out of the garden should not be difficult, anyway. The pierced design in the stone of the walls gave it good hand- and footholds for climbing. Jared went up in the corner nearest his sleeping room, where the branches of a satan tree would hide him as he reached the top.

But on top he had to sit and consider where to go from there. The candaglobes in the portico cast too much light into the courtyard for his liking. He would be seen anywhere he crossed. In the other direction, the roof of the temple stretched away from him in a thousand sloping planes, lighted only by the half-moons overhead. The tiles made slippery walking. He remembered that from the time in Middle School he had gone across the roofs on a dare to spy on the Shepherd's garden. But at least it was a route he could travel with little likelihood of meeting anyone else.

He pulled off his slippers and pushed one into each tunic pocket. Then he climbed through the branches of the satan tree and onto the roof above his sleeping room. The roof tiles were smooth and cool beneath his feet. He paused, staying low, to orient himself. The temple looked much different from up here. He conjured up corridors in his mind and planned how he would go through them to reach the school wing. He kept that picture before him as he set out.

Crossing the roof seemed to take forever. It was easier in bare feet than it had been in slippers, but was still treacherous going. Every time the building changed direction, the pitch of the roof changed, too. The shadows cast by Nightseye made distances and slopes deceptive. More than once he stepped over what he thought was a mere joining of roofs and found a sudden drop on the other side. Being a good deal older and more sedentary than he had been the last time he made this trip did not help, either.

Yet in a strange way, this experience was not so very different. There was the same night breeze cool on his bare face, and the same sweaty fear of being caught. He almost expected to hear Aaron Methuselah's rich voice calling up to him, "What are you doing, my son? Come down where I can have a look at you." And as on that other night, he found this new perspective so interesting he wished he had time to enjoy the view.

He passed around the courtyard where the pre-Marahn statue stood. The gaze of its lifted face seemed to follow him. He stopped for a moment to look down at it.

"The Lord willing," he whispered to it, "I'm on my way to help finish something you started."

The narrow, inhuman face regarded him with dreamy benediction. A high, musical voice in his head, speaking in accents much like Alesdra's, said, "Good luck."

His tunic hampered him. When a courtyard he had to pass was occupied and he tried to crawl, the skirt tangled around his knees. As he circled around the swimming pool where the instructors and stewards were splashing through some water game, the material of the tunic bottom caught under his hand. He lost his grip and went slithering, headfirst, down the roof toward the pool. He jerked the hand free and thrust both out in front of him, flat on the tiles, desperately trying to brake. He dug in his fingertips. Just over a meter from the edge, friction took effect. He stopped. Something went on, though, sliding with a soft hiss, and dropped over the edge. He heard the plop of the thing hitting water.

"Hey," someone said. "Who threw in the slipper?"

Jared buried his face against the tiles and prayed that in the moonlight the green of his tunic blended with the red of the roof tiles.

The men climbed out of the pool and stood shivering naked in the night breeze while they peered upward. They tried blocking out the light of the candaglobes with their hands.

"I can't see anything."

"Want to guess who it probably is? Son," an instructor called up, "you'd better go back to bed. School starts tomorrow."

Jared remained motionless until, an interminable time later, they wrapped their towels around them and went inside. Only then did he sit up. He blew on his palms. They felt scraped raw. He flexed his hands a few times to make sure they still worked, and before going on he jammed the tail of his tunic, front and back, into the waistband of his trousers.

At the school wing he slid to the edge of the roof. He eased over until he was hanging by his hands, then dropped to the ground. It was an inside courtyard, dark and deserted. He paused in the nearest doorway to pull his tunic out of his trousers and straighten it, then went in.

The corridor was empty. His bare feet came down without sound on the tile floor. He resisted the strong urge to slide along the wall; it was an effort to walk down the middle with the brisk stride of someone on a necessary errand. Without his beard he might be mistaken for a page, or so he hoped.

He checked behind him once at the door of 135 before darting sideways into the cubicle. The boy woke the instant Jared touched him. He turned over and stared up at Jared.

"Be quiet, Isaiah," Jared whispered.

"Mother?" It was an incredulous whisper.

"No—Jared. Isaiah, do you want to live?"

The boy's breath caught. "Yes, Father."

"Then get up and come with me."

The boy swung off the sleeping shelf. He dressed without a word and followed Jared back down the corridor into the courtyard. They climbed onto the roof the way Jared had done years before, up a satan tree whose branches reached out across the tiles.

It was not until they were off the ground that Jared started considering how they were going to get out of the temple. He had never left before, except by the orthodox ways. He climbed to the peak of the roof and risked standing to get a broad view.

The sea of tiles around him stretched off into blackness in every direction. He could make out the outside wall only dimly. It was separated from the temple itself by a courtyard never less than fifty meters wide.

He thought a minute. Was the guest house against the outside wall? He thought so. Only . . . in which direction was it? He had never been there before, though he knew it was near the stable/hangar area. He headed toward the flyer hangar.

Nightseye was dropping toward the western horizon and Tagalong slipping around behind it when they found the guest house. It was against the outside wall, and joined to the main temple by a covered walkway that was also the entrance to the stable courtyard. In front of the guest house sat the flyer. Jared regarded it with longing. If only he knew how to fly the damn thing. Since he did not, he took Isaiah's arm and they hurried across the walkway. Crouching low, they climbed over the roof of the guest house to the top of the wall. There they gathered their courage, then dropped over the far side.

The packed sand of the street sent a jolt of pain up through Jared's feet, but he did not fall. He looked around for Isaiah and found the boy brushing sand from his hands and knees. Jared now regretted losing his slipper more than ever. It meant walking half-bare-footed across Gibeon. He wanted to cross yards rather than follow the streets, too.

"Where are we going?" Isaiah asked.

"To a friend."

That was all he dared say right now. He hurried the

boy across the street and into the shadows around the bicycle shop.

Half an hour later they reached Roshdan House. Jared was limping on his bare foot. He had stepped on innumerable sticks and rocks in the dark, and stubbed his toe once. He pushed Isaiah out of sight and stepped into the lighted portico to pull the bell cord. After a few minutes he pulled the cord again.

There was a rustle of sound inside and the door opened a crack. A woman's voice asked, "What is your business, please?"

"I need to see Brother Levi."

There was a pause. "Father? Jared?" The voice sounded incredulous. The door opened and the young sisterwife who had escorted him back to the temple came into the light. She smiled. "You've changed, Father. Please come in."

"I have someone with me. Isaiah."

The boy came out of the shadows. The woman's eyes widened but she stepped aside for them to enter. She closed the door behind them and led them into the sitting room.

"Please sit down. Do you want a light?"

"No."

He felt rather than saw her speculative stare. But he did see her nod. She adjusted a window shutter so some of the light from the portico filtered into the room. "I'll bring Levi."

Jared settled back in a rhino-hide chair and rubbed his aching foot. What a very fine young woman that was. She let them in without question and seemed to find his preference for darkness unremarkable.

Levi soon appeared, carrying a small, shaded candaglobe. He sat down opposite Jared. After holding the candaglobe up to look at Jared and Isaiah, he put it aside and sat back in the chair finger-combing the sleep-tangled wildness of his hair and beard. "What's happened?"

"First, is there a place the boy can sleep?"

Levi looked at him a moment, then nodded. He raised his voice. "Storm."

The young sisterwife appeared. Levi explained what

91

he wanted. Storm held out her hand to Isaiah. Isaiah, however, continued to sit where he was.

"Go with her," Jared told him. "I want you to do all these people say, no matter how strange it may seem. Your life depends on it."

The boy sighed. Jared could guess his feelings. Here they were in the midst of something very exciting and perhaps dangerous, but Isaiah was not allowed to be part of it. Sky had brought her son up to be obedient, however. He stood and followed Storm out of the room.

The men waited until the two were gone, then Levi raised his brows at Jared. Jared told him what had happened.

Levi listened gravely, but when Jared was finished asked, "Are you sure so extreme a reaction was necessary?"

Jared shrugged. "I don't know, but I was afraid to stay. What do you think?"

Levi considered, pulling at his beard. "How will you reach Eridu now?"

"By train, I think."

Levi looked surprised, then frowned.

"I know," Jared said. "There's no train to Eridu until Tuesday."

"Beyond what you'll do until then, you're going to need an escort. You can take Storm—she's intelligent and good company, by far the best of my daughters—but what about the boy? Is he going with you?"

Jared had been too busy keeping his balance on his way across the roof to think much farther ahead. Also, the walk here with one bare foot had had too many distractions to leave much time for planning. Jared considered possible courses of action now.

"I won't take an escort. I don't want to endanger anyone else's life. For the same reason, and because I'll be less conspicuous and can travel faster without him, I want to leave Isaiah here."

"Endanger—? That sounds like madness. Raaman wants your office, not your life."

Perhaps. This loud scream of alarm in him could be madness. But it might not be. "Raaman has always claimed I'm too weak to be a Shepherd. When he finds I've run away, and taken the boy with me, what is that going to suggest to him but that I'm taking a panic measure to save the boy's life? That would suggest I'm breaking under the weight of what I know. He hates me already. With an excuse like this, what might he feel justified in doing?" He paused. "What happens to men who break?"

"No one ever told me." Levi's voice became thoughtful. "But I always wondered how Daniel Amalek happened to drown. It was ruled suicide, but Daniel was terrified of water. I can't believe he would kill himself that way." He stopped for a long breath. "Daniel had been for a buggy ride with Aaron Methuselah just one week before. He came back looking ill and was very depressed from then to the night he died. Jared," Levi said urgently, "let me send Storm with you. A man alone is the most conspicuous person imaginable."

"A man would be, yes, but I won't be a man."

Levi blinked.

"I used to pass as my sister. With no beard, with my hair shorter, and in women's clothes, I can do it again."

"You can look like a woman, perhaps, but can you act like one? Jared, have you ever traveled by yourself before? Bought meals and tickets? You can't hope to fool a close scrutiny."

"But who will be looking closely at me? Raaman will be hunting for a man and a boy."

"He's bound to find the boy very quickly. If I try to hide him here, one of my family, the children at least, will let word slip to someone outside."

"Don't hide him. Cut his hair, dress him up in girl's clothes, and keep him openly. You can say he's kin. Pretend he's ill and keep him in bed."

Levi nodded. "We could do that. Storm can look after him. Only she, and perhaps Sinai and Bird, need to know who he is. Will he cooperate?"

"Tell him his life depends on it."

Their eyes met in painful understanding. At Isaiah's age a promise of life would have been enough to talk them into doing anything.

Levi pushed himself to his feet. "We'll see to outfitting you in the morning. You look about Sinai's size. And while you're waiting for Tuesday, I can have Sinai and Storm teach you how to act like a woman."

It was a good idea, except that Jared felt he could not wait another day before leaving. He could not board a train here, either.

"We'll have to outfit me now. I'm leaving tonight."

Levi had started for the door. He whirled. "To go where? The train—"

"Raaman may have people on the platform here who can recognize me even in women's clothes. I'll board at Viridian. No one knows me there."

Levi stared at him. His mouth worked but no speech came. When he did manage to speak, it was in a strangled whisper. *"Viridian.* You're proposing to cross four hundred kilometers of prairie all by yourself?"

"Lend me a bicycle and enough backpack food for five days. I can make it. I'll just follow the road."

Levi shook his head. "Impossible. How can you even think of such a thing?"

"What else can I do? I'll be all right. The Lord will look after me."

Levi sighed. "It still sounds like madness, but how can I refute that argument? Very well, Father, let's go rouse Storm again."

Jared's transformation into a woman took place in the kitchen in the light of a single, half-draped candaglobe. He watched the dark locks fall around his feet and thought of Samson and Delilah. What remained on his head, a short, crisp cap of curls, felt light and strange. He ran his hands through it repeatedly, fascinated by the feel.

"You're lucky you were in that depilation fad," Levi said. "A beard would betray you instantly."

Storm handed him a stack of clothing. There was a pair of narrow, corded ranch pants, knee-high boots of rhino hide with a laced instep, a heavy pullover shirt with a high collar, and a supple leaper-hide jacket.

"The nights are getting cool," she said. "This shirt and jacket should keep you warm and be bulky enough to hide the fact that you have no breasts. I hope the boots fit well enough for you to tolerate them." She gave them a wistful glance as she handed them over. "Your legs need the protection the tops will give you against snakes and stinghoppers."

He changed into the clothes. Everything felt strange but comfortable. As a finishing touch, Storm handed him a flat, stiff-brimmed range hat. He turned around in front of Storm and Levi. They nodded approval. Even the boots fit reasonably well when the insteps were laced as tightly as they would go. Storm looked almost sorry about that.

"They're my favorite working boots," she said. "Well, you'll pass a casual inspection anyway."

"Show him," Levi said.

She opened a window shutter. Jared stepped in front of the opening . . . and stared. The Shepherd of Gibeon was gone. Instead, in the strip of window, mirrored against the darkness outside, was a slender, narrow-hipped woman. The face was almost Sky's.

Storm closed the shutter and turned toward the cupboards. "I'll pack your supplies."

She talked while she worked, telling him how to make camp, warning him against dangerous plants and animals, suggesting how he could act like a woman. Jared listened, though he doubted he would remember most of what she said.

A few points were memorable. "A woman is always respectful to a man. She never argues with him, never interrupts. When you meet other women, remember they're your equals. You can't expect them to obey you or serve you. You may have to obey or serve them, depending on the circumstances. Don't call a woman *sister* unless she's in a superior position, you are total strangers, or are around men. It's used as a group address sometimes, but usually *sister* is a formal address not used between close friends."

When the pack was finished, it was lighter than Jared had thought it would be. Storm explained that all the food was dried, ready to eat without cooking.

"You should be sure to drink water when you eat, though. You'll fill up faster that way without eating as much. You'll travel better on a light stomach, and sleep more alertly, too." She frowned. "Do you know how to handle any kind of weapon?"

"I once learned to throw a bolas."

She sighed. "Not much help if a wild rapa chooses

95

you for its next meal. But I'll give you one anyway. Keep hold of one end. Hit anything that comes after you in the eye with the weight on the other end of the cord."

Through dressing Jared and packing the food, Levi had kept silent. He let Storm take charge. When she had finished showing Jared how to put on and adjust the pack, however, he protested one more time. "Don't do this. We can hide you here until Tuesday and then find a way to put you on the train."

Jared shook his head.

"How much can you endanger us? Raaman can claim to be hunting a madman, nothing more."

"He ought to have some money, Levi." Storm left the kitchen.

"I don't know what he's capable of doing," Jared said. "I don't want to have to find out."

Storm came back with a handful of bills. She counted it into his hand: twenty hundred-unit notes, three thousand-unit notes, one two-thousand-unit note. "This was going to buy Levi a new bicycle for his birthday, so you have to give me something in return for it. Promise me that one day you'll tell me why you're doing this."

"I promise."

Levi took him by the shoulders. "The Lord be with you, Father." He hugged Jared hard.

Storm took Jared out the rear door to the bicycle rack. She backed one machine out and handed it to him. "There's one more thing. You make a handsome woman, so remember, a woman has the right to refuse the sexual advance of any man or woman. It's wise to have a polite excuse to give a man, but you'll probably find more insistent women than men."

Jared stared at her. This was something that would never have occurred to him. "Surely I'm not—"

"You *are* likely to interest at least one person along the way," she interrupted, "particularly anyone you meet on the prairie. If the advance comes from a real animal, don't be afraid to slap her. It may take that to discourage her. It's possible you won't meet anyone, of course; I'm telling you so you won't be surprised if it happens. That would be too odd to be overlooked.

Women may be angered, disgusted, or amused by sexual advances, but we've been receiving such overtures since Middle School, so we're never surprised."

Jared took a deep breath and let it out in a gusty sigh. "Thank you for warning me."

She fastened a small candaglobe to the light bracket on the handlebars of the bicycle. "This will show you only the road under your front wheel, I'm afraid. I wish it were stronger. I was out that road schooling a buggy rapa on Friday and it needs to be regraded. The surface is best near the edges."

She walked to the street with him and stood while he swung onto the machine.

"Thank you for everything," he said.

"It's our honor to serve you, Father. Be careful. Listen more than you speak. The Lord be with you."

He left her standing in the street looking after him. He turned a corner and was alone.

In minutes the last houses of Gibeon were behind him. Then he started to feel alone. With the moons down, the road stretching southwest before him was a dark strip on dark prairie, marked only by the dotted line of candalilies on either side. The breeze brought him no suggestion of humanity, only the scents of dust and animal musk, the squeals and barks of distant wildlife, and the high buzz of nightflies visiting the candalilies. Even Gibeon was out of sight behind him. He might have been the only human on the planet.

Now that he had time to reflect on it, Jared felt less confident than he had managed to sound to Levi. He realized he had been counting more on those stolen childhood excursions onto the prairie than on Divine protection to get him to Viridian. He wondered of how much value those excursions would be. They were so very long ago.

Four hundred kilometers seemed like four thousand. The time he would waste traveling made him grind his teeth in anguish. While he was crawling along this road, Alesdra Pontokouros could be refused permission to build her shuttlebox. The ship could give up and leave. Without the ship to protect her, she was too vulnerable to be able to blackmail the Bishop. Jared might save Isaiah, but what would become of those thousands of other boys? Five days. Could he make Viridian in five days? Perhaps less, if he pushed himself. He leaned forward over the handlebars and pedaled faster.

Chapter Eleven

RAAMAN WAS a study in unctuous solemnity. "Brothers, this is a serious matter."

The four Deacons and the temple's chief steward stood in the middle of Jared's sitting room. Levi was interested in their reactions. Raaman had lines of anxiety around his mouth and between his brows, not from his pretended concern but from a deeper fear that showed in his eyes in a periodic frantic flicker. The discovery of Jared's flight must have been a most unpleasant shock to him. Forest seemed at a loss how to react. He kept watching Raaman for a cue. The chief steward and Kaleb looked puzzled and skeptical.

"Maybe he's somewhere else in the temple," Kaleb said.

"He couldn't have left these rooms normally with the door blocked as it was."

Levi asked, "How did you happen to discover the Shepherd was gone?"

"I had a dream that he needed me. It was so real, so urgent, that I came and knocked on his door. When he didn't answer, I tried to go in. The door wouldn't open. I had a guard climb over the garden wall. She found the rooms empty and that chair fixed under the doorknob. I took a guard off both gates, located all the night pages, and used them to search the temple. We couldn't find the Shepherd anywhere."

Kaleb wandered into the sleeping room. "There's no sign of where he might have gone, or how?"

"No. All the rhinos and buggies are still here, as is the flyer. He didn't ask any of the night pages to find him an escort."

Kaleb came back. "There are some fouled clothes in the bathroom. It looks like he was ill."

"I know, and that's why I'm worried. We all know how peculiar his behavior has been these past few weeks. To find him gone with evidence of a recent and violent bout of sickness left behind disturbs me deeply."

Levi could just imagine it did. The first thing it told Raaman was that Jared knew more about Raaman's activities and plans than Raaman cared to have him know. The lean Deacon would have no way of guessing what steps Jared might be taking against him at that moment. Levi wondered if Raaman had discovered Isaiah Joseph's absence yet. Probably not, or he would certainly have mentioned it. Levi decided to keep everyone calm as long as possible.

"I'm sure there's a reasonable explanation, Brother Raaman. It's nearly time for the morning Praying. The Shepherd is a conscientious man. He hasn't missed a Praying for over ten years. I can't imagine him missing this one. In any case, the rest of us need to be there."

"What if he doesn't come?" Forest asked.

"We can worry about that if it happens."

Raaman said, "I think we should cancel the Praying and enlist everyone's aid in looking for the Shepherd."

"Cancel the *Praying!*" Kaleb was shocked.

"Certainly not," Levi said. "We don't need the Shepherd for the ritual; it's just customary to have him there."

"This could be a critical situation."

"I doubt that very much, but if it is, wouldn't you say we need the Praying even more? Let's all of us ask for guidance."

The prayer bell began ringing. Levi turned for the door. "Above all, let's not alarm our flock."

Jared did not come for the Praying. Levi, as the senior Deacon, led the ritual in his place, as he was required to do when the Shepherd was ill or away. None of the celebrants in the tabernacle as much as raised a brow. The boys listened to him with as little attention as they would have given Jared. Only one woman looked disappointed. Levi wondered if she had come to ask Jared for permission to use his seed.

At the close of the Praying, walking up the aisle, Raaman hissed, "Well, Brother Levi?"

"Surely we can wait until after breakfast to start panicking."

"Why aren't you more concerned?" Raaman frowned. "Do you know where he is, perhaps?"

"No, I don't." That was true enough. Jared could be anywhere along the road to Viridian by now, or even dead, struck down by a wild rapa or one of the great raptors. "I'm just not convinced there's any need for concern. I've seen much more peculiar human behavior than this during my tenure as Deacon."

But events would not wait until after breakfast. In the middle of the meal, the dormitory steward came to the head table. "We have a boy missing. I didn't notice until someone said his place at the table was empty. I've just checked his room and he isn't there. No one has seen him since last night."

Raaman's eyes brightened with interest. "Which boy?"

"Isaiah Joseph."

Raaman turned to look at Levi. "Well. That's interesting, don't you think?"

School opening was delayed while everyone searched the temple for the Shepherd and his sister's son. Levi made one more protest for sanity. "Perhaps the two of them, being kin, went for an early walk and have been prevented from coming back."

"Walk where? Prevented by what?" Raaman challenged. "Who escorted them?"

With a sigh, Levi let him take charge. All normal temple business was canceled for the day. Everyone in the temple was questioned about everything they had seen and heard the evening before. Runners were sent to bring back the four night guards so they, too, could be questioned. By the time the last one left, it was midday. The Deacons took their noon meal on trays in the meeting room where they had been conducting the interviews.

Raaman sat at the apex of the triangular table,

toying with a sheet of notes. "So much for reasonable explanations. We have a Shepherd and a boy who haven't been seen since last night, who are nowhere within the temple walls, yet who were not seen leaving. We have a slipper"—he held it up—"retrieved from the pool. The size matches that of other footwear in Jared Joseph's rooms. We have a third-year boy who saw Isaiah Joseph walking down the corridor last night with what the boy thought at the time was a page."

"Do you really think they got out by climbing over the wall?" Forest Timna asked.

"Yes."

"The wall is three and a half meters high," Kaleb said, "and built smooth to make climbing impossible."

"The top is only a half-meter above the roof of the guest house, and we know he must have used the roof to reach the school wing."

Levi shifted in his chair. "I find it difficult to believe Jared Joseph would climb across roofs in the middle of the night with a boy, jump over a wall which has gates he is perfectly entitled to walk through, and run off into the night on one bare foot." Only because Levi had seen Jared last night and heard him confess to it did he believe it. He still found it hard to accept. The whole thing seemed like part of some mad dream.

"The Jared Joseph we've known and respected wouldn't do that," Raaman said, "but the man we've seen these past weeks has been . . . different. He's obviously a very disturbed man. We can't begin to guess why he abducted the boy, and even less where he may have taken him. There could be serious consequences, though. We need to find him and put him in the care of a healer as soon as possible."

"I won't believe Jared would hurt the boy," Kaleb said.

That was not the serious consequence Raaman had in mind, Levi knew. Innocent Kaleb. Levi envied him that lack of knowledge. With the Lord's grace, Kaleb and thousands like him would be able to remain innocent, be able to sleep nights . . . be able to face sons and grandsons of their families without flinching when begged for a trick or prayer to help them survive the

Trial. With more luck, there would never again be a Trial.

With a start he focused on Raaman again. "Did you say something about keepers?"

"They can find him for us. Theirs is the best-coordinated search system on Marah."

"But he hasn't been gone three days yet," Kaleb said. "The keepers won't classify him as a missing person."

"We won't have him hunted as a missing person." Raaman's solemn expression looked practiced. "He did take the boy, remember."

Kaleb was on his feet. "You can't make him a fugitive on a criminal charge!"

Even Forest's expression protested.

"Kaleb is right," Levi said. "It's unthinkable."

Raaman was all earnest concern. "It's for his own good. We have to find him. Afterward we can drop the charge."

"No. I forbid it," Levi said.

Raaman shrugged. "You're too late. I've already had a warrant issued." His satisfaction showed in his eyes.

Levi and Kaleb stared at him in horror. Levi searched for his voice. Sound was there but the words, a hundred variations of shocked protest, were stuck trying to force their way out all together. He was not surprised, however. He almost expected Raaman to do something like this.

He picked one sentence. "You've overstepped your authority, Raaman Midian. As senior Deacon, I'm next after the Shepherd. When Jared returns, I'll see that he knows every detail of your conduct and deals appropriately with you." He stood. "And now, as this meeting seems to have outlived useful function, I'm going to try doing a little work in what remains of the day." He strode out of the room.

He was nearly to his office when he heard Raaman behind him. "Levi, take a walk with me."

Levi frowned, eying the door of his office. "I have a great deal of work waiting."

"This is important."

Levi sighed. He might as well hear everything Raaman had to say. "Very well."

They walked in the courtyard with the alien artifact and sat together on a bench at its base.

"You're fighting me, Levi. Why?" Raaman's puzzled tone sounded genuine.

Levi folded his hands in his lap. "I know what you're trying to do. I won't support any action to depose or destroy Jared."

"Have you considered what he can do to *us?* You see what's happening. You must. He's breaking. At best he's taken the boy off to hide him until after puberty. At worst, he can say the wrong things to the wrong people and destroy us."

Levi turned to look at him. "Could he, if the Trial is truly the Lord's will?"

That caught the lean Deacon without an answer. He stared openmouthed at Levi.

"The problem with secrets is keeping them. David Moses should have found another way to conduct the Trial, some way so we would never have to worry how people of lesser faith might react if they learned the truth."

Raaman found his voice again. "The question is not what David Moses should have done, but what we can do to protect ourselves now. Aaron must have been in his dotage to tell Jared in the first place. We can't let Jared tell anyone else."

The words chilled Levi. In addition to Raaman's hatred of Jared, he heard a man speaking out of fear for his position and reputation. Self-preservation and ambition were deadly motivations in an opponent like Raaman. Levi tightened his folded hands and prayed Jared had a speedy journey.

Chapter Twelve

MONDAY WAS Sky's home day, but she arranged for the younger children to stay with the family next door and used the day to show Alesdra the Old City. Part of it had been preserved from mining operations and was open to the public. Touring the ruins, Alesdra was able to forget temporarily the Bishop and the still-recessed Grand Council. She even forgot the *Rose*. Instead, she and Sky wandered through the diggings and speculated about the vanished former inhabitants of Marah.

The buildings had once been slim and graceful. Their lines reminded her of the ancient statue in Gibeon. The taller ones were only fallen rubble now, though some of the lower structures had been buried intact. Excavated, they looked as they might have looked when they were first abandoned.

They lay along the sweeping arabesque curves of the streets, built of metal and stone, red stone, golden, and translucent ivory like Gibeon's artifact, with narrow, arched doorways and oval windows. The walls were covered with murals put on by some process that was not painting but color impregnated into the material of the wall itself. There were fanciful landscapes and nature scenes, depicting creatures that had not walked the planet for millennia . . . mammals, hooved and horned, maned and tailed, striped and spotted. There were a few creatures she recognized, the large, ostrich-like hoopers, and smaller versions of rhinos and rapas.

On other murals, laughing groups of the child-delicate aliens worked together at sleek machinery and lounged in groups around banquet tables and picnics. They were dark people, skin color ranging from amber to dark tea color, with short caps of shining blue-black hair. Their garments wrapped them in folds that shone or clung or glittered in a rainbow of colors.

Where the walls were not turned into galleries, they were covered with plastic or metal in bright colors. The door handles and control knobs of machinery were cleverly shaped wonders that drew the hands to touch and caress.

Their guide was a golden young woman from the historical society that stood watchdog on the exhibit section of the city. She invited Alesdra to touch whatever she wanted.

Alesdra drew her hand down the sinuous curves of one door handle. "You mean for five hundred years you've been tearing down walls like those and melting handles like these to make bicycles and sewer pipe? What a sacrilege. Someday when this planet is open for travel, a million archeologists are going to tear your throats out."

The guide nodded unhappily. "I know. The historical society keeps trying to save as much as possible, fighting the mining companies every millimeter of the way. Saving this is worth it for the knowledge alone. We know so little about them."

"What do you know about them?" Alesdra asked.

The guide's almond eyes brightened. Alesdra had obviously touched a sympathetic nerve. "Well, for one thing, they had a unique life-style. They lived in apartments so small they had to live alone, or perhaps with just a child, but there's only one kitchen facility per building. Their commercial buildings are full of machinery that takes many people to operate. You've seen the murals. All taken together, we're guessing they socialized at meals and work, then withdrew to spend much of their other time alone. We think they created then. At least, when you see a picture of a sculptor or painter, he or she is always isolated." Her face became animated as she warmed to her subject. "They were true artists, applying artistry to everything they did. We've been going mad trying to find how they came to annihilate themselves so horribly."

"Haven't you found any libraries?"

The guide's golden forehead furrowed. She rubbed

105

the crease between her eyes. "Oh, yes, but it doesn't help us much when we can't translate. We need a Rosetta stone. My recurring nightmare is, we'll find the key to their language one day, but before we can use it, a mining company will melt it into a stirrup." She glared off toward the mining section of the city. "They'd destroy everything, given a chance, never let us learn who and what the pre-Marahns were."

Sky looked puzzled. "Should we live without metal for the benefit of archeologists and museums, though?"

Alesdra looked from Sky to the impassioned face of their guide. Sky had a point. The colony did need metal, and there must be countless cities still buried around the world. Still, when Alesdra looked at those walls, the thought of such beauty destroyed forever seemed like criminal waste.

"When the last of this is gone," the guide said, "these people will be truly dead. At least now they can live in our imaginations."

Sky touched the control knobs of a machine. They were too narrow for her hands. "I've often tried to imagine what it must have been like for the women those last years. What a desolate world, without men or hope or future, just sitting around with all these pictures of the past, waiting to die."

The guide shivered. Alesdra, however, could imagine an even worse scene. She saw them slaving in their laboratories, searching desperately for a cure before the last boy reached puberty. And when the search failed, and the last boy had become a man and died, then she saw them suiciding, or dying one by one of old age.

The image filled her with despair. Here she stood in the ruins of a civilization that had developed this deadly virus, the musty scent of the millennia sharp in her nose, and she presumed that her civilization could produce scientists to find a cure the pre-Marahns failed to find.

She hated considering the possibility of failure. It would mean the shuttlebox was almost useless. People could only come to Marah through it, never leave. She could never leave. She was gripped by a sudden longing for the weathered hills and cobalt skies of Sahara.

"Homesick, Alesdra?"

Alesdra took control of her face again. She had not been aware her feelings showed so much. She raised a wry brow. "Are you sure you aren't a telepath?"

"Telepath? Oh . . . read minds. No, I'm not that." Sky smiled. "An instructor in school once told me I had healer potential. It lets me feel what others do."

"Can you feel that I've had enough of sad old ruins for today? Let's go home."

Sky nodded.

They thanked the historical society guide and climbed up out of the excavations. They walked back to the parking area in silence. They were still silent as they swung onto their bicycles and started pedaling back to Eridu. For once, Alesdra welcomed the suffocating heat. The effort to breathe and move kept her mind occupied.

Beside her, Sky hardly even sweated. She glanced sideways at Alesdra. "Do you really find Marah so unpleasant?"

"I find the steam heat in Eridu unpleasant; otherwise, it's a nice-enough world. I suppose it's a matter of not having been my choice to stay."

"That makes a difference?"

"Certainly. Healing is a wonderful calling, but how would you have felt if you'd been forced to become a healer just because you showed a talent for it?"

Sky sent her a sly sideglance. "I'd probably not have been aware of being forced. So few of our so-called decisions are the result of active choice on our parts."

Alesdra grimaced. "Are you talking about predestination? I thought your religion teaches free will."

"It does, but having the capacity is not the same as exercising it. And sometimes, I believe, we're bent to one decision or another to serve purposes beyond our understanding."

That remark made Sky sound like Jared in his more sanctimonious moments. Alesdra snorted. Trash.

She voiced the thought. Sky replied, and they rode the rest of the way to Ashasem House in a heated debate of free will versus Divine will versus conditioned responses. Not until they were parking the bicycles did Alesdra realize that most of Sky's passion had been assumed. Before she could become indignant about being goaded into an argument, Alesdra noticed the depression threatening her in the Old City had evaporated.

"You occasionally practice healing as a hobby, I see." Sky grinned.

Alesdra threw her arms around the other woman and hugged her. "Thank you." She could understand Jared's fondness for his sister.

With their arms around each other's waist, they crossed the portico and pushed open the front door.

Sabrina, Daria, and Seabright were waiting for them in the sitting room. Sky and Alesdra stopped in the doorway in surprise and exchanged glances. It was not even four o'clock yet. The sisterwives should still be at Peace Hall. What were they doing home, looking the way they did? The grim set of the sisterwives' faces made them look, for the first time since Alesdra had met them, like police officers.

"What's happened?" Sky asked.

"Isaiah's been abducted," Daria said.

"Abducted?" Sky stared at them in horror. "Who—"

"Your brother took him," Sabrina said. She handed Sky a sheet of message paper. "This came by radio about midafternoon."

Jared had taken Sky's son? That sounded incredible to Alesdra. She read the message over Sky's shoulder.

Sky threw it down. "This is ridiculous. Someone panicked down there. I'm surprised Gibeon took the accusation seriously enough to call us."

Seabright said, "They took it seriously enough to broadcast to every Peace Hall on Marah."

"*What?* Why? According to that"—she pointed to the paper on the floor—"they've been gone just a matter of hours. What evidence is there Jared took Isaiah by force?"

"Men don't wander off by themselves normally," Seabright said.

Alesdra bit her lip. True enough. She looked at Sky. Did Sky have an explanation?

"Can you explain it?" Daria asked.

"Sky," Sabrina said, "it's too strange. First he asks you to send Isaiah to him. He was acting distracted and strange for weeks. Now he's disappeared with your son."

Sky glanced toward Alesdra. Alesdra had told her how Kastavin's death affected Jared. Uncertainty flickered in Sky's eyes. "I can't believe he would harm Isaiah. Poor Jared. What could have driven him off like that?"

The others frowned at her. "Poor *Jared?* What about Isaiah?"

"Isaiah is safe; I'm sure of it." Sky sounded confident. "I'm worried about my brother." Worry lines pleated the skin between her brows. "I feel pain and fear . . . and danger. He could die."

Chapter Thirteen

JARED ACHED all over. His neck hurt from forcing himself not to look back. His hands were stiff from gripping the bicycle's handlebars. The straps of the pack cut into his shoulders and something hard in the pack itself ground against his spine. His buttocks felt bruised to the bone. He would not have been surprised to find the ischia protruding through the skin and penetrating the hard surface of the bicycle saddle. But all that was as nothing compared to the pain in his legs. Every muscle of his thighs and calves was tied in a separate white-hot knot. They trembled uncontrollably. He could hardly force himself to push down the pedals.

He had ignored Storm's instructions to ride and walk alternately. Nor had he rested more than the time it took to eat a quick meal at midday. The road stretching before him kept reminding him how far it was to Viridian, and how much farther to Eridu. So he had pushed himself, willing the distance to be shorter, willing himself across it in an impossibly short time.

Finally he could not pedal himself another meter. He

stopped the bicycle. He tried to swing off but his leg was so tired he could barely lift it. Jared had to lower the bicycle to the ground to step clear of it. He loosened the pack's straps and eased it off his back, wincing at the pain that lanced down his spine when he flexed his shoulder blades toward each other.

The pack fell to the ground and he followed, lowering himself gingerly. Once on the ground, he sighed and stretched out his legs before him. He began massaging them.

He should have followed Storm's advice. He berated himself for not doing so. Tomorrow he was going to be so crippled he would be lucky to be able to crawl, let alone pedal eighty kilometers.

According to the odometer on the bicycle, he had come only a little more than sixty kilometers today. At that rate he might reach Viridian in a week or so, but hardly in five days. He should have stayed in Gibeon and taken his chances boarding the train. Raaman might not be hunting him at all.

He was considering turning back—sixty kilometers was a long way, but much shorter than three hundred forty—when he became aware of the two-beat sound of a running rapa. It was approaching from the east . . . from Gibeon.

He looked around swiftly. There were no rock outcroppings here, no brush or trees to hide in. He sat there exposed on the roadside. He fought the urge to run—after all, there was nowhere to run to—and sat where he was.

The rapa was a tall copper king, ridden by a woman in ordinary riding clothes with a triangular green patch on the shoulder of her jacket. The keeper halted her mount. As his forelegs touched the ground, she vaulted off his back.

"The Lord be with you, sister," she said.

"And with you." Jared remembered to keep his voice pitched higher than normal.

The rapa stretched down his head to sniff Jared's pack. Jared steeled himself not to flinch away from the unmuzzled jaws and moved the pack to his other side.

"Hoosh," the keeper said.

110

The rapa jerked his head back and squatted on his haunches.

"Have you been traveling this road long?"

Jared had been thinking up an identity and story to explain his journey. Even so, he almost forgot it now that he was confronted with questions. He struggled to remember the town he had picked as his origin. For a moment of agony, he could not think, then it came in a rush.

"From Samuel's Ford." That was far enough away that most people around here would not have been there but close enough that someone might elect to travel from it by bicycle rather than waiting for a train.

"Have you seen anyone today?" the keeper asked.

"Two ranch wagons coming from the south."

"Anyone going the same direction you are?"

Jared shook his head.

The keeper squatted on her heels beside him. "What's your name, sister?"

"Handaroch Michal Virtue Shem."

"I know some Shems up toward Samuel's Ford, kin of my mother's fraternal sister. Might they also be kin of yours?"

Was this more than the usual do-you-know-so-and-so between strangers? Jared forced himself to meet the keeper's eyes. "Possibly, though my mother came from Joppa. Are you looking for someone?"

"A man and a boy, probably traveling unescorted."

"Unescorted?" Jared clucked in pretended amazement. "Why do you want them?"

The keeper shook her head in reproof. "You should know no criminal charges against a man are made public until his hearing."

Criminal charges! Jared stared at the keeper. What criminal charges? What excuse was Raaman using to have him hunted? For once he wished law and custom were less protective of men.

"I haven't seen any man or boy. How do you think he's traveling?"

"We don't know." The keeper stood. She frowned down at him a moment, then asked, "Are you carrying a radio?"

Jared shook his head.

"Bad practice. You never know when you might need to call for help."

"I trust in the Lord."

The keeper's eyes narrowed. "What did you say your name is?"

Jared kicked himself mentally. That was a foolish thing to say; it was a priest's kind of remark. "Michal Shem."

"From Samuel's Ford. Where are you going?"

"To Viridian, to catch a train for Southmarch."

"Why not take the train all the way?"

Jared shrugged. "Impulse." He smiled. Inside, he held his breath, praying she would accept his thin story. He willed her to turn and pick up the reins of her rapa.

She turned and picked up her reins. "The Lord be with you, then, Michal Shem. And if you see a man and a boy alone, call a keeper on the first radio you reach."

She swung onto the rapa and urged him to his feet. She waved as the king moved forward.

Jared watched her until she was only a dot in the distance, then flopped back and lay breathing in long, trembling breaths. So he was a criminal fugitive now, on some unknown, unknowable charge that he would not learn unless he were caught. How soon that might be worried him. He had passed as a woman . . . maybe. He could not say for certain the keeper had believed him. She might start thinking over their encounter and come back anytime crying, "You're no woman."

The road had been a bad choice. It was too obvious a route. He needed to get off. If this keeper did not discover who he was, another surely would. He would be harder to track across the prairie. Cross-country would be shorter, too.

Viridian would also be harder to find. The only guide he would have would be the imperfect memories of that ride to Viridian he and Sky had planned but never taken after Middle School.

The herd trails would be rough. It meant abandoning the bicycle and walking. Right now that thought bothered him very little. His immediate concern was knowing which trails to take. He tried to remember what Sky had said about navigating. At this time of year, the tail of the constellation called the Basilisk pointed straight toward Viridian. But what about during the day? Rapas were not night predators, but he did not like the idea of stumbling over trails alone at night.

Storm had put a map in Jared's pack. He dug it out and opened it. He traced the Viridian road with his finger. If he cut cross-country but touched the road at intervals, he could keep going in the right direction and still stay out of sight. He would do that.

He took a breath. It was time to be brave now. Clenching his teeth, Jared forced himself to his feet. Muscles sent knife stabs of protest up his legs and back. When he pulled the pack on again, he winced at the touch of the straps on his shoulders. Last of all, he picked up the bicycle. He did not attempt to mount it, though. He just pushed it.

He walked off the road with it and out across the prairie to a gully left by some vanished stream. He abandoned the bicycle there, covered with rocks and brush to hide it.

Once he was free of the machine, Jared turned until he matched the position of the sun to where it had been when he was on the road. He then set off in that direction.

Walking was painful. His legs protested every step. The boots Storm lent him were intended for riding, not hiking, so although they fit reasonably well, the little they slipped on his feet was enough to rub his heels raw. Still, it was more comfortable than riding the bicycle. He stretched his stride as long as he could. The sun was nearing the horizon, and he needed to reach a place to camp for the night, preferably near water. His canteen was almost empty.

A short time later he found a trail going the same direction he was. Trails usually led to water sooner or later, he remembered. Hoping it would be sooner, he followed the trail.

It was sooner. As he knelt on the muddy edge filling the canteen, he studied the water hole as a possible campsite. There were a few trees clustered at one end that would give good shelter. On the other hand, all kinds of animals drank at water holes, including wild rapas. Walking had taken some of the kinks out of his legs. Perhaps he should keep moving as long as possible. The farther he went today, the less distance he would have to cover tomorrow.

He decided to keep going. But first he would rest here a bit. He walked around the water hole to the trees. He eased off his pack by the base of a tree and lay down beside it. He closed his eyes.

Later he could not remember dreaming, nor any other awareness of passing time. It seemed as if he had just closed his eyes when he felt hot air on his face and smelled something like rancid meat. He woke to find himself staring into the reeking, cavernous jaws of a rapa.

Jared yelled in fright. The rapa jerked back, startled. Jared took advantage of the movement to roll away and onto his feet. *Watch out for the hind claws.* Sky's repeated warning came back to him from childhood memory as clearly as if she were standing beside him.

The rapa recovered and leaped for him. The dewclaws on the insides of its hind legs looked a meter long. Jared leaped, too . . . for the nearest tree. He swarmed up it like a climber lizard. Only when he was well out of the rapa's reach did he look back.

The rapa was a blue queen, he saw, and not alone. Two kids were wading in the water hole. The rapa stretched up on her hind legs, reaching as high as she could with her small forelegs. The closest she could come was half a meter below Jared's feet. He breathed a sigh of relief. She hissed in frustration and dropped down to take out her anger on his pack. It shredded beneath her hind claws.

Jared watched its destruction with mixed emotions. He would rather it happened to the pack than to him, but he hated losing his food. He hoped it was only squashed, not destroyed.

That hope ended as the rapa stopped tearing and bent down to sniff. She pulled the remains of the pack apart with her foreclaws, voicing a low, chuckling cry. Her kids climbed out of the water to join her. While Jared sat helpless in the tree, the three of them devoured his supplies, then took leisurely drinks before wandering off.

It was then that Jared realized the light was brightening. This was dawn, not sunset. He had slept straight through the night. That made him pause for thanks that the rapas were diurnal. If they had been night hunters, he might have wakened in the belly of that queen.

Climbing down, he noticed what he had not on the way up—dozens upon dozens of stiff, aching muscles. However painful the process, the tree climb demonstrated they were still functional. He noted the various aches, groaned once, and then tried to ignore them as he knelt to assess the damage to his pack.

After sorting through the remains he counted his possessions. He had the clothes on his back, the money Storm had given him, a knife, the small candaglobe that had hung on the bicycle, a canteen, and the bolas. He took the bolas and wrapped it around his waist where it should have been in the first place. How its cord escaped being slashed by the rapa's claws he did not know.

He stood, stuffing what he could into his pockets. The candaglobe would not fit. He had to leave it with the pack. Well, it would be lighter traveling without the pack, he reflected wryly, and there was little danger now of weighting himself with heavy meals. He took a long drink from the water hole, slung the canteen over his shoulder, and started walking.

Doing so was not easy with stiff legs and a blister on each heel, but Jared thought of the Bishop computing his figures of boys who must die, thought of the Grand Council convening, thought of Alesdra appearing before it. He pictured her calling her ship to tell them they had no sale and envisioned the ship leaving. The thoughts made him push on in spite of sore muscles and blisters.

He wondered just how long he could go without food. There were autumnberry bushes at intervals, some with berries the leapers and birds had missed, but it seemed like a limited, time-consuming diet. There was plenty of game around him, but the difficulty was catching it. He had grave doubts about his ability with a bolas.

115

He unwrapped the bolas from his waist and practiced throwing it at brush and rocks he passed. It confirmed his fears. He almost always wrapped it around something, but never the target he intended. He kept practicing.

He ate berries when he saw them. He drank his water, refilling the canteen at every opportunity. He pulled off his boots and soaked his feet while he rested, then struggled back into the boots before setting off again. When darkness made him stumble, he found a tree and wedged himself into high branches to sleep. He had no way of knowing how far he had come. While it felt like a hundred kilometers he was afraid it would be only forty. It was when he looked up to check the stars that he felt a faint glow of satisfaction. The tail of the Basilisk pointed straight before him. He was on course, at least.

His stomach was growling when he climbed down from the tree at dawn. He ignored it and picked pieces of leaf and bark out of his collar and hair. His stomach was disciplined to fasts; it would quiet down before long.

He started walking again. Gradually he became aware that in spite of the pain in his legs and feet, he felt oddly euphoric. Urgency was driving him on, but he was enjoying the march. He almost enjoyed the pain, too.

He tried to think why. He was alone on the prairie. He passed herds of rhino and leapers, flocks of hoopers. He saw rapas, usually alone but sometimes paired. But no other people. There was no feeling of loneliness, though, only this strange satisfaction, this contentment.

It occurred to him that he had never before in his life been really alone. There had always been someone near, in the next room at least—Sky or his mother or members of the family, fellow students, fellow instructors, pages and stewards—always someone to wait on him, to protect him, hover over him. Here there was no one to see or hear him. He could strip to the skin and walk naked if he liked, shout at the sky. He could do anything he liked without fear of interference, cautioning, or reproof. Being alone was a completely new feeling, and one he rather liked.

Coming over a rise, he stopped and stared in amazement. Below him, along both sides of a winding stream, a field of phoenix spread down a narrow valley as far as he could see. It was a blanket of color, with the flowers running from new-blooming yellow to the orange and scarlet of age. Some had dropped their petals and were starting new buds. A small herd of rhinosaurs nibbled the flowers a short way down the valley. The close-growing stems, each with its collar of leaves, reached to the beasts' bellies, making the rhino look as if they were floating on a flower-covered green sea. He drank in the scene with delight. There had been patches of phoenix around the ranch station while he was growing up, but nothing like this.

What sights he had been missing while he was cloistered in the walls of Gibeon temple. It was annoying to think that a woman, merely man's helpmate, could see something like this anytime. She could go where she wanted, when she wanted, be alone as much as she liked. She could join a family or leave it, change jobs, change towns. She could walk cross-country like this, see such sights as these, sit down and enjoy them as long as she pleased.

Of course they were not quite *that* free; women had ties and obligations, too, but they were more free than men, their masters. Only a woman would likely be walking this trail this way, never a man. And that, he thought, wading through the phoenix blossoms, was a great pity.

"What do you mean, there's no sign of him?"

Raaman Midian glanced at Levi Dan and back to the chief keeper standing before him.

The chief looked past both of them at the office wall. "We haven't found him or the boy anywhere. We've checked all the roads in every direction. All riding and buggy animals are accounted for. I have keepers at the railway station and so far they haven't seen an unidentified man and boy boarding a train. On the chance they boarded the eastbound yesterday morning, I radioed Cyrene. The train didn't stop between here and there and the Cyrene keepers didn't find them on board when the train arrived there, so unless they jumped off at a hundred and thirty kilometers per hour, the Shepherd was never on the train."

That relieved Levi. Each day would take Jared farther from Gibeon and closer to Eridu.

Raaman frowned in thought. "Perhaps he's hiding in town."

"In which case," Levi said, "there's no need to be concerned about the boy. Whoever might hide them will see neither of them comes to harm."

"Shall I stop the search, then?" the chief asked.

"No."

Levi sighed. "Why not? Let Jared come back when he will."

"I've had troubled dreams over this. We have to find him." Raaman tried to catch Levi's eyes.

The chief bowed her head. "We'll continue the search."

When she had left, Raaman repeated, "We have to find him."

"We don't know that he's breaking."

"I'm sure."

"But you have a special interest. I hear you've started circulating a petition for a Shepherd election."

Raaman had the grace to flush guiltily. "This temple can't function properly without a Shepherd."

It was true the court had been a shambles that morning and the Deacons were at a loss trying to take care of the petitioners who would normally have appealed to the Shepherd. Levi was neglecting many of his own duties while trying to watch Raaman.

Raaman frowned at the far wall. "I don't understand how he could just disappear. He could have left the road, but it would be suicide for an unescorted man to cross open prairie."

Levi said nothing.

"He must be traveling in disguise, wherever he's going."

Levi kept very still.

"The question is, what kind of disguise? And where is he going? He must have some objective in mind." He focused on Levi. "What kind of disguises could a man and boy use so they would be overlooked?"

"I cannot imagine."

The narrowing of Raaman's eyes told Levi the lean Deacon knew he was not trying to think of an answer. "Then I'll ask the brothers at supper to help me. I don't know why you fight me in favor of Jared, Levi. I'm much better suited to the office than he is."

Levi pulled at his beard. Raaman was probably right. He had enough charm mixed in his will of steel to manipulate almost anyone for any purpose he needed. But Levi liked the gentle man Jared was, and he had never quite forgiven Raaman for being one of Aaron Methuselah's favorites. Still, he wondered, just a little, if he should give in to Raaman.

He, too, was having troubled dreams, filled with the weeping ghosts of dead boys and angry shouts of accusation. He watched Isaiah Joseph struggling against health and energy to continue playing the role of a sick girl. How long could he continue the act? And last night Sinai, who sometimes had visions, climbed shivering into his bed and clung fiercely to him.

"I keep feeling that something is ending, Levi. It's like the walls of this house are shattering and falling in on us. I look at you and my sisterwives and think, This is the last."

Levi found himself afraid of the future. He was happy with most of his life, he realized now, contented, satisfied with his family and his work. He had never spent much time thinking what Marah would be like with as many men as women, what changes it might make. Now he tried to imagine such a thing and could not. What terrible process might he have started by helping Jared?

Chapter Fourteen

FASTING WAS euphoric only to a point, Jared found. After that there was just hunger. Two and a half days did not sound all that long; he had often gone three and four days on a fast. Of course, he had been living quietly in the temple at the time, too, and not marching cross-country with all the speed he could force from himself. The autumnberries he found were inadequate. Satan fruit was out of the question this early in the year. He would just have to try catching game, though he hated the thought of wasting time hunting, and of eating meat raw. Still, raw was better than nothing. He reached a compromise decision. He would not hunt. He would keep walking, but if game appeared in his path he would take it as a sign he should eat. Then he would stop to hunt.

It was at that point he began noticing what kind of game he saw most often. There were great herds of rhino and leapers and flocks of hoopers, but even if they had not been so large it would be wasteful to kill one for a single person, he would not have known how to catch them. He was no match for leapers, nor for a rhino, for that matter, if the beast were aroused. Even the hoopers, big dumb birds that they were, turned green-black eyes on him suspiciously, fluffing their useless black wings, ready to outrun him. Game birds and lizards were something he saw off in the distance. He timed his rest stops to put him beside autumnberry bushes so he could pick fruit and eat it while he rested, but it was a monotonous diet. More and more he looked longingly at the birds flying overhead.

He watched for ones that might come within range

of his bolas. He also watched the ground for coveys of ground birds. He knew from childhood experience that prairie runners and all their cousins who preferred running to flying usually darted off into high grass too fast to be caught, but there were sometimes slow birds, or crippled ones. Just thinking how the plump little birds tasted doubled his hunger pangs. In preparation he filled a pocket of his jacket with rocks.

In the next couple of hours he stumbled into several coveys, two of prairie runners and one of rockbirds, but there were no slow or crippled members among them. His rocks landed well behind the fleeing birds or were deflected by clumps of grass. The only creature who profited from his efforts was a big copper rapa king who happened to be in the flight path of the rockbirds. The rapa snapped one up in his mouth and trapped another with a hind foot as the birds burst through the grass at him.

Jared dropped to his stomach. The rapa looked big enough to take on a rhino. He had no desire to attract the carnivore's attention. While he lay there he prayed that the rapa would leave all or part of one bird. But his prayer was in vain. The king gulped down both birds —feathers, feet, and all. Jared was left to sigh in frustration and had to wait until the king moved on before getting up. Only after the rapa was gone did it occur to Jared that he could have thrown the rocks at him. That might have driven him away from the second bird. He grimaced in disgust at his failure. There was more to surviving on the prairie than there had seemed when he was out with Sky.

He gave up hunting and concentrated on covering as much distance as possible before sunset. The stiffness and pain were working out of his muscles, making walking much easier. He was finding a rhythm, too, that let him move at a steady pace for longer periods of time. His feet were so swollen he could hardly pull off his boots for periodic soakings in streams and water holes, but that served him in its way. At least the boots no longer slipped on his heels.

Toward sunset he started climbing the highest ground he could find. From the top he hoped to see part of the Viridian road and verify that he was still headed in the right direction. Halfway up the slope he heard the low chittering of prairie runners. He stopped and stood still, holding his breath, turning his head from side to side, trying to identify the source of the sound. It was coming from above him.

Jared took two rocks from his jacket pocket and, hunching low, began easing up the slope. He tested each step before he shifted his weight, making sure there were no slippery stones underfoot, nor dry grass. Every meter he stopped and listened for the birds again. Their noise continued undisturbed. Near the top he thought he saw their motion in the grass, pecking at the ground. Then the leaves of a scrubby bush scraped across the sleeve of his jacket with a sharp hiss. One of the birds squawked in warning.

The grass exploded with running birds. Jared stood and hurled a rock at the nearest. The rock missed. Instead of disappearing into the grass, however, the covey suddenly flung themselves skyward in a flurry of wings. Jared was so startled he forgot to throw his other rock. He stood staring after them in astonishment. The birds were capable of flight, but he had never seen any of them fly before. Why had they now?

When, a moment later, he lowered his gaze, he saw why. Staring back at him from across the crest was a tall woman in ranch clothes.

Her face mirrored his own surprise. She recovered with a laugh. "Well, sister, it seems we've done each other out of supper. I'm Jerusha Teman."

Jared felt his throat close. The Temans were a linear family on one of the outlying ranches in the northern part of Gibeon parish. Their ranch station was just a few days' ride from the Kedar ranch. He had met some of the Temans before.

He took a breath to open his throat. "I'm Michal Shem." Perhaps she was not one of the Temans he knew. "Am I on your land?"

She shook her head. "According to the brands I've seen on the local stock, this is the Talusah ranch. Some of my sisterwives and I are passing west, headed for Viridian."

"So am I."

"Will you join us for supper, then?"

He should not. Some of her sisterwives might recognize him. But the invitation of food was too much to refuse. He told himself he might as well see how successfully he could play the role of a woman.

They had set up camp not far away, around a spring pond. When he saw the camp, Jared nearly changed his mind about eating with them. The group of women did not look formidable—there were only four more—but around the camp and pond were tethered at least two dozen rapas . . . kings, queens, and a few yearling kids.

Jerusha saw his hesitation and grinned. "Impressive, aren't they? They're a new cross we've been developing."

Jared looked at the rapas more closely. They were as tall as plains rapas but slimmer and more finely boned, and instead of plain blue or copper, their hides carried variegated patterns, the aurora, clouded, and spotted colors normally seen only on timber rapas.

"We imported timber kings from the Becher forest intending to breed them to our queens, but we found out why no one has tried this cross before; timber and plains rapas won't breed to each other. The pheromones are wrong or something. So we found a way to collect semen from the kings and bred our queens by AI. We wanted to get the speed and agility of the timber rapa while keeping the size and mild temperament of the plains rapa."

Jared eyed them. One queen hissed at him. "Have you been successful?"

"We've managed to keep the size."

Jared kept well away from the tether lines as he walked into camp.

The four women around the fire looked up. Had he ever met any of them before? He could not remember. The weathering of their faces made their ages indefinite, except for the one by the cooking pot. She looked young.

The darkest of the group said, "That's a bad choice of game, Jerusha. It's too much meat for us and not enough for the rapas."

Jerusha grinned. "Pay no attention, Michal. My sisterwife has a strange sense of humor. This is a guest. Michal Shem. So show some courtesy. Nile is the one of questionable wit, there, Michal. The one who's the

123

color of a copper rapa is Summer. Next to her is Patience, and by the cooking pot is our baby, Bathsheba Manasseh. She's a sisterwife, too. Her grandmother's brother brought his sister along when he became one of our family men and there have been Manassehs in the Temans ever since. These are only a handful of Temans, of course; we left dozens at home. Sit down and help yourself to stew. It's meatless, I'm afraid, thanks to me."

"Well, you were too busy rounding up strays for anything as minor as hunting," Nile said. She regarded Jared with raised brows. "Passing, sister?"

"She's headed for Viridian, too."

Bathsheba filled a wooden bowl with stew from the pot and handed it to Jared. Meat or no meat, it was delicious, and hot. He had to force himself to eat slowly enough to keep from burning his tongue.

No one asked further questions but Jared could feel their eyes flicking toward him while they ate. Naturally they were curious. He tried to remember what Storm might have said about normal female behavior in situations like this. Men exchanged confidences freely, at least among men of their own ecclesiastic rank. He did not know about men who were complete strangers to one another; he had never met a man who was a complete stranger. How much information did women share with each other? Was he expected to volunteer answers to their unspoken questions?

While he was considering that, he had another thought. If these women were questioned by keepers hunting for him, they might mention a woman who had kept silent about herself.

"Would you like more?" Bathsheba asked.

He handed her the bowl. "Please. Thank you." They might not connect the object of the keepers' search with a woman who talked freely, though.

After he cleaned up his second helping and drank half a mug of strong tea, he gave them the same story he had told the keeper, that he was from Samuel's Ford, headed for a new job teaching in Southmarch, traveling cross-country on impulse. He dressed it up with a few true facts, that his subject in teaching was religion and law, that he had started on a bicycle, that he had left

124

the bicycle to walk. The excuse he gave for that was that the wheel had bent beyond repair in a rut. He told them about the rapa that destroyed his pack. They exchanged looks at that. Nile shook her head.

"How much cross-country experience have you had?" Jerusha asked.

"I grew up on a ranch."

Nile's brows quirked. "Must have been a long time ago."

Jared felt himself flushing. "Yes."

"You're either very brave or utterly foolish to give in to an impulse like this," Summer said. "Do you intend to keep on?"

He nodded. "I have to reach Viridian and have no radio to call for help."

"It's a long walk."

He laughed ruefully. "I know that." He looked beyond the circle of firelight at the rapas. "Would you sell one of them?"

Nile snorted. "That answers the question—she's utterly foolish."

"Michal," Jerusha said, "if you bend a bicycle wheel on the road and abandon the machine and the road, then lose your pack in a careless camp, you'll kill yourself on a rapa."

"These are hardly broken," Patience said. "We're trailing them to Viridian instead of shipping them by rail so we can school them on the way."

Summer held up her hands for silence. "Family conference."

The five drew to the far end of the fire circle where they talked in low voices. Once Nile cried out, "She'll be killed." Jerusha said, "Hoosh." The conference went on.

When they came back, Summer had a proposition. They intended to be in Viridian in five days. Michal could travel with them, but she would have to help with camp and herd duties on the way to pay her keep. Otherwise, Summer would use her radio to call the nearest ranch station and Jared could beg or buy help from the family at the station.

"Michal" agreed, though Jared on the inside wondered if it might not be wiser to take help from a local family. It would be slower, but safer. Going with the Temans meant riding a rapa.

He wondered about pushing rapas that fast. His family had always spoken of trailing as a slow process. "The rapas don't break down at the pace you're riding them?"

"We've been changing mounts five times a day, so each will be ridden some each day. We backpack instead of using a pack animal or wagon that might slow us down. If we go too slow, the rapas will start looking around at the game and want to hunt."

If they did not hunt, how did the rapas eat, Jared wondered. He would have asked but he had a sudden fear it was a question to which any ranch-raised woman should know the answer. So he swallowed it. No doubt he would see for himself soon enough.

They asked a few more questions, mostly trying to establish if they had mutual acquaintances. When they were convinced they did not, the conversation drifted off in other directions, to the prices they hoped to get for the rapas at the sale they were taking them to, to ranch business like speculation on winter weather and stock losses, and then, somehow, to babies.

Bathsheba objected to that. "Who cares about babies?"

There was a silence while her sisterwives eyed her, then Patience said, "You'll feel differently ten months from now."

From which Jared gathered Bathsheba was pregnant. He stole a look at her waistline. Her shirt and ranch pants were a little snug. He also gathered Bathsheba was not pleased by it. She greeted Patience's remark with a derisive snort. It shocked Jared. He thought women loved children.

"Having a baby is different from being pregnant," Jerusha said. "I hate being pregnant, but I adore my children."

Nile said, "Not everyone does. But remember, Ba, you only have to have this one, and you can always let it be raised by those sisterwives foolish enough to want it."

Bathsheba looked at Jared. "Do you like your children?"

Jared imagined how Sky would answer. "Yes, of course."

"What do you have?"

No need to lie there. "A son. He's fifteen."

Jerusha and Patience launched into enthusiastic descriptions of their children. Nile spat into the fire and, pushing to her feet, stalked off into the darkness. Summer bent her head over the stirrup leather she was mending. Jared thought he saw tears in her eyes.

He poked Bathsheba. "Is Summer not able to have children?" he asked in a whisper.

"She had a son. He failed the Trial last year."

Jared went hot and cold with guilt. The boy would have been at Gibeon temple. He could not bear to look at Summer again.

Eventually the talk died out and the fire was coals. The Temans reached for blankets and started rolling up in them to sleep.

"Would you care to share with me?" Jerusha asked Jared.

He thanked her. He noticed Patience frown but thought nothing of it, at least not until he was slipping into sleep and was suddenly awakened by the feel of a hand working its way up his thigh.

"Want to tangle, Michal?" Jerusha whispered, her lips against his ear.

Storm's warning came back to him. He rolled away from Jerusha's warmth. "I want to sleep. That's all."

He waited tensely to see what she might do, but she only said, "Another time, perhaps," and turned her back to him.

He curled up by the coals of the fire.

The prod of a booted toe in his side woke him at dawn. Sitting up, he was surprised to find himself covered by a blanket. The source of it was explained moments later, when he saw Patience and Jerusha crawling from under the same blanket, giggling and tussling with one another.

It reminded him of home. He had not seen women in an open display of affection for many years. This was not a public place, of course, and they had no way of knowing he was an ecclesiastic who must officially condemn sexual relationships between women.

He felt a boot in his back again. "How long does it take you to wake up, Michal?" Nile said. "This isn't the city. There's a trail waiting for us."

Jared scrambled to his feet. "What do you want me to do?"

Nile raised a brow. "Sisters, she's a morning baritone."

Jared hoped his flush would be taken for reaction to Nile's remark. He cleared his throat and tried the question again in a pitch above his normal tone.

"Stir up the ashes and put some dry grass on them to see if we still have a live coal or two," Bathsheba said.

There was. After smoldering a few minutes, the grass caught in a burst of cheery flame. Bathsheba set him to feeding the fire with small branches while she started tea and reheated last night's stew for breakfast.

As the scents of the stew and tea began filling the campsite, Jared came fully awake. He realized he felt wonderful. The last pain was gone from his muscles. Around him was a bright, clean dawn with dew jeweling every rock and blade of grass. Even the rapas, growling up out of sleep, hissing at each other, seemed part of new beginnings.

"Michal! Do you want to eat or not?"

He realized belatedly that Bathsheba was shoving a cup and bowl into his hands. He started to eat slowly, savoring the novelty of stew for breakfast, but when he saw the others inhaling their food like starving rapas, he followed suit. Then he helped Bathsheba clean and pack the pot and utensils and bury the fire.

"Michal," Summer called as the last of the fire was smothered by rocks and dirt, "see if you can ride this one."

It was a tall aurora queen, all sun golds and reds in color and green-eyed with anger. She swiped a hind foot at him. Jared stepped back. The dewclaws had been clipped, but the beast still looked dangerous.

"I'm taking a saddle away from someone, aren't I?"

"Nile rides bareback very well. You're sure you've ridden rapas before?"

He nodded.

"All right. I'll just remind you of a few things, then. Remember, if you want to stop her, don't lean back on her as you would on a rhino. That only helps her counterbalance better. Lean forward. That will weight her forehand and slow her down."

She held the reins and a hand cupped over the queen's near eye while she legged Jared up past the reaching claws into the saddle. When he was settled with his feet in the stirrups, she gave him the reins.

The queen bolted. Jared started to pull back, then remembered and leaned forward. Only he leaned too far. The queen dropped her forehand and sent him somersaulting off over her shoulder.

He rolled sideways and scrambled to his feet. Claws missed him by centimeters. He found, though, that he had somehow managed to hang on to the reins. He and the queen circled each other at the length of them, she hissing, he dodging not only claws but swinging tail. Her muzzle saved him from only her teeth.

"Now see if you can get back on by yourself," Summer called.

Jared looked back at them. All five were standing at the edge of the camp, obviously enjoying the show. Not one of them made a move to help him. The message was clear—he took care of himself or he did not come with them.

He worked his way down the reins to the queen's head. The motion triggered memories of watching his mother school green rapas at home. Reaching up, he covered the queen's near eye with his hand. Hooking two fingers over the edge of the muzzle at the same time, he pulled her head down. Half-blinded, she yielded to him. That lowered her forehand until her forefeet were on the ground and made it impossible for her to stand on just one hind leg. In the moment that both hind legs were firmly on the ground and before she could jerk her head up again, he put a foot in the stirrup and swung on. This time he kept his weight forward so she could not start running.

The Temans cheered.

Jared grinned. Sky would have been proud of him. He was rather pleased with himself. He wondered how

129

the Temans would react, though, if they knew they had just seen a man mounting this half-wild rapa?

Sky. Thought of her wiped the pleasure from the morning. From her his thoughts skipped down the sequence to Eridu and Alesdra Pontokouros.

When he rode back into camp and accepted the pack Nile had worn up to now, he only half-listened to Summer's trailing instructions. One sisterwife would lead all the muzzled rapas tied along a single lead line. The rest of them were to range up and down preventing trouble. Jared hoped Alesdra was not fighting with the Bishop. When did the Grand Council convene? Tomorrow, he thought. He prayed Alesdra would not be brought before it too soon, nor put off so long she became discouraged and sent her ship away. As the rapa group started out of camp he wondered what would be happening in Eridu in five days, what would be happening when he finally reached there by train.

He wondered all day. He kept his place at the rear of the drive. He changed mounts when the others did. He listened to the women call back and forth to each other, but his mind was always ahead. Every kilometer they walked, he wanted to jog, and when they jogged, he wanted to run.

"You don't talk much," Jerusha said once.

"Riding keeps me busy," he replied.

Jerusha laughed and sent her rapa running up the line.

The sun passed zenith and started its slide toward the western horizon. Jared watched its progress. Could they possibly reach Viridian in less than five days? He felt like cheering each time Summer moved the drive into a fast jog. She was doing it more often as the day progressed, too. Was she feeling his mind pushing her?

Then, about midafternoon, Summer circled the rapas beside a stream. The other women vaulted off their mounts. They began pulling rapas off the lead line and staking them out, each well separated from the others.

"We're stopping to camp already?" Jared said.

Bathsheba looked up at him from saddling another rapa. "We have to hunt food for the rapas or they'll be eating each other and us, too. Haven't you noticed how restless they've been? They're hungry. We weren't able to feed them yesterday. That's why Summer has kept them moving."

It would take a great deal of game to feed twenty-eight rapas. "Feed them what?"

"Leapers."

Jared bit his lip. "Everything around here is ranch stock."

Bathsheba looked surprised. "We know that. Summer radioed the ranch station for permission to hunt. They'll send the bill to the Teman ranch. Change to a fresh mount."

Jared obeyed, though he had doubts about his value on a hunt.

As it turned out, he need not have worried. It was hardly a hunt. They located a herd of leapers not far from the campsite. Summer, Jerusha, and Nile handed the reins of their rapas to the others and walked up to the edge of the herd with their bows ready. Some of the leapers raised up, small forelegs folded across their chests, propping themselves on their tails, but the majority never stopped nibbling grass or the leaves off brush. The women fired seven arrows, dropping seven leapers. It was only the death cries and the smell of blood that alarmed the herd. With warning barks they jerked up their heads and bounded away. The women tied ropes around the hind legs of the dead ones and used the rapas to drag the carcasses back to camp. That was the hard part, keeping the rapas from turning on the meat they pulled behind them. In camp everyone went to work quartering the kill, then unmuzzling the rapas and tossing each a portion of meat.

The rapas tore into the leapers with chuckles of contentment. Jared watched. He was of two minds. A part of him remembered how deliciously plump the leapers had been and regarded the rapas' meal enviously. The other part of him wanted to be on his way again, riding hard for Viridian.

He closed off the latter. Riding hard indeed. Riding was giving him a whole new set of stiff and painful muscles. Tomorrow was time enough to face the idea of hours in the saddle again. Tonight—well, tonight he wished he had some of that leaper meat.

131

"Michal, would you rather eat or watch the rapas?"

He turned to see Jerusha holding up thick slabs of meat.

"Help Bathsheba start a fire and we'll cook these for supper." •

Chapter Fifteen

THE ASHASEMS were a family of keepers, but for the time being there was little peace in the household. All week they spent their spare moments on duty hanging over Sabrina's shoulder in the radio room, keeping track of the manhunt in the south. At home they debated it endlessly—at meals, during housework, even playing with the children. But the most serious discussions were always held after the children were in bed. They sat or sprawled on the lawn in the darkness and heated the humid night still more with words. By Friday there were three camps: Sky on the defensive, her sister-wives on the offensive, and Alesdra trying to stay out of it.

"No sign of the man, negative, not found, no trace," Daria growled in disgust.

"How can a man alone evade an entire keeper network?" Seabright asked.

"Incompetent keepers."

"Or he's being helped," Sabrina said.

"I hope so."

Seabright scowled at Sky. "You don't sound like you want him found."

"Not until I know why he's hiding."

"Don't you care at all about Isaiah?" Sabrina was outraged.

"Jared wouldn't hurt any child, let alone a boy, and certainly not Isaiah."

"No?" In the dark, Daria's voice sounded like raised eyebrows. "You left him. If he hates you for it—"

"I won't believe that. It's Jared who's in danger. I keep dreaming he's being chased by a black-robed figure."

Alesdra felt she would have sided with Sky, if she had allowed herself to become involved. She lay on her stomach in the grass, smelling its lushness and the scents of flowers around the yard, trying to shut out the voices. She would rather have listened to the sounds of insects and songs of nightbirds. She wanted to keep out of local problems. She had a ship full of planet-hungry people still orbiting Marah, a captain wanting to know whether to stay or go, and the Grand Council assembling without any word of when she was to appear before them. She had no time for anything extraneous. Damn Jared Joseph. Damn him for mentioning his sister and making Alesdra interested in meeting her, and damn him for running off with that boy. If it turned out the two of them were only taking a get-acquainted lark on the prairie she would personally fly south, without a flyer, and strangle him.

She knew the Council had assembled today. It had been announced all over the city. But there had been no message for her regarding a time to be heard before them. She had checked twice at Solon House to be sure. The house steward had assured her such a message would be sent on the moment it arrived. Alesdra had tried to see the Bishop and been refused an appointment. There seemed to be nothing to do now but grit her teeth and wait some more.

Captain Deyoe had not been at all happy to hear about further delay. "Are you sure this is worth it, Ponto?"

"Yes." Alesdra had crossed her fingers as she answered. "Surely it won't be more than another week before we have an answer from them one way or the other."

"The eagerness with which they've greeted you suggests an answer to me already."

133

"Please, Skipper, don't maroon me yet."

Captain Deyoe had reluctantly agreed to wait another week. Perhaps the shuttlebox crew had helped persuade her. The captain had mentioned they were dying to try their sterile construction method. Alesdra carefully refrained from mentioning they would be dying indeed if it failed to work.

That thought gave her pangs of uncertainty. What if their plan was unworkable and some of the boys died? They were all so young, hardly older than Kastavin. Could she bear seeing that kind of anguish again? Perhaps it would be better to send them on and have them warn the rest of the galaxy that Marah was a plague planet.

She considered it but chose not to mention her doubts to Captain Deyoe just yet. She broke communication.

That had been just before supper. So with her own concerns to think and worry about, the Ashasems had to intrude this damned abduction/runaway. She felt like getting up and going to bed. But it was hot in the house and she was reluctant to leave Sky alone. Alesdra disapproved of three against one. Three against one and a neutral was much better.

"Chased by a robed figure?" Sabrina said. "What do you think it is?"

"Conscience," Daria said.

"Stop it, please." Sky sounded weary.

"Explain him, then."

She sighed. "I can't."

Unless, Alesdra thought, feeling guilty of disloyalty even as she thought it, Jared had become unhinged by Kastavin's death.

"What do you think, Alesdra?" Sabrina asked. "You must have an opinion."

Not one she cared to express aloud. That would make it sound like four against one. Picking a blade of grass and tearing it into short pieces, she tried to think of a way to say something honest that would not commit her one way or the other. "He impressed me as a man of duty. I'm sure he has a compelling reason for whatever he's done." Real or imagined, sane or mad. "I'm waiting to hear his defense before I judge him."

Daria chuckled. "A diplomatic answer."

Sky sighed.

Sabrina started to say something but was stopped by the jingle of a bicycle bell in the street. "Messenger."

They turned toward the sound. A slight figure parked a bicycle and came up the walk toward the front door.

"We're in the side yard," Sabrina called. "Do you suppose it's about Jared?"

Alesdra was afraid it was.

The messenger came around the house and stood silhouetted against the light from the street. "I have a message for Alesdra Pontokouros."

Alesdra jumped to her feet. She took the message and ran for the house. She tore open the envelope and read the message by the light coming through a window. It was from the Grand Council.

"I'm to appear before the Council on the morning of Monday, November 12."

Monday! That was much sooner than she had dared to hope she might be called. Monday was only three days away. The *Rose* might have its answer on the shuttlebox within a week, after all.

The realization gave her an uneasy twinge. In a week she could know whether to order construction started or to tell the *Rose* good-bye. She could know whether she might someday leave Marah, or whether she would be living here the rest of her life. It would all depend on how well she sold herself and the box to the Council on Monday.

She felt something like a cold sweat start on the back of her neck.

Chapter Sixteen

As MUCH AS he disliked the idea, Levi had to admit Raaman was right; Gibeon did need a Shepherd. All week the men of the temple had been nervous and uncertain. Pages and stewards usually efficient in their duties seemed to need constant reminding what to do next. The Middle School instructors distractedly taught classes of boys who heard almost nothing of what was said. Discipline was disastrous. Though said before a well-filled tabernacle, morning and evening Prayings had become nothing but rote recitations, and could be giving the celebrants little of the reassurance they came for.

The meeting with the city commissioners that afternoon was a farce. Raaman had sat silent throughout. Forest Timna kept watching him for leads and, getting none, spoke only when he had to and then in stammering uncertainty. Kaleb Eshban had to be questioned two or three times before he would answer. The rest of the time his glazed eyes suggested a man whose attention was all on his own thoughts. Levi suspected he himself seemed none too attentive.

Only the commissioners appeared untouched. They sat with calm, placid faces, patiently repeating questions, reading their proposals and reports in slow, clear voices. Levi found that as annoying as the Deacons' behavior. Were the women completely insensitive to what was happening to their temple and town?

Constance Amalek suddenly stopped reading and, after looking at each of the Deacons, folded the petition and put it away in her notebook. "Perhaps it would be

136

best to present this another time, when the Deacons can give it their full attention."

Levi looked sharply at her. Her voice was mild and her face properly respectful, but he had a peculiar feeling, as if he had been scored by an invisible whip.

"We do seem to be intruding secular affairs at an improper time," Esther Heber said. "Good Deacons, shall we adjourn this meeting for today?"

"Perhaps it would be best," Levi said.

Forest frowned. "But . . . the city has to be run. There are—there are things to be decided. We have to tell you what to do."

"Be at peace, brother," Cirrus Ishbak said. "Everything will be done. You may concentrate on priestly things."

Again Levi felt the touch of that invisible whip. He watched the four women pick up their papers and leave. All at once he had the strange impression that they were not insensitive to the present situation at all. On the contrary, they were very much aware, but were indifferent. Somehow, it did not touch them. Levi found that a deeply disturbing thought.

As if by common consent, the Deacons remained seated, and when the door closed behind the commissioners, Raaman said, "Stop fighting the election, Levi. I've sent a radio message to the Bishop about the situation here. Unless you agree to an election, he may order one."

"He can't," Kaleb said. "Only Gibeonites can order a Gibeon election."

"He may consider this a special situation."

Levi doubted it. The parishes were jealous of their autonomy regarding local affairs. He debated, but knew it was his emotions that rebelled against Raaman, not his reason. They did need leadership, definite leadership. "I'll support an election, but only if Brother Kaleb will agree to nominate me for candidacy."

Raaman arched a brow. "With the idea of being elected and then stepping down the moment Jared reappears?"

Levi hoped the guilty flush he felt was not visible on his face. "Candidacy is my condition for supporting an election."

"I'll nominate you," Kaleb said.

Raaman stood and turned to leave the room.

"Wait a minute," Kaleb said.

Raaman stopped. His mouth was a knife slash in his face. "What is it? I need to visit the keepers and learn what progress they've made finding Jared."

"I have something to tell you about him."

Raaman said nothing, but his brows rose.

Kaleb folded his hands together on the table before him. "Several days ago you asked if anyone might know of a disguise Jared could use."

Levi stopped breathing. His muscles went rigid.

Raaman sat back down, suddenly very attentive. He leaned forward. "And you've thought of something?"

Kaleb nodded. He looked down at his hands. "I've debated whether or not to mention this. He's the son of my mother's fraternal sister, after all."

Raaman nodded. "Almost kin. I understand your reluctance, but remember, we only want to help him. You're not betraying him by helping us find him."

"Probably not, but I feel like I am. Though I don't understand what he's done, nor why, I feel he must have good reason. I've known him since we were children and always loved him. It's only because I do believe we need to find him that I'm telling you."

"I appreciate your loyalty to him. What disguise do you think he's using?" Raaman's voice vibrated with eagerness.

"Even after my mother left the Kedars to join the Eshiah family she occasionally went back to the ranch for visits. Sometimes she took me with her. One time just after I'd become a temple scribner and Jared was in his last year of Middle School, she and I went to the ranch with him for New Year's. One evening Jared didn't come to the family Praying. He wasn't at supper, either. We searched the entire station and couldn't find him. No one had seen him, we found out, since he said good-bye to his sister Sky that morning. She was out checking on some hooper flocks. Then someone said they had seen Sky riding out, but Jared had not said good-bye to her. It was confusing. One person said Sky's rapa had been copper, while someone else insisted it had been blue."

Raaman sighed. "I hate to seem impatient, Brother Kaleb, but is all this narrative necessary?"

Kaleb sighed in his turn. "Perhaps not. We finally found him, sneaking into the stables with Sky and two rapas, one blue, one copper. Jared was wearing Sky's clothes. He looked just like her."

"A woman," Raaman breathed.

Levi stifled a groan of despair. Fighting to keep his voice offhand, he said, "He might pass as a woman while he was a boy, but as a man he could never—"

"Jared Joseph could do it," Raaman said. His eyes glittered. "He has no beard to give him away. It would be a perfect disguise. Thank you, Brother Kaleb."

He rushed from the room, followed by Forest Timna. Kaleb looked after them, then leaned forward until his head was pillowed on his still-folded hands.

"May the Lord forgive you," Levi said. There was no anger in him, only weariness.

Kaleb did not move. "Then I was right? Did you help him leave?"

"Yes. He has a good reason for what he's doing, I assure you."

Kaleb sat up. "Why didn't you tell me? Did you think I was Raaman's puppet, too?"

The bitterness in his voice made Levi wince. "I was afraid you might want to know the reason."

"I do, but I won't insist you tell me."

"Thank you." Levi smoothed his beard. He remembered with a pang what it had done to his respect for Aaron Methuselah to be told about the Trial. If Kaleb felt about Jared as he claimed, what would learning of the thing Jared permitted and participated in do to those feelings? "If the Lord is merciful, you will never have to learn the reason for his behavior."

Kaleb regarded him with a worried frown. "Have I hurt him very much by telling?"

Levi could only shake his head and sigh. "I don't know. We'll just have to wait and see."

Chapter Seventeen

THE GAIT of Jared's mount had become increasingly irregular over the last kilometers. When it was too much to ignore any longer, he shouted for a halt and vaulted off. The clouded queen dropped to her forelegs and shifted her rear weight off her right leg. Jared walked around in front of her, keeping a hand on her and gently scratching her hide as he moved. Her eyes followed him but she stood quiet. She did not even move as he ran his hands down her leg and picked up the foot.

Summer brought her rapa jogging down the line to halt beside him. "What's wrong?"

Jared's finger traced an irregular dark area on one pad. "She's lame."

Summer leaned down to look at the foot. "Ah, she's picked up a stone bruise. Change mounts. She looks quiet, so see if you can bandage that foot and put a little padding over that bruise before you put her in the line." She raised her voice. "Bathsheba! Bring the medical kit."

The young sisterwife came back to join them. She pulled a roll of gauze from her backpack, then stood holding the queen's head and murmuring in a low voice while Summer showed Jared how to wind the gauze around the queen's foot and between the toes to cover the bruise.

"Finish off by tearing it lengthwise for a short way like this, then wrap each end around the leg separately and tie them together." Summer dropped the foot and straightened. "You can do it yourself next time." She handed him the roll of gauze. "Put her back in line and choose another mount."

He took a black spotted king. Clipping the reins to the sides of the muzzle and putting on the saddle, he was struck by how much easier the whole process was than on that first day. Saddlings then had been long successions of hissing struggles punctuated by striking claws and lashing tails. He wondered if the rapas were gentling down this fast or he were simply becoming more adept.

He scratched at a big spot on the king's neck before taking up the reins. The king leaned into the scratching hand, making a low chuckling sound in his throat. Still scratching, Jared put a foot in the stirrup and swung on. The chuckle sharpened to a hiss and the rapa crouched under Jared's added weight. The wicked head started to snake around.

Jared snapped the king's nose with the free end of the reins. *"Hoosh."*

The king flung up his head, but then straightened around and stepped out at a walk.

Summer nodded approval. She rode off toward the front of the line. In a minute they were all moving again. Jared watched the clouded queen for a while. Freed of his weight, her lameness improved until it was almost imperceptible. Still, it worried him. Lameness was one accident he had not anticipated, and it was one that would delay their arrival in Viridian. Not only did lame animals move slower, a lame rapa was one they could not use, and it was the frequent changes of mounts that let them travel as fast as they had been.

He was not aware of Jerusha riding beside him until she spoke. "Don't worry. Animals go lame on the trail. It can't be helped. No one will accuse you of abusing her."

He smiled at her misunderstanding. "I'm not afraid of that. I'm wondering, will we still reach Viridian on Wednesday?"

"I hope so. The sale starts Thursday and we have to have our animals on the sale grounds before midnight the night before." Her brows lifted. "Is it so vital for you to be there by that date?"

He wanted to tell her it was vital for him to have been in Eridu days ago, but he only said, "Yes."

She shook her head in amazement. "You don't act like a woman with a deadline to meet."

That was because he often forgot his purpose for hours at a time. He was ashamed to admit that to even himself. Out here, though, forgetting was easy. There was only the swing of the sun and moons across the sky to mark time. There was no temple clock, no routine of praying, no court, no hearings of petitioners. The women talked about other concerns—the rapas, the upcoming sale, hunting, children. The affairs of men never intruded. In fact, thinking about it, since he had joined them men had never even been mentioned. The things that drove him out here seemed to belong to a world as distant and alien as those Alesdra came from. He had to keep reminding himself he was Jared Joseph, Shepherd of Gibeon, not a foot-free woman named Michal Shem.

He came out of his reverie to find himself riding alone. Jerusha was ahead, slapping her bow across the muzzled nose of one rapa that had been edging up on the swinging tail of another. The rear rapa backed off the other's tail.

Jared checked the other rapas in the line near him. He saw no other impending trouble. The closest ones were the yearlings and most of their energy was used up just keeping pace with the older animals.

He rode forward to check on the clouded queen again. She appeared to be moving easily. He could see the bandage was fraying from contact with the ground, but it was not yet flapping loose. He slowed his king and let the others pass him until he was riding behind the line again.

About midafternoon Summer pulled the radio from its carrying case on her saddle and extended the antenna. She was asking the local ranch station for hunting privileges, Jared supposed. She talked for a long time, and when she returned the radio to its case, she ran her rapa up the nearest rise. She stopped on top, standing in her stirrups to gaze out across the prairie. It was several minutes before she sat down again and came back to join the drive.

She pointed south. "Head that direction."

"What is it?" Nile asked.

"A lake, a herd of leapers, and, according to the Azariah ranch station, several hands to help us pick out some animals for slaughter."

Bathsheba whooped. "Company!"

Jared had never heard of the Azariah ranch. This must finally be the Viridian parish.

"How soon?" Patience called back from her place up the line.

"Several hours yet. I could just see the lake from the top there."

They took the rest of the afternoon to reach the lake. Jared started to worry whether there would be time enough to hunt before dark. From the comments called back and forth between the women, he gathered they were concerned, too. But when they reached the shore of the lake they found a campfire already built and halves and quarters of leapers stacked like cordwood beside it. Three women sitting around the fire stood and came to meet them.

"Ruth!" Nile shrieked. She hurled herself off her rapa into the arms of one of the women. "Did you know it was us?"

The woman grinned. "After your trail boss gave the names of everyone in the crew. But we can talk later. Your rapas look ready to eat through their muzzles."

The Azariah hands helped remove the rapas from the lead line and take them to the lake for a drink before staking them out for feeding. With nine people to do it, the job was over quickly, then there was time for introductions and conversation.

Ruth was Ruth Methuselah. She and Nile had become friends one winter when Nile was ill and had been sent to Middle School in Gibeon to put her near the healers. The names of the other two slipped by Jared unremembered except for the matronym of the smaller woman. It was Shem.

"Michal's a Shem," Jerusha said. "Maybe you're kin."

It would have been suspicious not to play the game so Jared went along. "My people are from Samuel's Ford and Joppa. I had a cousin move this way. Do you know a Bethel Shem?"

"No. Do you know Benjamin Shem from Cyrene?"

They tossed names back and forth for several minutes without producing one in common. At the end of it they laughed and shrugged. With three million people on Marah and only four hundred matronyms, relationships between two people of the same name were often very distant. They might have had a common ancestor seven, ten, or fourteen generations ago. He was not worried about the woman named Shem.

But he wondered about Ruth Methuselah.

"You came from Gibeon?"

She nodded. "After Middle School there was no trade or profession I was particularly interested in, so I came down to take a job as a ranch hand here for a while . . . and we ended up staying and joining the family."

"We?" Nile's brows went up. "Do you mean who I think?"

Ruth smiled. "Of course I brought Enoch with me. I'd never be happy living anywhere without him. He's joined the Azariahs, too."

Jared drifted away from the group toward the feeding rapas. He knew Enoch Methuselah. They had been in the same class in Middle School. Their rooms were across the corridor from each other. It was Enoch, in fact, who had dared Jared to climb over the roofs to spy on the Shepherd's garden.

"Enough talk," he heard Jerusha protest. "I had at least a week's worth of trail dirt on me to start with and now I'm all bloody from carrying meat. Since we have a lake full of water, I'm going swimming. Who's with me?"

They all were. Hats and jackets dropped on the ground, followed by shirts, boots, and breeches as the women stripped to the skin.

"Hey, Michal, aren't you coming, too?" Jerusha called.

The water looked clear and inviting. It was probably cold, too. This was no longer summer, after all. He would not have minded a cold swim; he and Sky had often gone swimming in weather much like this. There was always a campfire to stand over afterward, to warm everyone up and dry them off. But swimming would certainly reveal more secrets than he cared to have them know.

"I want to re-wrap that queen's foot before dark."

Jerusha came over to stare more closely at him. She stood before him, nut-brown, lean and firm of body despite the stretch marks on her belly that attested to several pregnancies. It had been some time since he had had occasion to see a nude woman. Jared felt his breath quicken.

"Wrapping a rapa's foot is a thin excuse. Why don't you really want to come?" She paused. "Are you afraid of water?"

That sounded like a better excuse. He looked down at his feet. "I'm afraid of water."

"Poor thing. Water can be such fun. I'd make sure you weren't hurt." She leaned closer. "I'd make sure you had fun."

He regarded her with a frown. "Wouldn't that upset Patience?"

"Oh, we aren't tanglemates, just sometime partners."

He thought of Sky. "But I have a tanglemate."

Jerusha drew back. "Have you vowed fidelity?"

In a way, he supposed so. "Yes, we have."

"In that case, please forgive me. I won't bother you again. You should have told me when I invited you to tangle that first night."

"I didn't think of it then." He had never heard that women vowed fidelity to one another. He wondered if the Bishop should be told. It sounded like a dangerous practice.

In the midst of the thought he came up short, wondering what he was doing. The Shepherd in him acted on reflex, it seemed. He laughed silently at himself.

Jerusha hugged him and gave him a quick kiss, then turned and ran for the lake. She hit the water in a long, flat dive. She came up with a scream. "It's *ice* water."

Jared stood enviously watching the women splash and wrestle and laugh with each other over the cold. When he felt tempted to join them, he turned away and went to the clouded queen.

She raised her head from her quarter of leaper with a threatening hiss. But he made no move to come closer or reach for it, so she went back to tearing at it. There was little left. She was at the point of chewing up bone.

She proceeded to do that, cracking the bone into pieces between her strong jaws.

He watched, admiring the efficient carnivore that she was. The bandage on her foot was ragged. Once in a while she shook it. The gesture seemed to be more one of annoyance at the flapping ends than of pain. He still had the roll of gauze Summer had given him earlier. When the queen had finished eating, he edged up to her, talking soothingly, and worked a scratching hand down toward the foot. She watched him, but made no move to pull away or strike at him. She let him cut off what remained of the old bandage and wind on a new one.

He was tying the ends when he heard a chuckle behind him. "You'll be an expert hand by the time we reach Viridian."

He straightened. Summer stood there pulling her shirt over her head. She looked past him to the queen. "They're all going to be footsore, I'm afraid. We'll have to bathe and oil them before we take them into the sale ring, but won't they be quiet, well-mannered mounts?" She grinned. "Quiet enough for even men, perhaps." She tucked her shirt into her pants. "Let's see how well the Azariahs can cook."

They started for the fire. Before they reached it, though, Jared heard the beat of a trotting rhinosaur. He looked up to see two figures riding toward them out of the sunset.

"Some of your sisterwives, Ruth?" Summer called.

Ruth stood by the fire rubbing herself dry. She looked around . . . and sighed. "One of them, and my brother. I'm sorry; I didn't ask him out. I don't know why he's here."

Around him Jared felt a sudden change in the atmosphere. The women seemed to diminish in size. Their chins lowered and their voices stilled. No one spoke a word while the two riders brought their mounts into the light of the fire and swung down to the ground.

The man turned from his rhino and opened his arms to them. "The Lord be with you, sisters. The Lord be with you, Nile."

Nile bowed her head. "And with you, Brother Enoch." Her voice was subdued as Jared had never heard it before.

He edged into Summer's shadow. Except for the fact the man had a beard, probably as false as the one Jared usually wore since he, too, had joined the depilation fad, Enoch Methuselah looked just as he had in school. His kinship to Gibeon's former Shepherd was evident in the same golden glow of color, the same richness of voice.

"When I heard a trail group with my sister's dear friend Nile in it was passing through our ranch, and since this is the Sabbath, I thought it would be fitting to come to greet you and conduct a Praying for you."

Sabbath? Jared counted days. It was. He felt instantly guilty for not having remembered. A Praying was a fine idea. He had not had any time for daily meditation since he had been traveling.

"Enoch, they've been on the trail all day and haven't eaten yet," Ruth said.

"Good. Praying is best done on an empty stomach. Introduce your sisterwives, Nile."

Nile did. As each was named, she bowed her head to the man. Jared did the same, and kept his head bowed. He hoped Enoch had not looked at his face.

But Enoch said, "Michal Shem, look at me."

Jared reluctantly lifted his chin.

"Take off your hat and come here."

Silently, Jared obeyed. Cold crawled through his bones.

Enoch stared hard at him. "I don't recall any Shems around Gibeon, but you look very familiar. When did you join the Teman family?"

He just managed to talk around the knot in his throat. "I'm not in the family; I'm just helping with the drive."

"You even sound familiar. It's strange. I hear your voice and for some reason it reminds me of Middle School. Do you live in Gibeon, by any chance?"

"No, brother." Jared slid the pitch of his voice up a bit more. "I come from Samuel's Ford."

"But you look—oh, I know."

Jared's blood congealed.

"Sky Joseph," Enoch said. "You look like Sky. Do you know her?"

Jared met his eyes squarely. "No, brother."

147

"Very well." Enoch shrugged. "The resemblance is remarkable, though. Kneel, sisters, and let us begin."

Jared retreated to Summer's side and collapsed on his knees. He forced himself to breathe slowly rather than gasp in relief. Enoch. Of all people to meet again in the middle of the prairie.

Minutes later his relief was replaced by irritation. Enoch's recitation was terrible. Every jumbled phrase and missed rhythm scraped at his Shepherd's nerves. When Enoch missed the order of the Litany, it took all Jared's self-control not to jump up and take over the ritual. Now he understood the pleading hint in Ruth's last words. Better no Praying at all than this. If the spirit had been there, the rest could have been forgiven, but Jared had been standing up before congregations too long not to recognize when the celebrants' tongues were the only part of them attending the ritual. It was obvious to him that the mind of every woman here was on something entirely different.

Finally, blessedly, Enoch was through. Jared climbed to his feet and stretched. He moved to help Bathsheba and the Azariah hands with supper, careful to keep people between himself and the man.

"Show me your animals," he heard Enoch tell Summer. "I understand they're an unusual breeding."

The two of them went off into the dusk with a candaglobe.

Jared glanced from time to time toward the circle of light that marked the man's location. Enoch looked the same as always, but he did not act the same. Jared remembered him as warm and witty. Now here he was ordering Summer to show him the rapas, rather than asking permission, telling them he was conducting a Praying instead of finding out first if the women were interested. When had his schoolmate become so officious?

By the end of the evening, Jared had added arrogant and pompous to the description. The man dominated the conversation during supper, ostensibly discussing genetics with the Teman women, but somehow managing to lecture on the subject instead. Much of his information was inaccurate. Jared remembered sitting up late at night with Enoch, the two of them huddled under the sheets with a candaglobe, coaching the other boy in genetics for their biology class. Enoch was very interested in the subject and talked of becoming a geneticist, but even with the coaching, and a few answers passed to him during tests, Enoch barely passed that unit of biology. Listening to the man hold forth now, Jared reflected that following Enoch's suggestions for breeding pairs was likely to result in a muddy-colored dwarf with the temper of a stinghopper. Jared wondered how the women could sit listening so attentively and never once correct the man. Surely they recognized he was wrong. Jared remembered what Storm said about never arguing with a man, but she could not have meant the policy to go this far. He would have corrected Enoch a number of times except for the fear of calling further attention to himself.

It was a relief when the meal was over. Enoch and his escort stood.

The women stood, too. "You've honored our camp," Summer said. "Thank you for coming. The Lord be with you on your ride back to the station."

"Thank you, sister." He turned and started toward his rhino, then stopped and came back to the fire. "I can't leave without saying one more thing. My conscience requires me to reprove you for the condition of your animals. They're magnificent rapas, but several are lame and all have hides in very dry condition. I saw signs of parasite infestation, too. It's shameful to let such good animals come to that condition. You can't get a good price for them this way. You should never have trailed them; you should have shipped them by rail from Gibeon. My best suggestion to you at this point is for you to rest your animals here several days. Treat the lame ones, bathe all of them, then move on very slowly."

Jared sucked in his breath. That was one remark too many. He took a step forward.

Iron fingers bit into his shoulder, holding him back.

"Thank you, brother," Summer said. "It's quite true about the rapas. The trail has been hard on them. Your suggestion is an excellent one."

She went with Enoch to help him mount his rhino,

and stood watching while the man and his escort disappeared into the darkness.

The hand let go of Jared's shoulder. Rubbing it, he turned to see who it had been. Nile was frowning at him.

"Why—" he began.

"Shut up, Michal," she said.

The Azariah hands looked at one another and started toward their own mounts, rapas tethered near the Teman group. There were farewells and hugs, particularly between Nile and Ruth.

"I'm sorry about Enoch," Ruth said.

Nile shrugged.

Eventually the Temans were alone around the fire. Not until then did anyone speak to Jared. It was Summer who started.

"I heard that hiss. Just what were you thinking of doing?" She sounded angry.

Jared blinked, puzzled. "I was going to tell him why you're trailing the rapas, for a start."

"Thank the Lord that Nile had the presence of mind to stop you. I don't know how it is in your family, but in ours we've been taught it's rude to criticize a man before his family. I make it a practice never, under any circumstances, to contradict *any* man."

"But what he said was unjustified. He didn't know the circumstances."

Nile grimaced. "Has lack of knowledge ever stopped a man from offering advice at any time on any subject whatsoever? After all, they're the Lord's appointed rulers of the universe; they'll tell you so. They can even show you scripture to prove it."

Summer smiled faintly. "Nile, as you may have guessed, doesn't like men, but you'll notice she's still polite to them."

"Do you like them?"

Her smile widened. She nodded. All the others but Nile did, too.

"We've all started our pregnancies with natural insemination, and we bed our family men for the pure pleasure of it. Even Nile will admit they're good company."

Nile scowled. "But why in Heaven can't they be con-

150

tent with that? Why can't they stick to being priests and leave the business of the world to those of us with better qualifications than a beard and a line of scripture?"

A hot flush crept up Jared's neck to his face. Many women throughout his life had sat smiling while he talked, had nodded at each of his suggestions, had said, "Yes, Jared; yes, brother; yes, Father." How many of them had been twitching with annoyance inside?

"But are we going to stay here and rest as he told us to, then?" he asked.

Five pairs of eyes fastened on him in surprise. "Of course not. We have to be in Viridian in two days. The sale is Wednesday," Summer said.

"Then we are contradicting him."

"No, we're just not obeying him. He'll never know. If he asks, his family will assure him we stayed."

"Merciful Lord," Patience said. "I wouldn't have thought Samuel's Ford was the end of the world, but in some ways, what an innocent you are, Michal!"

Jared tried to cover himself. "I know about being polite, it's just that . . . he spoiled the whole day."

"Don't they always?" Nile said.

Jared slept very little that night. He kept remembering his encounters with women over the years and wondering how he had appeared to them. It made him burn to think of what they may have been feeling behind their submissive faces. How often had he misjudged a situation and never been corrected? Travel was said to be educational. It certainly was, more than he ever dreamed.

Chapter Eighteen

LOOKING OUT across the Grand Council chamber, Alesdra found her nervousness and anger gone. It no longer mattered that she had waited weeks for this moment; the moment was here. She was Alesdra Pontokouros, liaison officer for the ramjet *Galactic Rose,* and she was going to sell these people a shuttlebox. She stood to the side of the rostrum, aware of the Bishop's long and formal introduction, but not listening. Instead, she watched the solons.

As in all rooms on Marah, the ceiling was low. It absorbed sound and gave voices a flat tone. It was still a large room, however, with each man and woman— about a third were women—seated at a desk. Alesdra had the impression of being in an office or large boardroom rather than in a legislative hall. The solons themselves were alert and attentive. Their eyes wandered from the Bishop to her with frank curiosity. There were frowns on only a few faces. Others looked interested.

The Bishop finished his introduction. "Brothers and sisters, Alesdra Pontokouros."

She crossed to the rostrum and mounted the two steps behind it. "Greetings. I want to thank you and Bishop Elias Jamin for this opportunity to appear before you. I hope that before the morning is over, you'll be glad of our meeting, too." Formal greetings were nearly always obligatory on occasions like this. She delivered them on behalf of IGC, the other colonies of Earth, and Captain Deyoe.

Once the greetings were finished, she began her sales talk. Every eye in the room fastened on her. Her voice became the only sound. She introduced her product, using IGC's name, Equipotential Transfer Portal. She outlined its uses in interplanetary communication and trade. She explained that IGC was not selling them the box itself but wanted to lease land on which to build it. She pointed out how it would make money for Marahns, in pay to local workers who helped build the box, in taxes and tariffs. And she told them how it could be used to clean their planet of their disease.

An intake of breath around the Council chamber punctuated that statement. A number of men frowned. She was not surprised. She had expected the idea to be met with some disfavor. But there was one man, in the front to the right, whose reaction did surprise her. His skin blanched. Panic stared back at her from his eyes. Why should he be afraid? What could be so terrifying about curing this disease?

She puzzled over it while she answered the obvious questions. "It will be impossible for you to be invaded through your portal. The box can't be more than three meters square, hardly large enough to contain much of an invasion force. Also, no portal on any other world will be able to reach you directly. On a strict schedule, half a day for sending, half a day for receiving, your portal reaches a central switching point maintained by IGC. Cargo and passengers are transferred within the switching point to the portals reaching their particular destinations. If anyone tried to invade you, they would only find themselves in IGC central. I don't know exactly how my crew intends to build the portal without being contaminated, but they assure me they have figured out a method. I know it will involve using local people for labor, all of whom will be paid in portal-use time. You'll be able to use the portal before the planet is decontaminated, as long as only trade goods or plants are sent through, items which can be sterilized without damaging them."

"What trade goods?" a woman asked.

Alesdra was ready for the question. She had been watching for commercial-quality items since she landed. "Candaglobes, for one. Many planets have tried to develop cold light. Most have failed. The candalilies themselves might be in demand to mark roads on other planets for night travel. And you have alien artifacts.

Every day you melt down objects from the Old City that collectors, archeologists, and anthropologists on other worlds would pay small fortunes for."

A man said, "Our ancestors came to Marah to escape the dehumanization and decadence of the civilization you come from. Wouldn't we be foolish to build a machine that allows that civilization to come after us?"

"You'll have absolute control over who enters and leaves the planet. If necessary, the portal can be surrounded by a fortified compound and all incoming passengers held until you decide whether to allow them on Marah or not."

There were other questions, and objections. She answered them as carefully as possible, or evaded them with professional skill. At least the wait had given her time to become proficient in the language.

When the questions became more directed toward what society was like on other worlds than toward IGC and the portal, the Bishop interrupted. "I think we have heard enough to let us form a judgment on this offer. We must now meditate and pray to the Lord for guidance in reaching a decision. There are advantages to be offered by this machine, it would seem, but we should remember there are many things offered us in life with the appearance of good."

It was an echo of Jared's sentiment on the temptation of children by satan fruit. Alesdra bit her lip. She supposed the objection was valid. The shuttlebox could be viewed as a kind of satan fruit. She wondered what the shaman's specific objections to the box were. No doubt he would list them next.

"Do we really care to risk contaminating the rest of the galaxy with the disease the Lord has seen fit to place on Marah? Is it good to have instant communication with cultures with morals so radically different from our own? Do we want to sell the fruits of our world in return for the fruits of others? We must ask ourselves if we really need things our own world does not presently produce." He turned to Alesdra. "We will consider your offer and notify you when a decision has been reached."

"When will that be?"

He spread his hands. "At the Lord's pleasure, sister. Be patient."

She bowed respectfully to him and let herself be escorted out through a side door. She found Sky waiting for her.

"How do you think you did?"

Alesdra pulled a wry face. "I think the women are interested. I'm not sure about the men. Living boys means less of a minority and therefore fewer privileges." She did not mention the fearful man. She remembered him, though, and wondered again at his fear. "The Bishop is against me."

"Oh, no," Sky protested. "I'm sure you're wrong. The Bishop wants to end the disease as much as we do."

Alesdra glanced at her. Dear Sky. She shook her head. "You give him the benefit of the doubt if you like. I can always hope you're right."

Sky sighed. It had a reproachful sound, but she said nothing.

They left the temple. At the gate, Sky stopped. "Let's drop by Peace Hall before we go home."

"Sabrina will bring home any radio messages that relate to Jared."

Sky grimaced. "I know. I think I'd prefer to see them for myself first."

They followed the street around the temple toward the keeper headquarters. Sky kept frowning.

"I'm really concerned about my sisterwives. For years we've been a close, loving family. Now suddenly I feel almost like an outsider. They've heard and convicted Jared of . . . inhumanity, I guess, without ever having met him."

"He's a man. Your sisterwives don't like men. Haven't they started all their pregnancies by AI?"

"But they never condemned Jared before. They always seemed very sympathetic when I talked about him."

Sky could be sensitive and perceptive, but she could be amazingly blind, too. Alesdra raised a brow at her. "He hadn't stolen your son, then."

Sky bit her lip.

They waved at the keeper on reception duty as they

155

walked into Peace Hall and down the corridor to the radio room. Sabrina was gone at the moment and Sky sighed in relief.

The operator on duty looked up at them. "There's been heavy traffic today. There's only one item that I transcribed relating to your brother, though." She picked up a stack of messages and handed them to Sky. "Read away."

Alesdra and Sky shuffled through the stack. Most of it was irrelevant, as the operator said. There were only a few messages coming out of Gibeon. One of those was to Samuel's Ford asking for information on a woman named Michal Shem. The same request had also been sent to Joppa. But there was one general call from Gibeon, and it made Sky take a sharp breath and clutch tight to the message sheet. Alesdra pried it away from her to read.

As she read, her brows went up. "Jared Joseph may be disguised as a woman? As he did when you were children?"

"Probably." Sky ran nervous hands through her hair. "I know he told you, but how could anyone else have found out?" Her eyes suddenly widened. "Oh. Oh, no, not Kaleb."

"Kaleb Eshban?"

Sky nodded. "He was there once when Jared was caught. But surely he wouldn't tell; he's almost kin."

"It only proves, never trust a shaman."

"Maybe they'll catch him soon, then, and get back your son," the radio operator said.

Sky sent her a look of despair. "That's what I'm afraid of." She walked out of the room, leaving the operator to stare after her in bewilderment.

Chapter Nineteen

ANOTHER RAPA was gimping. Jared frowned at the line. That made four now. A day or two of rest would cure all of them, but until they could rest, the lame ones were slowing them down more and more.

"Summer," he called, "there's an aurora queen back here that—"

"I see her," Summer pointed ahead of them. "Ride up that hill and tell me what you see."

He looked toward the hill. As if reading his mind, his mount swung around and headed in that direction. Jared clucked approval. These animals were becoming almost a pleasure to ride. He squeezed with his legs. The queen obediently stretched her legs and went up the slope in long, bounding strides. She stopped at the top by dropping into a crouch with such suddenness that Jared found himself wrapped around her neck.

He pushed himself back into the saddle. "You're almost too handy, beast."

He fancied he saw a humorous gleam in a green eye turned back toward him.

Scratching the queen's neck, he looked out across the rolling land. There was a road just ahead. His breathing quickened in excitement. It must be the Viridian road. Perhaps they could use it the rest of the way in. He followed the red strip with his eyes, speculating how far Viridian might be. He hoped it was close. The stock sale was the next day, and so was the next train for—

All thought stopped as he saw the rows of farm crops on the next hills. His eyes jumped to the southern horizon and found three tall radio towers protruding into the sky.

He spun the queen on her toes and sent her racing down the hill. "Viridian! Not more than fifteen or twenty kilometers away. We can be there tonight."

The women whooped in elation, sending the rapas dancing and hissing.

"Viridian," Jerusha sighed, " 'Thou glittering gem of the Nimrod/Thou cultural cradle of the south.' " She sat very straight in her saddle. "Let's *ride*."

"Let's be sensible," Summer said. "We don't want to cripple our stock at the last minute."

"After all, Viridian will wait for us," Nile said.

Jerusha grimaced. "You don't care about getting there, I suppose. I remember how you were the last time we were there. Viridian has a fine, fine women's club, Michal. We'll go there, have a long, hot bath and massage. We'll visit a shop and pick up something for evening wear, perhaps a simple one-piece suit in plush material, then we can go out to dinner and—" she extended her arms to the sides, putting her hands on the shoulders of imaginary partners "—and dancing." She started humming.

Bathsheba looked entranced. "Yes, let's."

Summer cleared her throat. "After we register the rapas for the sale, bathe and oil and feed them, and bed them down for the night."

Jerusha sighed. "That means about midnight."

"Perhaps a bit sooner if we stop talking and start riding."

Jerusha and Bathsheba wheeled their rapas away, whistling at the line to move. The other women exchanged smiles and took up their places again.

They struck the road ten minutes later. There were mounted and driven animals along it, so they kept the drive off to one side. Riding parallel, they followed it toward Viridian.

Women passing on the road stared. "Those are the biggest timber rapas I've ever seen."

One woman reined her copper king alongside Patience and spent some time asking about breeding and pedigrees. "Are they a consignment for the autumn stock sale?" When Patience nodded, the woman eyed the blue spotted king Patience was riding. "I think I'll come by."

A few women called questions to Jared. He referred them to Summer. "I'm just helping with the drive."

Viridian was close. He could feel it waiting for them. He had to restrain himself from urging his queen into a run.

"The Lord be with you, sister," a voice said.

"And with—" Jared began, turning. "You," he finished.

The speaker wore the brown shirt and triangular green patch of Viridian's peacekeepers. She paced her copper queen beside Jared's mount. "These are magnificent animals you have. Are they northern imports?"

Jared told his heart to slow down. The keeper was only interested in the rapas like everyone else. "No, they were bred on the Teman ranch."

The keeper looked thoughtful. "That's near Gibeon, isn't it? I seem to recall talking to rowdy Temans at other autumn and spring stock sales. You've trailed here this time; did you see anyone unusual on the way?"

Jared eased breath past the sudden tight place in his throat. "Unusual? No."

Ahead, he saw Patience glance over at the keeper with raised brows. She moved her rapa up beside Summer. Moments later Summer swung her rapa around and rode back around the end of the line to join Jared and the keeper.

"Admiring our stock? They're hardy and intelligent animals. They'd make good keeper mounts."

"They look like they would," the keeper agreed.

"I understand you're wondering about people we might have met on the trail."

"We're looking for a man, possibly traveling with a boy."

"Two males alone?" Summer stared. "No, we certainly haven't seen anyone like that."

"There's a chance the man is traveling dressed as a woman."

The line of rapas was on one side of him, the keeper and Summer on the other. Jared felt trapped. How had they found out about his disguise?

"What does he look like?" Summer asked.

"Late thirties, one hundred seventy-five centimeters

tall, slight build, complexion of medium yellow-brown, dark brown hair, light brown eyes."

There was no mention of what he was wearing. The keepers had not learned from Levi or Storm, then. The rest of it was description anyone who knew him could give. What were the charges against him, though? That was what he wanted most to know. What did he face if he were caught?

"How could a man think he would be taken for a woman just because he dressed like one?" Summer said.

The keeper shrugged. "Male arrogance, I suppose. Is your crew hired help or family?"

"Family," Summer said, "or hired hands who seem like family by this time. We'll keep watch for your fugitive." She regarded the keeper speculatively. "I don't suppose you can tell us what he's done."

The keeper smiled. "Not even what he's alleged to have done." She looked over the rapas again. "These certainly are nice animals. I hope you get a good price for them."

She swung her rapa back toward the road, urging her into a run. Summer watched her go with a thoughtful frown.

After the keeper was out of sight, she said, "Let's ride farther back, Michal."

They let ten or twelve meters open up between them and the line. Hairs stirred on Jared's neck. He did not think he was going to like what Summer must be planning to say.

"Would *you* care to tell me why the keepers want you?"

He tried to bluff. "What? You think I'm a man? That's—"

"Of course you're a man. It explains everything that's odd about you. If we'd known before there was a man pretending to be a woman, we would have suspected you right away. You're lucky people aren't very observant, otherwise that keeper would have seen she was describing you perfectly." She paused. "You are the man they're looking for, aren't you?"

Jared sighed and nodded.

They rode in silence for several minutes. Jared waited in agony. She knew. Now what?

He finally broke the silence. "What are you going to do?"

"Nothing. If I'd wanted to give you over, I would have done so when the keeper was here."

He turned in his saddle to stare at her. "Why didn't you?"

She thought for several moments before answering. "I'm not quite sure. Perhaps because you had to have help to do as well as you've done, which means some woman believes in you. Perhaps because you've worked as hard on this drive as the rest of us. You've earned your keep. And perhaps because you do seem almost like kin." She legged her rapa into a brisk jog. "Sisters, let's move them; we're almost home!"

By late afternoon they were in Viridian. They collected admiring stares as they circled the town to the sale grounds on the western edge. The rapas danced along on their toes, heads turning constantly, nostrils twitching.

Jared felt as anxious as the rapas acted. What a sense-assaulting place a town was. People laughed and talked. Bicycle bells jangled. Wagons clattered. But it was not only noisy; it smelled. He had always thought rapas smelled strongly musky. Now he found people had an odor, too, sharp and acid. As they neared the sale grounds, the smell of people was replaced by that of animals.

It was going to be a big sale, Jared saw. Row after row of rapa stalls spread across the grounds between high pens holding herds of leapers and rhino and flocks of black-and-white hoopers.

They halted at the sale office. Summer dismounted and went in. She came back with a woman carrying a tablet and scriber.

The woman's brows went up at the sight of the rapas. "Small consignment."

Summer smiled. "With luck, we'll whet the buyers' appetites enough that they'll come to us for more."

The woman counted. "Four yearling king kids, fifteen kings, nine queens." She wrote on her tablet. "You can put them in stall row G. You"—she pointed her scriber at Summer—"come in and give me the description and breeding of each animal, and pedigree papers, if any."

Summer handed the reins of her rapa to Bathsheba. "Start looking after them."

They led the rapas around the grounds to stall row G. After Patience located the wash floor and an oil dealer, they went to work. Each rapa was taken to the wash floor, hosed and scrubbed, then gone over for cuts and parasites. They applied medication where necessary. When the rapas were dry, medicinal-smelling oil was rubbed into their hides. Some of the rapas were startled by the sight of water spraying out of what looked like long snakes and objected strenuously to the washing process. Jared and the Temans ended up as wet as their animals.

Twenty-eight rapas used a great deal of oil. Inevitably, some of it ended up on the applicators as well as on the applicatees. Not because the rapas objected to it, though. On the contrary, they enjoyed it so much they leaned against whoever was tending to them, hoping to be rubbed harder.

Summer reappeared as they were finishing.

"You've missed all the fun," Nile said.

Summer grinned. "I had to make arrangements for feeding these beasts. Get them back to their stalls. The meat wagon is coming."

A quarter of an hour later all the animals were stalled, tearing at huge quarters of rhino meat. Jared looked down the row. The colorful hides gleamed in the candlelight. He nodded. They looked good, which was nice. He would have hated to get so wet and messy for nothing . . . and sore. His arms and shoulders ached from rubbing.

Belatedly he thought, Candlelight? He looked up. It was night. When had the sun set?

"There are a couple of stalls we can sleep in," Summer said.

Patience sighed. "Point them out."

"I'm for the women's club and a long bath first, then food for myself," Jerusha said.

Nile and Bathsheba seconded the idea.

Patience shook her head. "I don't even care about eating. The rest of you can rowdy around if you like. I'm going to sleep."

"Michal, want to come with us?"

162

Jared shook his head. Summer indicated she was staying on the sale grounds, too.

"But you'll be missing the best part of the trip."

"They're old ladies," Bathsheba said. "Let them stay."

The three raced one another toward the street. Patience smiled indulgently, then picked up her pack and started toward the empty stalls Summer pointed out.

Jared and Summer stood watching the rapas a while longer. When they became hungry, though, they went looking for food, too. They found a little cafe near the sale grounds and ate a small meal there. Later they walked back to their animals.

Except for a few people moving in the distance, they were alone on the stall row. The atmosphere was quiet and peaceful. An aurora king stretched his neck over the top bar of his stall. Jared reached up to rub around the tympanic membrane on the side of the wicked head. The rapa leaned into him, chuckling.

"What will you do now?" Summer asked.

"There's a train leaving for Eridu tomorrow. I need to be on it."

"Be careful. They may be looking for you on trains. It won't be like traveling with some gullible ranchers."

He stopped rubbing. The king bared his teeth and hissed. Jared slapped the animal's nose. The king's head jerked back over the bars into the stall.

"I don't think you've been gullible," he told Summer. "It's just that you're kind people and I'm very clever."

Summer grinned. "You're beginning to sound like a woman. A man would never say that; he'd just act like he thought so." She paused. "You're an unusual man."

Was he? Jared found that hard to believe. "Maybe I'm just the first one you've ever had the chance to know as something other than a priest."

He left her considering that and went to stretch out in the stall near Patience.

He must have fallen asleep immediately. He was not aware of Summer coming to bed, nor of the other three returning at whatever hour they did. He just found them asleep all around him when he woke.

The sky was still dark. He wondered what had wakened him. A moment later he consciously heard what his ears had detected while he was still asleep, a temple prayer bell. The long years of habit had pulled him out of sleep at the first chimes. He lay listening, wanting to answer the summons. It seemed like months since he had attended a morning Praying. He felt guilty knowing he would not be there again today.

The bell seemed to go on forever, and when, at last, it stopped, Jared was fully awake. He was awake and unable to go back to sleep. Perhaps he ought to go. He did not know what time the train arrived. It left Gibeon about dawn.

He quietly got to his feet and made his way to the stall door, stepping over sleeping Temans. He paused a moment in the aisle to look back at them. There was a strange pain in him, a reluctance to leave. He made himself turn his back on them and walk away down the stall row.

Viridian was larger than Gibeon, but still small enough for everything to be within short walking range. He reached the station in minutes. The ticket window was just opening when he arrived.

The ticket agent's nose wrinkled as she regarded him.

"One way to Eridu," he said. "Second class."

"That'll be five thousand."

He counted out the two-thousand note and three thousand-unit notes. "When does the train leave?"

"Ten noon." She handed him a second-class ticket.

Nearly four hours to wait. What could he do until then? He remembered how the ticket agent's nose wrinkled. He counted the rest of his money. Two thousand left. What could he do with two thousand units to make himself more socially acceptable? After a minute of reflection he grinned.

The receptionist at the women's club did not wrinkle her nose; she was too well trained. "A bath costs five hundred units. Clothes cleaning is another five hundred."

That would leave him enough for meals on the train. "I'll take the bath and clothes cleaning."

"Would you like a massage, too? It's only five hundred more."

"Just the bath . . . a private bath."

"This way, please."

Following her through the corridors to a bath cubicle, he was amazed at his temerity in coming here, of all places. But he appeared to be passing as a woman here, too. Still, he was careful to be submerged to his neck in soapy water when the attendant came for his clothes, and when she left, he climbed out of the tub to lock the door behind her.

He made the bath long and hot. He soaped and scrubbed until he nearly bled. It was only when he heard the attendant knock on the door and announce his clothes were back that he climbed out. A week and a half of trail dirt swirled away down the drain.

He opened the door just wide enough to reach out for his clothes and quickly shut it again. The clothes were still warm and spicy-smelling from drying. His boots and jacket were oiled to a fine gleaming patina. Even the flat-brimmed ranch hat had been brushed until it looked almost new.

There was a long mirror on the back of the door. When he wiped the steam from it, he found himself facing a person leaner and darker than the one he had seen reflected in the window of Levi's kitchen. The youthfully soft face he knew was replaced by one with a sharp jaw and sunburned skin pulled tight over jutting cheekbones. The face looked familiar, though. It looked like his mother's.

After he paid for the bath, he walked back to the railway station. The sun was high overhead. It had to be near noon. He felt his breath quicken. Soon he would be on his way.

In the door of the station, though, he stopped short. Without moving too fast, he turned and walked back out. Keepers! He flattened against the side of the building. Two of them stood at the door to the platform, and with them was a thin-bearded man in green. Jared had caught only a glimpse of the ecclesiastic but it was enough for him to recognize one of Raaman's trusted pages. The page would also know Jared, with or without a beard.

It could mean only one thing—they had found out he was in Viridian and planning to take a train out. Speculation on how they found out was put aside for the moment in favor of thinking what he could do now. Even if he went around the station to the platform, he would still have to board from the platform. The keepers would see him.

In the distance, he heard the shrill whistle of a train. He bit his lip. Perhaps if he walked through at the last moment he would pass them before they realized who he was. Better yet, perhaps he could walk through with a group. But the trouble with that was, he could not count on a group. He might be the only passenger boarding.

"Michal," a voice said. "I'm so glad we caught you. How dare you leave without giving us a chance to say good-bye?"

He focused his eyes and found himself looking into the indignant face of Jerusha Teman. Beyond her was Summer, looking solemn.

"Our rapas don't go into the ring until midafternoon, so I thought Jerusha and I could come down and see you away."

The sound of the whistle was growing louder. Jared could hear the hum of the engine, too. Inside the station people were starting to stir.

Jerusha put an arm around his waist. "You look beautiful without the trail dirt. You must have gone to the women's club, after all. Why didn't you come last night? It would have been the bath of your life."

A corner of Summer's mouth quirked. Jared could imagine her thoughts. It would have been a surprising bath indeed.

With a last blast that blended into the squeal of brakes, the train coasted into the station. Jared turned for the door. "I'm glad you came. It would have been terrible getting on alone." He put his arm around Jerusha.

Summer joined them. Arms wrapped around each other, they walked through the station. Jared bent his head toward Summer as they reached the door to the platform, using her head and the brim of his hat to obscure the page's view of his face.

"We're going to miss you, sister," Summer said, loud enough for the keepers to hear.

"And all the lovely nights we could have had together," Jerusha added in a whisper.

Jared looked down the string of low, sleek cars, past the engine, along the tracks toward Eridu. "If I ever come back, I'll visit you."

"Please do."

Jerusha threw her arms around him and kissed him on the cheek. Mindful of the keepers and page watching, he hugged her back, then turned and hugged Summer, too. She was stiff in his arms.

"I hope we helped," she said.

"You have."

He stepped back from her and swung across the narrow space between the platform and the car's entrance. A steward directed him to a second-class compartment. He took off his hat and sat down, and looked out the window to find the women still on the platform, talking to each other, smiling and waving . . . and standing between him and the keepers. They remained there, blocking the keepers' view while mail and cargo were unloaded and loaded. They were still there when the train moved out of the station.

Only when Viridian was well behind did Jared relax. He sat back in his seat and sighed deeply. He found there was a lightness of spirit in him that he had not felt since leaving Gibeon. He was on the train. Eridu lay just two days away.

He looked out the window at the prairie streaming by. At last he was traveling at a speed that ate up distance. It was far better than walking or riding a rapa.

"Are you a rancher?"

Jared looked toward the voice. It belonged to a small boy. He was one of three children and two women who also occupied the compartment. The boy stared at Jared intently.

"Are you a rancher?" the boy repeated.

"Forgive him," one of the women, presumably the boy's mother, said. "We come from Simeon, where there are farmers and fishermen, but no ranchers. He's very curious."

"Yes, I'm a rancher," Jared said.

"Do you ride rapas?"

Jared felt uncomfortable under the boy's stare. Could he ask the mother to keep the boy quiet? Jared had little experience with young children. He had even less idea how a woman would talk to them. On the other hand, if the keepers were looking for him on the train, it would be for a man traveling alone, not with a group. Perhaps he could hide among these women and their children.

"Yes, I ride rapas."

"Tell me about them."

The officious note, so like the one he had been shocked to find in Enoch Methuselah's voice, bristled the hair on Jared's neck. The boy needed to be taught more courtesy. But instead of offering correction, Jared talked about rapas.

He wondered if he would burn in Hell for the tales he spun. They were half-truths compounded of childhood memories and more recent experience. There were also pure fabrications. He watched the women for signs they were catching him lying, but neither gave any indication of disagreeing with him. The boy's mother was occupied with a fussy toddler. The other listened with as much interest as the boy did. The third child, a girl about the boy's age, slept by the second woman.

Jared invited the boy to sit beside him and wear his hat. The boy did, until he fell asleep, then Jared took off his jacket and covered the boy with it. Anyone looking into the compartment would see three women, each with a child beside her.

"Thank you," the boy's mother said. The child she held was finally dozing off as well. "Now we can have some peace."

"If you've come from Simeon, this has been a long trip."

"Yes. I thought they were never going to run out of energy."

"Where are you going?" he asked.

"River Rest."

That would give him company almost halfway to Eridu.

Jared kept up the conversation with them. He learned they were mechanics. They were moving to new jobs at the flyer plant in River Rest. When they asked about him, he called himself Naomi Azariah and told them he was on a buying trip, looking for king timber rapas to bring back for a new breeding program on his family's ranch.

The girl's mother shuddered. "I don't know whether to call you brave or foolish for wanting to work with creatures like that."

"They're not so bad when you learn to know them."

While they talked the train approached the West River country and the land outside grew greener and more hilly. Jared estimated they must be nearing Nimrim.

A steward opened the compartment door, announced, "The dining car is open for supper," then went on.

"Would you like me to help with the children?" Jared asked.

The boy's mother gave him a grateful smile. "Take Matthew."

They woke the children and headed for the dining car.

They were in the middle of the meal when the train pulled into Nimrim. Through the window Jared could see several keepers strolling the length of the platform, peering into the train. He made himself keep eating and would not let himself look at the keepers.

The train was still in the station when the meal was finished. On the way back to their compartment, they passed a keeper in the corridor.

Jared flattened against the windows to let the keeper by. He pulled the boy with him. "Let her pass, Matthew," he said.

He smiled at the keeper. He kept smiling as he talked to the women and children, but it felt like part of a mask until the train was underway again.

The tracks followed the shore of the Crystal Sea as they headed north. The inland sea was a large one, so wide its western shore was below the horizon. Instead, the water merged into the sky. At sunset sea and sky were one great conflagration, a vivid flood of scarlets and golds.

They watched the spectacle until the last reds had faded into night, then moved to give each child room to sleep lying down. The women fell asleep not long after. Jared dozed, but every change in the sound of the wheels woke him. He waited through the two stops the train made during the night almost without breath. At both stops keepers were on the platform and one walked the length of the train peering into each compartment. Jared pretended to be asleep, but behind his closed eyes, his mind raced. Did they suspect he was on this train, or was this normal procedure in any general hunt? And what were the charges against him?

There were keepers at River Rest, too. Watching the women and their children disembark, Jared felt naked.

Not long after, his fears were justified. A keeper looked into the compartment. She regarded him speculatively. "You're a rancher?"

He nodded.

"Name?"

"Naomi Azariah."

"From?"

He hated giving out checkable information. Not answering would be worse, though. "Viridian." At least there were Azariahs in Viridian.

"Bound for?"

"Eridu." His seat ticket gave away that much.

"Are you traveling alone?"

"Yes. What's the matter?"

The keeper smiled a bland, professional smile. "We're hunting a missing person. What did you say your name was again?"

Steadily, he said, "Azariah Naomi Bethel Azariah."

"Thank you. Sorry to have disturbed you."

The keeper left but Jared still felt her presence. He did not like this. He had had to give her too much information on himself. He wished someone would take the other seats in the compartment. He hated being alone.

Just before the train left, two women, one young and one middle-aged, and a young man in ecclesiastic green came into the compartment. While the women shoved luggage under the seats, the man sat opposite Jared.

"The Lord be with you," Jared said.

The man flicked a glance at him. "And with you, sister." He was carrying a Testament. He opened it and began reading.

170

The older woman reached out to touch Jared's jacket lying folded on the seat beside him. "That's nice. Is it leaper hide?"

The man looked up. "If you want to talk, go somewhere else, sisters. I'm trying to read."

The woman's mouth tensed, then formed a smile. "I'm sorry, Boaz." She produced a periodical titled *The Bicycle Crafter's Yearbook* from her carryall and began reading.

The young woman looked Jared over with interest, then glanced at the man. She grimaced. With a silent sigh, she settled back and closed her eyes.

It looked as if he would be getting no companionship from this group. Jared turned his attention out the window. On the passenger side of the train were the fertile hills of the West River country. Farms spread out over them in variegated patchworks of color and texture. On the corridor side of the train he could see the West River and, across it, more hills. Beyond the hills was a faint line of red marking the edge of the Edom Desert. By noon they were following the shore of the Red Sea. Its rusty waters looked so close the waves seemed to lap at the roadbed.

He ate lunch alone and came back to a compartment as quiet as the one he had left. The young woman was gone, leaving the older woman with the man.

Jared leaned back in his seat. His full stomach, the silence, and the warmth of the compartment combined to make him drowsy. He tried for a while to just doze. He wanted to be awake when they came into each station, but his lack of sleep the night before overtook him. He half-woke about midafternoon and realized he had slept through at least one stop. He considered getting up and walking around, but the effort was too much. He closed his eyes again.

Someone was calling him. He looked around his rooms in the Gibeon temple wondering who it could be. The voice was outside his door, accompanied by an insistent rapping.

"Father Jared."

"Who is it?"

"Father, you're late for evening Praying."

Late for Praying? He had not even heard the prayer bell. "I'm coming."

"Jared. Jared."

"I'm—" He broke off. The voice was real. He opened his eyes to find himself looking up at the sky-blue shirt and triangular green patch of a keeper.

He turned his head. Outside it was nearing sunset and the train was stopped at a station.

"Jared Joseph, I must ask you to come with me," the keeper said.

Past her, the ecclesiastic and the young woman stared at him wide-eyed. Another keeper waited in the doorway. Jared tensed. What would it take to push past them?

The keeper leaned closer. "Please, Father, don't resist."

Jared regarded her for a minute in silence, then sighed in resignation. Picking up his jacket, he stood and followed her off the train.

Chapter Twenty

"JARED HAS been captured," Raaman announced with great satisfaction and relief. "The keepers caught him on a train headed for Eridu."

"Did they?" Levi regarded Raaman thoughtfully. Surely this one piece of news was not why the lean Deacon had sent to Roshdan House for him. It could have waited until morning. "Did he have the boy?"

Raaman frowned. "No. The keepers tell me that as far as they've been able to trace him, Jared left Gibeon alone. That has to mean the boy is hiding here."

"Here? That's impossible."

Raaman shrugged. "I don't know. I haven't started

looking for him yet, but I'm sure when we do, we'll find someone with an unaccountable fifteen-year-old child."

Raaman was right. Perhaps it was time to find a new hiding place for Isaiah.

"I've ordered the keepers to give Jared over to the local temple for keeping until we send for him."

Neck hair rippled on Levi. "Give him to the local temple? Which temple?"

"Gaza."

Once inside the temple, Jared would be under the power of the Shepherd. Anything could happen to him. Levi had a vivid memory of Daniel Amalek floating face down in the swimming pool. "Was that all you wanted to tell me? This is why you had me brought from home?"

"Not quite. I really wanted to see your reaction when I told you." Raaman paused. "You seemed less surprised about where he was caught than you might. Why do you suppose he was going to Eridu?"

"His sister lives there."

"Then why go alone, without the boy?"

Levi shrugged. "I'm not a seer, Brother Raaman."

Raaman pursed his lips. "Someone had to give him the women's clothes he was wearing."

Levi breathed carefully. He tightened his mouth as if he were angry. "I suggest you don't try to blame me for it. I've served the temple faithfully in every required capacity. I've administered the Trial impartially. Do you really think I would help a man destroy the position I've spent my life building? I think your fear and ambition are disturbing your logic, Raaman. You'd better calm yourself if you hope to defeat me in the election."

Raaman's nostrils flared. "What election? You and Kaleb vote against every date Forest and I propose." His voice was acid. "I know what you're waiting for. You think Jared will vindicate himself somehow so it won't be necessary to hold an election at all. You can't get away with that, Levi." He smiled thinly. "Unless you agree to an election, and it's held before Jared is returned, Jared won't live to come back or vindicate himself."

Levi looked at him for a long moment. That was no idle threat, he felt sure. Even if Raaman had not hated

Jared so much, he had to be afraid ever to let Jared make a public answer to the question of why he had run away. Jared might tell the truth.

Levi countered with the only weapon he had, bait for Raaman's ambition. "Bring Jared safely home and I'll not only agree to the election, I'll support you."

He left Raaman to consider that.

"They caught him in Gaza."

Sabrina burst into the sitting room, leaving the house door open behind her. Outside, her bicycle toppled over with a crash. She stood with feet spread, fists on hips, staring around at her sisterwives and children. "He pretended not to know what the charge against him is. He even pretended to be shocked when they told him."

Alesdra felt the sudden tensing of the atmosphere as palpably as coils of a line being thrown and tightened around her.

"Isaiah?" someone asked.

"He was alone."

Seabright's eyes blazed. Daria hissed. The children looked frightened. Every attempt had been made to keep them from learning what was troubling their mothers, but the older ones had somehow found out.

"Does that mean Isaiah is dead?" Daria's eleven-year-old daughter asked.

"Of course not," Daria said.

"He just wasn't with Sky's brother," Sabrina said. "Will all of you please go to the dormitory?"

"But we want to hear—"

"Go," Daria said. "Now."

Reluctantly, they went. Seabright went to make sure they were not hiding around a corner somewhere listening. She shut the front door on her way back. "What do you have to say, Sky?"

Sky's face was taut, bloodless around her mouth. "Is Jared all right, Sabrina?"

"Jared!" Sabrina was outraged. "Isaiah *is* probably dead, you know. Don't you care about *him?*"

"No," Daria said. "Only Jared . . . always Jared." She spat the name.

Sky came to her feet. "Stop that! How dare you accuse me of not caring about my own son. If I thought

174

for one moment Jared had harmed him or allowed him to come to harm, I would damn my brother's soul to Hell!"

Alesdra coughed. "Before the massacre starts—Sky, why don't you take a walk outdoors with me?"

She took Sky's wrist and dragged her out of the house into the dark yard. "Are you still feeling he's in danger?"

Sky was breathing hard. "Yes, more than ever."

"Can you contact the flyer pilot?"

Alesdra felt Sky looking at her. "The Bishop has to approve all flyer flights. He'll never allow us to fly to Gaza."

"If he knows. I've been here long enough to learn something of how people get around restrictions on Marah. When the Gibeon flyer took me from the Gahan ranch station to the Gibeon temple, the pilot made a side flight of her own to pick up a woman and take her to a hospital. It wouldn't take long to fly us to Gaza. The pilot could do it tonight and be back before morning."

Sky considered. "I try to be ethical. I was always honest with Jared. I don't like the masks we wear so much of the time. If we want to use the flyer, we ought to ask permission."

"How much are you afraid for Jared?"

Sky was silent for several moments. She sighed heavily. "Yes, I can reach the pilot. Her name will be listed at Peace Hall. I know one of the substitute pilots personally, too."

"Let's go see one of them."

Chapter Twenty-one

JARED WAS shocked every time he thought of the charge against him. Yet, he supposed he should have expected it. What more natural thing to charge him with than abduction? Raaman was very clever.

"You're a stubborn man, Father."

Jared looked around at his inquisitors and felt guilty for not answering. They had been so impeccably polite. They had fed him dinner, brought him water and tea. They sat around him in their chairs looking and acting not like inquisitors but just ordinary, if rather tired-looking, women. He had seen each of the three as an individual at first, but now they all looked alike. They all sounded alike. How could anyone remain so polite for so long? He wondered what they were really thinking and feeling.

He sighed. "I am stubborn. I'm sorry for the inconvenience it causes."

His apology appeared to startle them. They stared at him for several minutes without speaking. One finally said, "You can stop the inconvenience. Answer our questions so we can all go home."

He looked down at his hands in his lap. "I can't. I'm sorry."

"Why not, if the boy is all right? Tell us so we can check on him. Don't you think his mother is worried?"

He hoped Sky would know him better than to think he would hurt the boy, but even if she were worrying, talking would give her more to worry about. "He's safe. That's all I can tell you." He looked up at them again. "This is . . . a temple affair. There are men who would use the boy as a weapon against me if they could find him."

"How could they do that?"

"He's my son."

They frowned. "Men don't have sons."

"Some of us do."

"What kind of temple politics makes a Shepherd run off dressed in women's clothes?"

He looked down at his hands. "I'm sorry; I can't say."

"You're sorry." The keeper did not sound as if she believed him. "You keep saying that, but you won't help us or yourself by answering the questions."

The annoyance in the comment was the first genuine emotion he had heard expressed. Jared spoke to that keeper directly. "I *am* sorry. I'll tell you I was going to Eridu to see the alien woman there. Do you know about her?"

"The one from the Terran ship? Yes, we've heard. Why were you going to see her?"

"If I could have reached her—" He broke off, struck by a sudden thought. Perhaps he could still talk to Alesdra. He leaned toward the keepers. "If I could talk to her, it would be possible to help every boy live through puberty. Will you send her a message for me? Tell her I'm here and that I need to see her."

They stared. "Help every boy live? How?"

"She has a machine that can bring people to cure the disease. Will you send for her? Please?"

They regarded him speculatively. "Perhaps if you were to answer a few questions first we could consider it."

He bit his lip. "Perhaps I can answer your questions after I've seen Alesdra, but not until then. Pontokouros is her last name. She's probably staying at Solon House."

The keepers exchanged looks. One of them sighed. "You won't help us until you've seen the alien and we can't send for the alien until you answer some questions. We seem to have reached an impasse." She rose. "This is enough for one evening, I think. Rachel!" she called.

A woman opened the door and looked in.

"Pick another woman and escort the Shepherd to the temple."

Jared stared at them. "The temple? Why am I going to the temple?"

"For detention, of course."

"But you have detention quarters here."

They frowned. "For women, not men. Men are always detained in the temple. You know that."

A temple was the last place he wanted to go. "I'd rather stay here."

"You're a man, a Shepherd. We can't lock you up here. It's unheard of."

"Besides," another keeper added, "our Shepherd has specifically requested that we give you over to him. There's also been a radio message from the temple at Gibeon seconding the request. Not to give you over would be flagrant disobedience."

Giving him over could be fatal. Jared felt sweat breaking out under his arms and on his lip. Those men had too much to fear from him.

But the look on the women's faces was adamant. He sighed and stood. It looked as if he had no choice.

Rachel and another uniformed keeper walked him across the street to the temple. Peace Hall faced the main gate. The street was deserted. Nightseye and Tagalong were bright ellipses overhead. He looked up at them. In a few days they would be full again. What a great deal had happened since the last time they were full.

Ahead of him the temple gate loomed like a mouth, opening wider at every step Jared took toward it. The keepers greeted the guards. In another few steps the gate had swallowed them. Jared looked back over his shoulder all the way across the courtyard, watching the arch grow smaller again. What a tiny glimpse of street and town could be seen through it. He had never noticed before what a restricted view temple gates gave.

They stopped under the candaglobes in the portico of the main doors and waited while Rachel pulled the bell cord. "We've brought the Shepherd from Gibeon," she told the steward who opened the door.

The temple doors swallowed him, too. Two silent stewards took him through the labyrinth of silent corridors to a small room. There he was given a tunic and trousers of ecclesiastic green.

"The Shepherd will be coming to see you presently," one steward said.

The men left. There was a lock on the door. Jared heard the bolt slide home with a solid thunk.

For some time, he remained standing in the middle of the room looking around him, at the room, at the clothes laid out on the sleeping shelf. There were differences, like the color of the stone, but ignoring those, he might have been back in Gibeon temple. It was so much the same. He knew without looking that the door at the far end of the room opened into a small, enclosed garden. Its walls would be of solid stone, the outside walls of other rooms, and there would be no trees in it. Temple detention rooms were made to keep men in comfort, but to keep them *in*. There was a steward outside the door to reinforce the lock on it, he also knew.

Slowly, he changed into the tunic and trousers. The tunic felt long and smothering around his legs. It restricted his stride. He fingered the material with a hollow feeling growing inside him. He was more than swallowed up by the temple; he was entombed. How stupid he had been to be caught that way. He should never have let himself fall asleep. For his carelessness, he almost deserved whatever happened to him here.

He heard the bolt on the door slide. The door opened to admit Gaza's Shepherd. Watching the man cross the room toward him, Jared felt the hollowness in him keep growing. The Shepherd was old, very old. That was unusual in an office whose burdens were as heavy as a Shepherd's. Worse, Gaza's Shepherd moved with a brisk stride, and he had a sharp, lean face that reminded Jared of Raaman Midian.

The Shepherd folded into a chair of woven rhinohide straps. "So you're Jared Joseph. I'm Hawk Benjamin. You've led us a long chase, my son."

Jared sat down on the sleeping shelf. "Not long enough."

"Where were you trying to go?"

Jared looked at him and away. He shrugged. "It doesn't matter any longer." He paused a moment, then looked back at the Shepherd. "Brother, Raaman Midian hates me. He covets Shepherdhood with such greed he cares about nothing else. He isn't to be believed or trusted."

White eyebrows arched. "Indeed? I've spoken with him at some length and found him reasonable. Having now seen you, I tend to agree with his evaluation of you. He said you were weak, that you were about to break. I don't know what else would drive a man to do what you've done."

Jared wanted to tell him about Raaman's attempt at poisoning, but could think of no way to keep the words from sounding like those of a sick man illogically afraid of everything and everyone. He looked down at his hands. "When am I to go back?"

"I don't know. Brother Raaman said he'd send for you when he's ready."

That sounded unencouraging. But maybe there was something Jared could try. "And you'll send me when he asks."

"Of course."

Jared sat up straight. "I want to be heard on reasons why I should not be sent back."

The Shepherd looked amused. "Very well. I won't deny you your legal rights. I'll call the Deacons to hear you in my rooms in the morning."

"I want a public hearing."

The old man's smile faded. "That I will deny you."

"It's my right to be publicly heard. Even a man has that choice."

"Not in this case, not with what you might say." The Shepherd smiled again. This time it was thin and not at all amused. "I'll poison you before I'll let you be heard in public. But I sincerely hope that extreme won't be necessary. I knew and admired Aaron Methuselah. Whatever his reasons for choosing you as his successor, I respect them. Behave yourself and I promise you'll have nothing to fear while you remain in Gaza. I'll do all I can to make you comfortable."

"Thank you." Jared knew he sounded bitter. He made no attempt to hide it.

The Shepherd regarded him with glittering eyes. "If you fear this Deacon of yours, I can see that you don't have to go back. You can remain here. Your contacts

with people would, of course, be somewhat restricted."
The Shepherd coughed. "But you would be alive."

Entombed. Jared remembered two men who had died in detention while he was an instructor in Gibeon. One had been serving a sentence imposed by the court and had no family to keep him. The other had been in sanctuary, shut up forever to escape what he thought the law would inflict on him. Jared remembered them, half-mad creatures, and shuddered. "No, thank you."

"Don't be hasty." The Shepherd stood. "I'll leave you to meditate on it." He walked to the door. "The Lord be with you."

Jared paced rather than meditate, but after several hours decided there was little he could do about escaping tonight. He stretched out on the sleeping shelf and was aware of nothing more until the prayer bell woke him in the morning.

A hand touched his shoulder. "The Shepherd requires all men in the temple to attend Prayings."

Jared sat up, his mind working. So there were at least two times a day he could get out of the room. That was something to plan around.

Walking to the tabernacle between his guards, Jared tried to count how many times he had heard prayer bells. It must have been almost every day of his life since he was fifteen. They had always brought a feeling of warm familiarity, sometimes of anticipation, but this morning the bell was shrill and irritating, and the anticipation was compounded of fear and desperation. From now on, prayer bells might be marking the chances he had at escape.

He sat at the front of the tabernacle, to the side of the Middle School boys, and listened to the Praying without hearing any of it. It was as if it were spoken in a foreign language, sounds without meaning. He watched the boys, instead, and thought of Isaiah, of boys everywhere who could be dying within the next months because he had allowed himself to be caught and trapped here. He must make a move to escape just as fast as he could. Every day he delayed was another day of risk for boys like these.

"The Lord be with you," the Shepherd said. He left up the aisle, followed by his Deacons.

The other celebrants started to follow. It was then, turning, that Jared saw the two women at the back of the tabernacle, women in Eridu keeper uniforms. His heart bounced off his ribs. Sky! He wanted to shout with happiness. She looked wonderful. He did not know the taller, black-haired woman with her.

Jared hung back, waiting for the boys to leave ahead of him. He managed to be one of the last people out of the tabernacle.

Sky and the other keeper remained standing where they were. As Jared and his guards came opposite them, Jared pretended to stumble. He fell hard against the man on his left, shoving him into the women.

He and the guard went down. The women kept on their feet and bent to help the men up. Jared found his face close to Sky's.

"Are you all right?" she whispered.

"Get me out of here," he murmured in reply.

Then he was standing again and the stewards were pushing him out of the tabernacle ahead of them. Jared went without further resistance and without looking back. He paid little attention where they were going until they crossed a courtyard they had not crossed coming from his room.

He stopped. "Where are we going?"

"To the dining hall for breakfast."

The last meal he had eaten in a temple had been poisoned. That unpleasant memory ruined his appetite. "Take me back to my room."

"But it's time for breakfast."

"Does the Shepherd require everyone to attend every meal, too?"

One of the stewards frowned. "If you don't eat now, there's nothing more until lunch."

"That's fine."

He must be very careful, he told himself, to eat and drink nothing brought to him. The water from the sink tap should be safe, but he could trust nothing else.

With the door to the corridor locked behind him again, he felt a little safer. If he could not get out, it was also hard for anyone else to come in. He stretched out on his sleeping shelf and began considering plans for escaping if Sky were unable to find a way to get him out of the temple.

Some time later he heard voices in the corridor. "Take him back to Peace Hall? Why?"

The Shepherd's voice replied, "The keepers say the mother of the boy he abducted is over there. She wants to see if she can make him tell her where the boy is."

"I'm surprised you gave permission."

"I'm sending you with him."

The bolt slid back. The Shepherd came into the room, close to Jared. He kept his voice low. "I'm sending you back to the keepers for more interrogation. Reuben, my personal servant, will go with you. Reuben knows about the Trial, and he has orders to bring you back here immediately if you start to say anything regarding that or any other temple secret. He may bring you back in whatever condition you make necessary to your most efficient silencing and removal." The Shepherd paused. "You understand me, I hope."

Jared nodded. He crossed to the drawers under the sleeping shelf and took out his women's clothes. "I'll return these while I'm there."

Two keepers met them at the outside door of the temple. They raised brows at the steward but did not object when he insisted on coming to Peace Hall with them.

Jared had come across the street last night dragging his feet. He went back at an eager pace that the others had to stretch to match. Something tight in his stomach loosened as they came through the gate. It vanished entirely when they had threaded through the traffic of the street and crossed the portico of Peace Hall.

Inside, he and the steward were taken down the corridor toward the room where Jared had been interrogated the night before. At the door, Jared was admitted but two husky keepers barred the steward.

"The Shepherd wants me to stay with him," the steward protested.

"We aren't going to hurt the man. You'll have to wait outside," was the reply.

"I'm to stay *with* him. It's the Shepherd's orders." The steward tried to push past the keepers.

The two women took him by the arms and gently

183

but irresistibly backed him away from the door and down the corridor. He disappeared from sight as the door was shut.

"Sit down, Father."

The speaker was an older woman with a gold star in the middle of her insignia patch. She would be the chief keeper. She sat in a chair beside a desk, sipping from a cup of tea. The two keepers who brought him from the temple stood behind her.

"Yes, please, sit down, Jared."

He whirled toward the sound. It was Sky. The other Eridu keeper was with her. "Kiri Sky!" He opened his arms and took her in.

She felt thin and smelled dusty. He loved the feel of every bone and, for today at least, thought dust was a fine perfume. He hugged her until her ribs gave. He never wanted to let go. "Kiri Sky, Sky of mine." How easily the old pet address came back.

"Excuse me," the chief said in a dry voice, "but this is supposed to be an interview between a frantic mother and the evil abductor of her child."

Jared reluctantly loosened his hold and stepped back. He kept one of Sky's hands, though, so that she had to stand beside him as he sat in his chair.

"It's good to see you, Jared," Sky said. Her fingers tightened around his. "I've been so worried about you."

"Sisters, I wonder if we haven't been maneuvered into this." The chief sounded amused. "What was that excuse you gave me for insisting we bring this man back from the temple?"

"Sanctuary," the keeper with Sky said.

Jared started. He knew that voice, that accent. He looked up into a face framed by curling black hair—a face no longer death-pale but tanned golden brown—and into cool green eyes. It was Alesdra Pontokouros.

"In the Middle Ages of Earth," Alesdra went on, "criminals could take refuge in churches and be safe from prosecution for their crimes. I suggested that there was danger here of Jared disappearing forever into the safety of the temple."

Jared stared at her. "I was on my way to see you. What are you and Sky doing together? Why are you wearing that uniform?"

Alesdra brushed at her shirt. "I borrowed it from Seabright Ashbel so Sky and I would look official when the flyer took off with us. I'll tell you about it some other time."

"Right now I want to hear where the boy is," the chief said. "You will tell his mother, won't you?"

Sky's hand tightened again. Jared looked up at her. She smiled encouragement.

"He's at Roshdan House in Gibeon, in the care of one of my Deacons and his family. But don't tell anyone else, and when you go after him, be careful not to let any men know."

"There really is a danger to him?" the chief asked.

"Yes. I don't know which men I can trust, except Levi Dan. I was poisoned once before I escaped from Gibeon and I've been threatened by the Shepherd here. If the wrong people find Isaiah—" He left the sentence hanging.

The chief pursed her lips. "Hawk Benjamin is my grandmother's brother, and a close friend of my family. I trust him completely."

"Women should never trust men. We keep some terrible secrets from you."

Everyone stared at him with expressions ranging from concern to disbelief.

Alesdra said, "Was one of those secrets the reason you were coming to see me, perhaps?"

He hesitated. It was not a question he wanted to answer in a room full of women. "May I speak to you alone?"

"You want to keep the secrets, too, is that right?" Alesdra said.

"You'll trust Alesdra, an alien you've only known a few weeks, but not me?" Sky said.

He looked from his sister to the others. Tell everyone? That was impossible, unthinkable, and yet . . . Alesdra's and Sky's last words echoed loudly in his head. They had the same resounding thunder Levi's words had had the night Jared decided he had to save all the boys. He could feel them turning him as Levi's words had turned him. Men and women on Marah had secrets from each other. He had learned some of the women's secrets and it was a shock, but not a killing one. Perhaps it was time women learned about men, too.

A marvelous calm flowed through him. It was like the time he led his first Praying. He had been almost sick to his stomach with nervousness, but as he stood, and began reading, all fear went. The words poured from him with melodious certainty.

"I guess it's time we stopped lying to each other," he said. "You lie by exclusion, never letting men know what you really think, and we—" He looked at Alesdra. "You once wondered why resistance to the disease hasn't bred through the population. It has. No Marahn has died of the disease for over four hundred years."

A keeper turned toward him, puzzled. "How can you claim that when—"

But Alesdra said, "So that was why that solon was afraid. He knew virologists would discover that if they came here. Just how do the boys die?"

Jared looked straight at her. "We men have been poisoning them at puberty."

He expected a scream in reaction, or a babble of voices. Instead, there was only silence. The women stared at him in disbelief.

After several minutes the chief cleared her throat. "The original message said you were possibly unbalanced, but I had no idea you suffered from such delusions."

"I know our family man. He wouldn't do something like that," another keeper chimed in.

"He may not be. Most men don't get involved. They also think the disease kills the boys. But the Bishop and Shepherds all know the truth. Most of the Deacons do, too."

"Jared, why are you saying this?" Sky said. "You're a Shepherd. You couldn't harm any child. You couldn't possibly poison hundreds of boys. What reason would you or any other man have?"

"Power," Alesdra said. Her voice was flat. "He isn't mad. I've seen enough of what people will do to gain and keep power to believe what he's saying. It answers so many questions I had. How do you do it, Jared?"

He told them. He told them about the poison, about

the quotas handed down from Eridu each year, about the Trial procedure. And while he talked, he saw them begin to believe. Their faces went pale. Horror grew in their eyes. They stepped back from him.

"Jared, I thought I knew you," Sky said. "How could you do this?"

He met her eyes. The repugnance there cut him to the bone. "I had to; I'm a Shepherd."

She jerked her hand out of his. "You're a butcher. To think I sent Isaiah to you because I thought he would be safe."

"I would never have let Isaiah be harmed."

"My sisterwives have been right about you all along."

She spun and started for the door.

He could have accepted almost anything but that. He could not let her leave. "Sky, I wanted it all to stop. I didn't want—"

But the slamming door cut him off.

There was a knife in him, twisting and cutting. He was bleeding internally. "I wanted all the boys to live," he whispered.

"Why did you wait until now to try stopping the Trial?" the chief asked.

"Because I never knew what torture it was until now, not until I saw Kastavin die. After that—I couldn't let it go on."

"Poor Kastavin," Alesdra said. "Perhaps his death has meaning after all."

After his confession there seemed to be nothing more to say. One of the keepers looked as if she wanted to strike him, but she kept her distance. They all kept their distance. They just looked at him without expression, without speaking.

Jared had no idea how long the silence lasted. It seemed to go on for an eternity. He heard the sounds of buggies and wagons and bicycle bells in the street outside, the murmur of voices in the corridor. In the distance, doors opened and closed.

And then, at last, a keeper asked, "What are we going to do with him?"

The chief drew a breath like a sob. "More important yet, what are we going to do with the rest of them?"

Chapter Twenty-two

THE NIGHTWATCH OFFICER had control of the bridge when Alesdra called the *Rose*. He seemed surprised to be hearing from her. "Do we have an answer on the shuttlebox already?"

"Not exactly. Will you get the captain for me?"

"She's asleep."

"This is important."

Her communicator went silent. While she waited, Alesdra looked out through the window slit into the street. Incredibly, everything looked quite normal. Even the keeper office looked the same, except that she was the only person in it. Jared had been taken to a detention room. The chief was in the corridor talking to the steward.

"Go back and tell Hawk I'm keeping Jared Joseph here."

"You can't. He's a man."

"He's also violent. He attacked one of my keepers. You or the Shepherd might be his next target, and I refuse to allow you to assume that kind of danger. He stays here."

"No, he must come back with me."

"Rachel, show this man back to the temple, please."

The sounds of the steward's protests faded down the corridor.

The chief came back into the office. She looked aged. "I had a son," she said. "Hawk Benjamin wept at his death along with my family. His tears seemed real." She shook her head. "Don't make us sound too barbaric to your ship, will you?"

Captain Deyoe's voice came over the communicator, yawning. "What is it, Ponto?"

"We've had a very dirty nuclear accident and I don't know how far the fallout will spread."

The captain's voice came sharply alert. "Nuclear—oh. Ponto, don't go figurative on me when I've just waked up. What's happened?"

Alesdra told her.

"Good God," the captain said. "Is there anything I can do?"

"Hope we avoid a bloodbath."

"We can drop you some sleepers."

The number of weapons the *Rose* carried would not even arm all Gaza's keepers. "No, thank you. Why I wanted to talk to you"—she hated to bring it up but felt she had to—"is to tell you that this may tie up the shuttlebox question indefinitely."

The captain sighed. "More and more delays. Or are you suggesting maybe we should forget about this planet and go on?"

"It's . . . something to think about." She hoped the captain would not think very hard. "I can't very well ask you to wait around for the years it might take to settle this mess."

There was a long silence. Alesdra wondered whether the captain was just thinking or was asking Connie Melas and crew how they felt about it. The ramjet was well stocked with provisions, but the ship was not large. Its hold was finite. The longest they could wait was the point at which they would have just enough supplies to last them to the next planet.

Captain Deyoe came back. "We've been here this long; we'll wait at least another week or two. By that time we should be able to assess the situation down there."

"Thank you, skipper." She felt weak with relief.

The captain chuckled. "We need to get you off that planet. You're developing a terrible accent. *Rose* out."

Alesdra clipped the communicator back on her belt and turned to find the chief, her two subordinates, and Sky watching her. Sky's eyes were red and swollen.

"They aren't going to get mixed up in this, are they?" the chief asked.

With no weapons, no fighting experience, and no personnel with the physical condition of these whipcord women?" "No."

The chief sighed with relief. Alesdra wondered what these Marahns thought the ship was like. "Sit down, sisters," the chief said.

They dragged up chairs to make a circle with hers.

"I've been thinking, we need to publish a statement of policy along with the news of what the men have been doing. The people to write a policy like that are the solons . . . the women solons, of course. Someone needs to fly to Eridu and tell them what we've learned and start them working on plans to deal with the men."

"Excuse me. May I express an opinion?" Alesdra asked.

"Please do. I could use a disinterested viewpoint."

"I agree with what you've said, but I think that should be the second step. The first should be planning to deal with the women's reaction to the news. I would guess they'll feel much as you did—disbelief, followed by belief, then anger. Some are going to be killing mad. Not all men are guilty, but there will be women who blame them all. You have to arrange protection for the men before you let this news out."

"Why?" Sky said. "Given a chance at power, all of them would be willing to become guilty."

Alesdra shook her head. "You sound like your sister-wives. You don't really believe what you're saying. You're just angry because you don't know Jared quite as well as you've thought."

"I don't think I know him at all," Sky replied bitterly.

The chief touched Sky's arm. "Peace." She looked back at Alesdra. "Do you have any suggestions how we can protect the men?"

"Think about it. How did your ancestors do it those first generations? By sequestering them in a fortified location. You still have one easily defended structure in every town."

Understanding came. "The temples!"

Alesdra nodded. "You need to contact every keeper radio on Marah. Don't tell them the whole truth—you never know who may be listening—but tell them there's a danger to the men. Have them—"

"Just a minute," a keeper interrupted. "The whole

continent isn't going to take Gaza's word for a thing like that."

"She's right." the chief said.

"Who would they obey?"

"The Bishop."

Alesdra thought. "We have to go to Eridu anyway. You come along and see the chief keeper there. Tell her everything, then we'll make a call on the Bishop."

For one moment in the anteroom Alesdra wondered if the scribner were going to deny them an interview with the Bishop. but he was only a scribner, while they were two chief keepers and a grim-looking alien. He showed them into the Bishop's office.

The Bishop frowned in annoyance. "What is the—" He broke off as he recognized Alesdra. His brows rose at her keeper's uniform. "What is this?"

Eridu's chief told him. What he heard shook the Bishop to his soul. "A Shepherd betrayed the secrets of his office? Merciful Lord. How could Aaron make such a disastrous choice for his successor?"

"Is that all you're concerned about?" The Eridu chief became agitated. "You ought to be wondering how Marah's women are going to act when they learn."

His eyes glittered. "They won't believe you. The Shepherds will all tell them these are lies spread by this satan's agent." He pointed a sharp finger at Alesdra.

"They'll believe, and some will come asking for your blood. They'll want the blood of innocent men, too. We want you to help us protect the men by asking all temples to cooperate with such orders as the keepers may give, and by sending all keeper stations a message we'll dictate to you."

The Bishop drew himself up. "This is rebellion. I am the Lord's devoted servant. I have followed His will all my life, and done nothing but follow His will. The Trial is a Divine ritual."

"No woman is going to believe that. I've respected you all my life, Father, so I'll make this a request rather than an order. Please come with us to the radio room and make the broadcasts we've asked for."

"I won't be ordered about by women. You are commanded by the Lord, by scripture, to obey me. 'Thy desire shall be to thy husband, and he shall rule over thee.' There are no husbands on Marah, but there are Shepherds, appointed by the Lord to lead you."

Alesdra had a sneaky admiration for the spirit of the Bishop. He was a tough, unquenchable old man.

Eridu's chief never raised her voice. She remained quietly polite, but her eyes met his unwaveringly. "So was King Saul also the Lord's appointed leader of his people, and he was thrown down by the Lord when he presumed too much."

"You presume too much." Elias Jamin's voice shook with anger. "Leave this office, sisters. Leave this temple before the Lord's wrath destroys you."

The chief sighed. "If we leave without having sent those broadcasts, Father, we leave you to the wrath of Marah's women. How long do you think four gate guards, if indeed they remain faithful, and a few stewards can defend this temple?"

The Bishop considered that in silence. He sat looking from one to another of them. He looked at Alesdra. "Do you believe I would murder innocent children?"

"I've seen men do worse and think they were acting righteously."

"Does your ship know about this?"

"Of course. If we should happen to disappear into this temple, they'll broadcast the news on all planetary bands."

The Bishop shriveled visibly before them. "That's blackmail."

"A time-honored weapon of diplomacy, Father," Alesdra said. "Will you send the messages now?"

She felt sorry for him. His power was being stripped away not by age nor failure to keep command, but by no more than Jared's emotional reaction to Kastavin's death. Still, she did not regret what Jared had done. The society of this world needed to be shaken. It only remained to see it was not shaken apart in the process.

Elias Jamin stood and slowly walked toward the door.

Gibeon's chief keeper came to the temple just before evening Praying. The Deacons were waiting for her.

"What's this danger the Bishop talks about?" Raaman asked her.

"I'll try to be brief so I won't delay the Praying. I don't know the exact nature of the danger. I only know I've been ordered to move all men in this parish into the temple. Will you see to arranging accommodations for them?"

Levi glanced toward Raaman. The lean Deacon looked back with a frown.

"We'll arrange for them," Levi said. "The Bishop said you would have several directions for us. What are the others?"

The chief licked her lips. "I've been ordered to send all boys in Middle School here at the temple home to their mothers."

"What?" Forest blinked. "If the men are in danger, aren't the boys, too?"

"I don't know," the chief said. "It would seem not. I do know the Bishop's orders were very emphatic. All boys must leave the temple."

Men inside, boys outside, and a danger to the men? Levi felt a chill rising in him.

"We'll accommodate the men," Raaman said, "but the boys must stay as well."

The chief seemed to grow in height. "I was told you might react this way." All apology had left her voice. "I was told to give you a message. I don't understand it, but I was assured that all Shepherds and most Deacons would understand. Jared Joseph has revealed all of David Moses' vision."

Levi's hands crushed each other in his lap. *No.* Jared had told someone other than the alien woman? That was madness.

He saw his horror reflected on Raaman and Forest's faces. Only Kaleb looked puzzled.

"What does that have to do with keeping the men here and sending the boys home?" Kaleb asked.

"I don't know. But there was one more part to the message. I was advised that any Deacon who did not understand the message is to be particularly protected." She raked her eyes over the rest of them. "Will you see that no harm comes to this man? And will you please go after the boys? The Bishop says I can't leave the temple without them."

Levi rose. "I'll bring them to you at the main doors by the tabernacle."

Raaman moved to block him. "No. The boys stay." There was fear in his eyes.

Levi regarded him coldly. "They go or I'll tell Sister Keziah the meaning of that message."

Raaman stared at him. His eyes said, "You wouldn't dare!" But Levi met the stare and after a moment, Raaman's eyes shifted downward. He turned away.

The chief said, "I have a personal message for you, Brother Levi. Sky Joseph is anxious to have her son back, so will you please send word to your family to give him to us?"

Forest's mouth dropped.

Kaleb stared in amazement. *"You've* been keeping him?"

Raaman said nothing. He turned slowly to face Levi. His face was a mask. Only his eyes carried expression, and what Levi saw there drew a cold claw down his spine.

Solon House was a mass of confusion. What danger, everyone wanted to know, men and women alike. Speculation ran in waves, none of it remotely accurate. Alesdra ate supper with the puzzled solons, then waited in the common room while the men were taken to the temple by keepers and the women gathered in small, murmuring groups.

"I don't understand," she heard repeatedly. "Did you see? The boys from Middle School are all being taken home. That doesn't make sense."

Alesdra wondered if the men were asking the Bishop the same questions, or if Elias Jamin had locked himself away in his rooms to avoid having to answer any questions. He had been a much older man when she and the chief keepers left him.

The trail of men across the street dwindled. At length, it stopped. Alesdra motioned to a steward.

"Are all the men out of the building?"

"I think so."

"Please check for me."

The steward left. When she came back a quarter of an hour later, she nodded. "They're all gone."

Alesdra took a deep breath and moved to the middle of the common room. "May I have your attention, sisters?"

She repeated the command several times. The murmur around her lowered and stopped as women focused their attention on her.

"Are all the women solons here?"

The women looked around. A few were missing, they said.

"Will someone bring them, please. You all know me. I've been asked to tell you about the danger to the men, but I need all of you here first. And we need to post guards at the exits so that the stewards and house staff, and anyone else outside this group, won't hear what's being said."

"This must be serious," a solon said.

Alesdra nodded.

The missing women were brought and the room sealed. While it was being done, Alesdra rummaged through her bag of training and knowledge for every scrap of the sales rep, politician, diplomat, and psychologist in her. There had never been a sale ahead of her like the one she now faced. Their faces turned to her in solemn expectation.

"Your Litany talks about tests of fire and trying of souls," she said. "Your world is about to be tested and tried as you've never imagined, and you will have to be the ones to lead your people through its Trial. The men can't help this time. Whether Marah survives or is destroyed will depend on how reasonable you can remain and how objectively you can act."

The silence that greeted her while she talked about the shuttlebox was cacophony compared to the silence around her now. The women hardly breathed. In as few and unemotional words as possible, she repeated what Jared had told her in Gaza.

The reaction was as she anticipated. They said nothing immediately, only sat in stunned, unbelieving silence. Then they started to turn to each other. At first they only stared. The first murmurs of talk started. Slowly, it grew in volume. It rose to a roar punctuated by angry

195

shouts. A couple of women started for the nearest doors.

"Stop them!" Alesdra shouted.

Someone did, and it started at least one knock-down fight.

Alesdra tried calling for order, but soon could not make herself heard or obeyed. For a while she let them yell at each other. Some were refusing adamantly to believe her. Others believed her readily indeed and were ready to condemn all men. Still others reacted more with hurt than anger. They wanted to hear what the men had to say. A few were ready to accept any excuse the men gave them. And every faction of belief was furiously arguing with all the others.

When Alesdra decided the intense reaction had gone on long enough, that it was not calming of its own accord nor accomplishing anything useful, she climbed on a table and shouted at the top of her voice, "DO YOU WANT THE WHOLE WORLD ACTING THIS WAY?"

Someone heard her. The women nearest her stopped, looked, and touched their neighbors. Those women looked at her and touched still more. Gradually, as slowly as the chaos had built, it died away to a few muttering voices.

"You're going to have an entire population of women feeling as you do once this news is announced. You need to decide now what to do about it, and what to tell them about how to deal with the men. Not all the men are guilty, remember. We've started by sequestering all of them together where they can be protected, but the next steps are your responsibility. I suggest you start by choosing someone to head this Council."

That was something they could deal with. They chose a woman named Hannah Isaac. She appeared to be very popular. The nomination was almost uncontested and the vote nearly unanimous. Hannah Isaac came forward. She was a small, fragile-looking woman with great dark eyes and skin almost as light as Alesdra's tanned color. She took Alesdra's place on the table.

"Well, then," she said, "what shall we do with our men, sisters?"

Alesdra quickly stopped wondering whether such a

small woman was capable of handling this emotional group. Hannah Isaac's voice had the firm certainty of authority. She answered by name everyone who spoke. When necessary, she could shout down the entire group. It was evident, though, that the discussion was more noisy than constructive.

Hannah pointed at Alesdra. "What do you think? You've seen other worlds. How would this be handled by other people?"

"A different way by every different people. Are you interested in my personal opinion?"

"She's an alien," someone muttered. "She can't know what's best for us."

"It seems we don't," Hannah said. "She can do no worse. Yes, I'm interested in your personal opinion."

"The guilty ones need to be punished in some way, probably, but I think each case should be judged individually. The men involved are involved in varying degrees. Some are only allowing the Trial to exist by not opposing it. Others are actually planning and execu— carrying it out. Some do it and believe it's actually Divine will. Others don't know and don't care. You can't make a general policy that will cover all the cases."

"But all of them who know are guilty. Guilty is guilty." Someone had called out from the back of the room.

"Is a man guilty who learns about it and is threatened with death himself if he tells about it or interferes in the process in any way? You ought to remember, your sons are going to have to live with the results of what today's men have done and what you women do about it tomorrow. Do you want your sons reviled for the sins of the previous generation?" She yawned. "Perhaps we should all sleep on the problem and come back to it fresh tomorrow."

"Perhaps so," Hannah said. "Why don't you go on to bed?"

Alesdra left the common room for the room she had been assigned what seemed like so long ago and never used. The sleeping shelf called to her. It reminded her she had not slept since the night before last. She was asleep almost as soon as she stretched out on it.

A touch on her shoulder woke her. She opened her eyes to sunlight flooding into the room and looked up into a face lined with weariness.

"Hannah wants you in the common room," the woman said.

Alesdra followed her back through the corridors. Coming into the common room, she saw they had not taken her advice and slept on their problems. The haggard, exhausted faces indicated that the women around her could not have seen any sleep at all. The solons must have sat up the entire night.

Only Hannah Isaac still looked energetic. "We've decided on trying the men one case at a time using tribunals made up of city commissioners and innocent men," she said. "We're writing up a formal statement now to broadcast and have printed up along with the facts of the Trial you've given us."

Alesdra nodded approval.

"Why I had you wakened, though, was to deal with another matter you forgot to mention last night."

Another matter? Alesdra frowned, trying to think what she could have forgotten.

"You came to Marah for a purpose and it isn't fair to you and your people to have to wait through our troubles for an answer to your portal proposal."

Alesdra took a sharp breath. She was not sure she was ready for this. She had never expected them to remember the shuttlebox, let alone take action on it. "Are you sure this is the time to consider that? You can take the matter up again when the situation is calmer."

"When will it be calmer?" Hannah asked. *"I* don't know. A proper solution may take years. So we took a vote just a few minutes ago. We feel that access to us from other worlds will bring in aliens that would be stressful under the best of circumstances. To add that stress to what we already have is more than we feel able to tolerate. So I'm afraid we must decline your portal."

The bottom went out of Alesdra's stomach. No, oh no! She fought to make her voice persuasive. "There will be aliens, yes, but aliens can provide new ideas about intersexual relationships and roles. They will

198

give you a chance to see how men and women in other cultures interact."

"I'm sure you're right, but I for one am afraid of that. I don't want Marah changing too much. Besides, you've been to many other worlds. You've seen how those people think and behave. When we need to know something like that, we'll ask you." Hannah paused, regarding Alesdra with genuine sympathy. "I'm truly sorry. Tell your ship to come back another time."

That could be a couple of hundred years! Much good it would do her then. "You—" she began, and broke off. Unfortunately, they *could* refuse the shuttlebox. It was certainly their right, and perhaps a correct action, from their point of view. Alesdra's throat was too tight for talking anyway. She turned and walked out of the room.

She left the building. The street was a broiling furnace but she hardly paid attention. She was having trouble seeing. The high walls of the temple across the street were blurred. She wiped at her eyes and activated her communicator.

"Pontokouros to *Rose*." She hardly recognized the voice as her own.

Captain Deyoe herself answered. "How are things, Ponto?"

Alesdra said it fast. "They've turned down the shuttlebox."

There was a pause. "Damn. Did you argue with them?"

"Yes." It came out with much more calm than she felt. "It . . . didn't help."

"And there's no chance they might change their minds soon?"

Alesdra sighed. "No."

This time the silence was very long. "Ponto, I'm sorry. Damn. What will you do?"

Her vision was blurring again. She blinked hard. "They're asking me to be a—an advisor of sorts . . . their mobile encyclopedia of comparative sociology. That should keep me busy and useful the rest of my life." She stopped to swallow. "I'm sorry. I shouldn't be bitter. At least I'm alive and it's a pleasant enough world. I'll miss you, though, skipper." Her voice cracked and she did not care. "I'll miss Connie. I'll even miss Leboyne. He ought to make a fair liaison officer, by the way. Better luck on—on—damn." Her throat was so tight she could hardly speak.

"Don't go to pieces saying good-bye yet, Ponto. We'll stay here a bit longer. I'll have to send someone down in a life-suit to retrieve the scout. I'll call you every day as long as we're here, and let you know before we leave."

It was only a short reprieve, she knew, but she was grateful for that much. "Thanks, skipper. Until later, then. Pontokouros out."

As she collapsed the communicator's antenna and wiped her eyes clear, she looked up to see Sky before her in the street. Sky wore her uniform and a radio on her hip and carried a keeper's patrol stick.

She held up the stick. "I'm part of the guard on the temple. How are things going inside?"

"They're writing up a statement for broadcast and printing."

"Then they've decided what to do with . . . the men? I suppose it's certain Jared will be prosecuted?" She watched Alesdra's face. "I thought so." She twisted the patrol stick in her hands. The radio on her hip crackled and murmured. "I wish *I* knew what to do about him. Men convicted of crimes are usually given to the custody of their families. If he has no family to take him, he'll be buried forever in some temple. I'll never see him again."

Alesdra looked more closely at Sky's face. It was as haggard as the faces of the solons inside. "You care, after all?"

"The Lord help me, yes." Sky grimaced and slapped the stick against her leg. "I remember our years together growing up, and when we were sharing rooms in Gibeon. We loved each other very much. I can't help but care. But I can't forget what he's done, either. That's inexcusable, monstrous. My sisterwives have told me not to involve myself, of course. They demand I repudiate him. They'll throw me out of the family if I don't." She sighed. "I can't decide what to do. I love my sisterwives, too."

"I wish I could help, really I do, but I suspect that

200

every Marahn woman with a family man or a brother she loves is going to have the same problem you do. Each of you is going to have to decide for herself."

"I might support him if it weren't for the threat of losing Daria and Sabrina and Seabright, and the fear that every time I look at Jared, I'll see the faces of a thousand dead boys between us."

Alesdra ached for her. "My shoulder is free to you for crying on anytime, Sky. I'll still be your friend whatever you decide."

She gave Sky a quick hug and went back into Solon House, leaving the Marahn woman staring after her with tortured eyes.

Chapter Twenty-three

THE WORLD fell apart on Sabbath eve. Jared could tell almost the exact hour. His detention room was small, not much larger than the school dormitory cubicles in Gibeon, just large enough for the sleeping shelf, bathroom, a table, and a chair. By opening the inner door, he could look out through the locked iron grille into a courtyard garden. Sounds from the street carried clearly into the garden, so although he had no outside window, he had communication with the world beyond the detention wing. And he could hear, on Sabbath eve, a swelling wave of voices pitched high in anger. From the corridor to the main part of Peace Hall he heard slamming doors and running feet. As he listened, the voices became interspersed with screams.

"There's fighting outside, isn't there?" he asked the keeper who brought him supper.

The keeper's skin was a muddy color. Her hands shook as she pushed the tray through the opening at the bottom of the grille. "The men have been killing our sons all these years, sister, not the disease. The women of Gaza are trying to break through the gates into the temple to get at the men."

Jared felt ill. He had never thought there would be violence or fighting. He left his supper untouched and sat listening.

The fighting went on through the night, and on through the Sabbath. Jared sat awake, unsleeping, not eating, praying. He listened to the shouts and screams and the incredibly incongruous dinging of the prayer bell. Inside the temple, the men seemed to be going about their routine unaffected by what was happening in the street.

In the afternoon the wounded began coming in. A keeper unlocked the grille of his door. "You're going to have to sleep on bare shelf tonight. We've finally built a double barricade across the street to the main gate so we can bring back the wounded. We need your mattress for them."

"Is there anything I can do to help?"

This keeper knew him. She regarded him with bitter eyes. "Haven't you done enough? You're lucky I'm sworn to keep the peace, no matter who breaks it, because, personally, I'd like to throw you out in the street and let those women tear you apart."

She dragged out the mattress and slammed the grille closed.

Jared wrapped his hands around the iron of the grille and looked after her with a strange feeling of elation. That had been an honest, unmasked expression of opinion.

But the elation lasted only moments. It was soon drowned by groans. Keepers and women with the keeper emblem pinned to street clothes carried in other women. The first ones were put in empty detention rooms. Later ones were laid on blankets and mattresses in the courtyard. Jared watched sickly. Fighting. There had never been anything like this before on Marah. Fighting was something Terrans did, not Marahns.

The chief keeper passed close by him.

"Let me help," he called to her.

She regarded him with distracted eyes for a moment,

then frowned as she focused on him. Finally she shrugged and motioned to the key keeper to unlock his grille. "Don't try escaping."

He had nowhere to go but into the street. "I won't." He walked out between the wounded. "What weapons are they using?"

"Staffs and rocks, mostly, but some dart tubes and bows and arrows."

"Here." Someone thrust a sponge and a pan of water into his hands. "Wash the cuts on those women."

He knelt beside the first woman and began sponging blood and sand from ragged cuts on her face and shoulders.

Jared washed cuts on other women, too. He helped hold a woman while a surgeon dug an arrow out of her shoulder. He handed needles and suture material to surgeons stitching cuts. He helped bandage an arm broken by the blow from a staff. He stood with a healer while she pulled a tiny dart from a keeper's neck and examined the unconscious woman.

"It's just narcotic. She'll probably wake up in a few hours."

They carried the woman into Jared's room and laid her on the bare sleeping shelf. The healer turned the table on its side and pushed it and the chair up beside the shelf.

"We ought to have someone watching her, but this will help keep her from rolling onto the floor."

"I'll watch her," Jared said.

He came to look in on her between other duties. In an hour she was moving, and in two, sitting up, groggy but coherent. In another, they sent her back into the fighting through the aisle created by the barricades.

Others went back as soon as they were able, too. The broken arms and concussions, and a woman shot in the chest with an arrow, were taken out the back of Peace Hall to the hospital.

Jared lost track of time. There were lulls. He noticed during one toward evening that there was no evening prayer bell. He slept a bit then, and struggled back to consciousness when the fighting resumed. He thought he ate once in a while but could not remember. He could remember only groans and blood, and endless orders. Wash this cut, bandage that one. Help the surgeon suture that one. Talk to that woman and see if that crack on her head has left her able to remember who and where she is. Get that one ready to move to the hospital.

Once he caught the chief's sleeve in passing. "I never intended this to happen."

She regarded him solemnly. "What did you think would happen?"

"I don't know. I suppose I didn't think about it. I just wanted to stop the Trial."

She looked at him with her forehead creased. She seemed to be struggling for something to say. At last she said, "Well, you did stop it, didn't you?"

It left him largely uncomforted. He turned away from her to work harder than ever. If these wounded were his responsibility, he was determined to care for them.

Inevitably, a few died. One came in dead, but another Jared watched die. He knelt with blood leaking through his fingers, trying to pinch off a gash in the woman's throat until the surgeon could suture it. The woman started gasping, her body arching with each effort. On the third, with a tired kind of sigh, she went limp. She did not take a fourth breath.

Jared stared at her in disbelief. Her blood still ran through his fingers, warm and liquid, but she was gone as softly as a shade thrown over a candaglobe. The eyes staring up at him were dull and empty.

"This one's gone," the surgeon said. She closed the eyes.

Jared regarded her for a moment, then put his hand over the still face and began reciting the prayer for the dead.

The surgeon stared. "What are you doing? You're not a priest."

Jared looked up. "I am a priest." He went on with the prayer. Now more than ever, the woman was his responsibility.

There was a sharp intake of breath near him. "The Judas Shepherd!"

He looked around. A woman with the pinned-on

insignia of a volunteer was struggling to her feet. She wiped blood from her eyes and forehead.

"You're the one who started this."

She picked up a patrol stick lying on the mattress beside her and came at Jared. He felt frozen on his knees. With the slowness of motion in a dream, he saw the stick swinging, saw people with horrified faces begin reaching for the woman. The stick filled his vision. Then vision disappeared in an explosion of stars and void.

He woke up on the sleeping shelf of his room. The keeper chief stood over him.

"That was a stupid thing to do," she said.

Jared's head reverberated with every beat of his pulse. It felt as if it weighed a thousand kilos. Reaching up, he found a large bandage across his forehead.

"She really laid your head open," the chief said. "The surgeon put in fifteen stitches. You'll have a fine scar as a souvenir of the day. Just what were you trying to do, may I ask? The idea of keeping you here dressed in those women's clothes was to protect you."

"I'm a priest and she was dead. She deserved whatever help I could give her. It's my fault she died." He tried to sit up. His head would not move. He felt the bandage. "That woman hated me," he said wonderingly. "I don't think I've ever been hated before, except by Raaman Midian."

"Get used to it," the chief said. "History may speak kindly of you, but no one now is ever going to thank you for what you've done."

Eventually, peace returned. There were no more wounded in the courtyard. The detention rooms filled with snarling women, prisoners detained for civil violence. Jared was taken from his room and told to get ready to leave for Gibeon.

"We need your space," the chief said. "We have all these women to deal with now as well as the men. There was also some fighting in the temple. A couple of men were killed in it. One was Hawk Benjamin. So we have that to sort out, too. You've made plenty of work for us."

There was nothing he could say in reply. Apologizing

205

seemed inadequate. He put on his leaper-hide jacket and walked to the flyer with his escorts.

The women talked to each other but only rarely to him during the flight. He noticed their conversation was more restrained than that of the Temans, but less so than he had heard women being around men before. Apart from being encouraged by that, he spent the flight watching the Nimrod Plains below, wondering what the towns they passed over were like. From the air, they looked quiet. What had happened on the ranches? How had Summer and the other Temans reacted to the news? He wondered if they knew there was a connection between the Judas Shepherd and Michal Shem, and if so, what they thought of him. He hoped Summer was not regretting having helped him.

The flyer landed in Gibeon in the street between the temple and Peace Hall. The street was deserted. There were only the Gibeon chief keeper and a subordinate to take him from the Gaza keepers. He looked around as thoroughly as he could in the time it took to cross to the door of Peace Hall. There were some chips in the temple wall, and here and there a dark stain, but the street was free of rubble. It looked as it always had. Gibeon felt different, though.

"We're going to keep you over here because we're just starting to sort through that mob in the temple," the chief said. "Five men have been killed over there already. I don't want to make it six."

"Thank you, Keziah. I'll try not to be any trouble."

"You mean *more* trouble. I hope not."

They put him in a detention room near the corridor end of the detention courtyard. "Don't show yourself too much or let it be known you're a man. We'll try to keep you anonymous as long as possible and give tempers every chance to cool down."

They kept him supplied with books to read, kept him fed. After he had been there a few days, they trimmed his hair.

"Don't want you to start looking like a man, after all."

They interviewed him several times, asking which men, to his knowledge, knew about the Trial and which did not. Otherwise he was alone. The guards rarely spoke to him. When other detainees out in the court-yard for exercise called to him, a guard would stroll near his door and suggest he move back.

It was something of a surprise, then, when one day a visitor was brought to see him. It was Storm Dan, wearing a keeper's uniform. She came in and shut the inside door.

"We meet again, Father."

"Not as I'd wanted to."

She shrugged and sat down in the chair. "It's only because I've joined the keepers and have become good friends with Keziah Aram that we're able to meet like this at all. She trusts me not to try killing you."

He sat down on the sleeping shelf. "Do you want to?"

"When the fighting was bad, I thought about it." She sounded wry but not angry. "I suppose this had to happen sometime, though, and bad as it seemed at times, it could have been bloodier."

"What is it like here now?"

"There are twenty dead counting . . . the men." She paused, biting her lip, then went on. "I don't know how many have been wounded. There are three hundred charges of civil violence against Gibeonite women.

"The worst thing has been the way families have been torn apart. Sisterwives were fighting each other. My mother—that's Sinai—and I have left the Roshdans. Mother sold Bird and Constance her share of the house. In other families the division of property will have to be settled in court."

Jared's head throbbed. The stitches had been taken out of his forehead but the scar was tender and he could feel it hot from temple to temple. "At least Levi has some of his family faithful to him. I'm assuming you and Sinai are the faithful ones? He's too fine a man to be abandoned."

Storm's face spasmed in pain. "Levi was one of the men killed in the temple."

Jared felt as if he had been kicked in the stomach. "Levi?" Oh, no, not *Levi*. "How?"

"He was poisoned." Her eyes filled with tears. "Kaleb Eshban says he thinks Raaman Midian did it in re-venge for Levi helping you. I came closer then to wanting to kill you than any other time."

Jared bowed his head. Levi dead. He felt numb. Levi. He would have preferred anyone else be killed, even Kaleb, but not Levi.

"Isaiah is safe. He's living with Mother and me at Keziah's house until we get word from your sister."

Fear invaded the numbness. "You haven't heard from Sky? Do you know why not?"

"She's been busy defending the temple in Eridu."

He stared at her in horror. He remembered the keeper who bled to death in his hands. Surely that would not happen to Sky. He would have had to feel it if something happened to her. But if it had, he would hate himself. He would give up even Levi's life for Sky.

Storm stood. "I'd better go. I'll let you know as soon as I hear anything from your sister." She patted his shoulder on the way to the door.

Jared sat for a long time staring at the opposite wall, willing Sky to be alive.

Keziah visited him later. "We're starting the hearings tomorrow. How much time do you need to prepare a defense?"

He could not think of any defense he could prepare. "I'm ready anytime."

Her brows skipped but she said, "Very well. We'll schedule you for tomorrow afternoon."

"Who will be hearing me?"

"A tribunal made up of the city commissioners and two men we know are innocent, Kaleb Eshban and Jonathan Heber."

Jared sat awake a good deal of the night wondering what might happen to him. There were no executions on Marah. Murderers were usually sentenced to personality modification, then given to the care of their families. Reparations fines were common at all levels of conviction, but reparations for all the boys he had helped kill, directly or indirectly, would be impossible to pay. Women were sent to work ranches if it were judged they needed to be separated from society. He had never heard of a man being sent. Men, again, went into house arrest in the custody of their families. But the mood now could change that. It was even conceivable a death penalty could be ordered, something scriptural, perhaps, like stoning. Jared shivered.

At noon the next day Keziah brought an ecclesiastic's tunic and trousers along with his lunch. He looked at the clothes but left them lying over the chair. They represented something he no longer felt willing or able to be a part of.

"I'd rather wear what I have on."

The chief keeper let him.

The walk across the street to the temple was as long as that he had made the first night in Gaza. It was to the rear gate this time, but as before, it gaped like a mouth before him. Traffic stopped for him. He was keenly aware of the hostile eyes watching him. The eyes were the only features alive in those stony faces, however. Their anger beat at him like summer heat.

He was almost at the gate when he heard a shout behind him. "Jared!"

He looked back. Storm Dan stood in the doorway of Peace Hall. "Sky is all right," she shouted. "She's—"

The rest of it was lost as a rhino-drawn ranch wagon rumbled between them.

Jared went on with his escorts. He did not mind about losing the rest of the message. What mattered was that Sky was all right. Knowing that, he could face his hearing in peace.

They came into the temple through the door near his garden. It meant they had to walk the width of the temple to reach the tabernacle. Jared knew every corridor and courtyard on the way, but they all looked as he had never seen them before. Men were everywhere, some cleaning, others simply sitting. They stared at him as he passed and their eyes were bitter as the women's outside. There were women in the temple, too. They wore keeper's uniforms and stood in pairs, patrol sticks hung on their belts.

"What did you want to do?" a man called at him as Jared passed.

"Are you satisfied at destroying our entire society?"

A steward spat at him. "That's for the innocent who are being destroyed along with the guilty."

Jared looked straight ahead and never answered back.

One of his escorts looked sidelong at him. "Are you sorry you ever started this? Is it worth the price we're paying?"

Was it? He considered the question. Around Marah hundreds of women and men had been killed. More were wounded. Families were breaking up. Years, perhaps decades, of social change, litigation, and criminal hearings lay ahead. He personally would have to bear hatred and hostility for the rest of his life.

There had been good things, too. He would never regret his time on the prairie, both alone and working with the rapas. He had enjoyed every minute of it. Someday, perhaps he could go back. He had had some honest conversations with women lately, like the chief keepers and Storm Dan. They had said things they really seemed to feel. Most of all, Isaiah was assured of growing up, and generations of boys to come would no longer face puberty in terror.

"Yes," he said. "It's worth the price." He had never felt such utter conviction. Marah was in chaos now, but one day a new stability would be achieved. It had to be no worse than the old one. "It's worth it."

"There's no guessing what the tribunal will do when they convict you," the other escort said. "You're the first to be heard."

Jared smiled. "It doesn't matter."

They passed through the courtyard with the alien artifact. It smiled dreamily at him.

No, the tribunal's sentence did not matter. It was all part of the price he paid, and all worth it.

The tabernacle doors were ahead.

He would not defend himself. He would make sure the witnesses gave correct testimony, but beyond that, he would not challenge the judges or witnesses.

The only thing he regretted, that had really hurt, was Sky's rejection. For days he had wished she would come to see him, send a message, even one reviling him. It was the feeling of being dead to her that cut to his soul. If her hatred was part of the price, too, the cost was dear indeed, but he supposed that he could come to accept even that, in time. He would go on loving her anyway, regardless of how she felt about him.

He turned through the doors of the tabernacle with his escorts. Starting down the aisle, he looked toward the altar. The city commissioners waited for him there, Esther Heber, Constance Amalek, Cirrus Ishbak, Jael

Midian, and two men, Kaleb and Jonathan Heber. His eyes slid to the defendant's chair, where he would sit to hear his accusers.

It was only then his stride faltered. He stared, first in disbelief, then with overwhelming joy. His feet leaped forward with his heart. Standing beside the chair, an ugly bruise across one cheekbone and her left arm in a sling, stood Sky, smiling at him.

About the Author

Lee Killough is a 5′7″ redhead who began her love affair with words and tales very early in her Kansas childhood. She started on science fiction in junior high school, after reading Leigh Brackett's *Starmen of Llyrdis* and C. L. Moore's "Shambleau." First published in 1970 in *Analog*, she has since appeared in a number of science-fiction magazines.

She supplements her writing income by moonlighting as a radiographer at Dykstra Veterinary Hospital in the College of Veterinary Medicine, Kansas State University, in Manhattan, Kansas. She shares her life and home with a big-eyed cat named Merlyn and a charming fellow named Pat, a lawyer turned business-law instructor, at whose insistence she first began submitting stories for publication.

She has taught riding—hunt seat—and ridden and trained horses. She is a compulsive book buyer, an insatiable reader, and a devoted Sherlock Holmes buff. She and Pat like to attend science-fiction conventions when their work schedules permit.

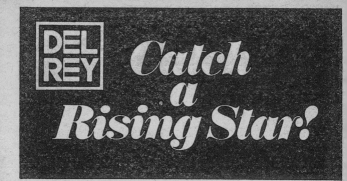

DEL REY *Catch a Rising Star!*